THE DEMON
HUNT

St. Martin's Paperbacks Titles by
KRIS GREENE

The Dark Storm

The Demon Hunt

THE DEMON HUNT

Kris Greene

St. Martin's Paperbacks

This is a work of fiction. All of the characters, organizations, and events portrayed in this novel are either products of the author's imagination or are used fictitiously.

THE DEMON HUNT

Copyright © 2010 by Kris Greene.

All rights reserved.

For information address St. Martin's Press, 175 Fifth Avenue, New York, NY 10010.

ISBN: 978-0-312-94423-0

Printed in the United States of America

St. Martin's Paperbacks edition / August 2010

St. Martin's Paperbacks are published by St. Martin's Press, 175 Fifth Avenue, New York, NY 10010.

10 9 8 7 6 5 4 3 2 1

PROLOGUE

When he was a little boy still studying the first circles of Sanctuary, Julius had loved to sneak off from his lessons at the Great House and catch the Saturday afternoon horror movies. There was something about the terror in the victim's eyes right before the monster got him or her that gave Julius an indescribable rush. But now that he found himself living in his own horror movie, he wished he had been more compassionate.

Julius was completely naked, his arms pinned above his head to a wooden pillar that overlooked the ocean—if the murky black waters below him could even be called that. Through the spill of white hair covering his face he could see the black liquid and the faces of the poor souls trapped beneath. They were the forgotten, spirits too weak or too vile to make the trip to either heaven or hell. Julius tried to close his eyes and imagine he was on a peaceful voyage across the Atlantic, but when he sucked in the cool air he tasted no salt, only death and sorrow. As the pinging of the dinghy a few yards off filled his ears, he feared that it would be the last thing he heard. All passengers on the *Jihad* had one-way tickets.

In all his years of training with the order he had never seen the likes of the things crawling from the ground at Sanctuary. Monsters, so hideous that they could only have been spawned by the pits of hell, had destroyed everyone in their wake, including the High Brother Angelo. When the battle had erupted, Julius's blade was the first to taste the blood of the order's enemies, laying low as many as he could before he was struck down by a goblin's ax. His terrified eyes watched as the foul beast reared back for the killing blow, but he could remember nothing past that. He had awoken as a prisoner on the *Jihad*, the Ghost ship used to transport departed souls to the Deadlands, and at the mercy of something far more fiendish than the brutish goblins—the ferryman Ezrah. Julius tried to call on his seldom-used magic to break his shackles, but there was nothing. He couldn't muster even a spark of the power passed on to him by his wayward father in the lands of the dead.

"You have no power here, so save your strength," Ezrah said as he stepped from the fog that was covering the deck of the *Jihad* with his hands folded behind his back. His skin was so transparent that Julius almost couldn't see him through the fog. However, the closer he got the more solid he became, as his skin darkened to it's original bronze color. He wore a thin breastplate of leather armor over a white tunic that stopped just above his knees. The single braid that hung from his shaved head blew softly on the ghostly winds that pushed the ship.

Julius craned his neck and watched the approaching specter with a fierce sneer. "If you've come to take me to the hereafter, then get on with it."

Ezrah smiled, and when he did so he looked almost human. "Hardly, brave soldier. I have come to offer you a bargain."

"After what you and your wraiths did to the order, I'd rather die than serve you!" Julius said venomously.

Ezrah gave him a look of amusement. "I think that the fact that you are here to even have this debate with me proves that death is just a relative term." He waved his hands through the mist and Julius caught a glimpse of himself being struck down by the goblin ax on the steps of Sanctuary. "Quite a few of your brothers have crossed these waters tonight and more will surely travel on my ship before it's all said and done. The only reason you still live is because I have need of a unique vessel such as yourself."

Julius averted his eyes. "There is nothing special about me. I am but a soldier and servant of the order."

"Come now, Julius. There are no secrets here. I know just who and what you are, mage."

"Liar. I am a child of the first order!" Julius shouted, jerking at his chains.

Ezrah laughed. "You are the child of a turncoat and a whore. It was only the mercies of Brother Angelo that saved you from becoming a victim of your own self-hate."

The truth in Ezrah's statement cut Julius like a knife. Outside of his parents, the secret of Julius's heritage had only been known to Brothers Angelo and David. Since he had been adopted by the order, he had used his hatred for his father and his people to mold himself into one of the order's most devoted followers.

"Save your tall tales for someone who has not peeled back the layers of your soul and seen what lies beneath." Ezrah took Julius's face and turned it toward him. "A thing of great power has been unleashed upon the world, and I will have it and my revenge on the ones who betrayed me and condemned me to this hell." Ezrah's eyes grew bright and in them Julius saw the vision of the crew members of the *Jihad* being locked below decks just before the agents of the church set the ship on fire. "Tell me, Julius, have you ever heard the screams of a man being burned alive? The scream of one man is more horrible than anything you can imagine and there were twenty in my crew."

"A fitting punishment for the agents of Satan if you ask me," Julius said with a smirk.

Ezrah thought about it. "Possibly, but we can debate what is fitting and not after you have done my bidding. Serve me and I will give you back the life stolen by the goblins."

Julius gave a maddened laugh. "You have wasted your power and your time, hell's spawn. In life or death I am loyal to my order and will not serve the likes of you. If I am to choose between your offer and death, I choose the latter." He then spat at Ezrah's face, but the saliva passed through him and landed on the deck.

"And who says you have a choice?" Ezrah raised his hands and called the fog to him. A ring of mist encircled Ezrah's feet and from the fog came ghostly shapes. "Be it as my champion or my slave, you will serve me."

Ezrah pointed his finger accusingly at Julius and the ghosts descended on him. Julius could feel the flesh being stripped from his back as the ghost rode him, the wounds spewing forth fog instead of blood. As the mist rolled from his back it thickened and lay across him like two sheets of chilled silk. Soon the vision of the *Jihad*'s deck was gone, replaced by the swirling forms ripping him limb from limb. When the spirits finally faded, Julius was gone, leaving behind something dark and frightening.

"What is your will, Master?" the shadowy figured asked in a distorted voice. The thing that had once been Julius knelt at Ezrah's feet.

Ezrah smiled like a proud father. "Bring me the spark and the head of Gabriel Redfeather."

CHAPTER ONE

"Redfeather, are you still with us?" Asha snapped Gabriel out of his daze. He had been sitting completely motionless for the last ten minutes and it unnerved her.

Gabriel blinked and looked around as if seeing the faces surrounding him for the first time. "Yeah, I'm good," he lied.

Ever since he had come into possession of the Nimrod he had been slipping into trances and seeing things through the eyes of the Bishop. For the most part the visions were jumbled and he could make no sense of them. The Bishop was trying to tell him something, but he had no idea what.

Gabriel ran his fingers through his thick black curls but it didn't help his appearance. His delicate hands were bruised and covered in blood, some of it his, but most of it coming from the friends he'd lost the battle the night before.

The fuel light on the dashboard blinked, but

they dared not stop until they were out of Manhattan or the sun had fully risen.

It was sheer luck that they had survived the initial onslaught of the dark forces, and in their present battle-worn conditions not even luck would save them from a second attack.

The forces of hell had nearly destroyed them along with Sanctuary. The stretch Hummer drew more than the occasional glance as it rumbled down the FDR en route to the Queensboro Bridge. It wasn't every day that you saw a modified Hummer with a religious emblem etched into the hood and doors. The cross sat in the center of three rings, which represented man, demon, and spirit. The ancient symbol once struck fear into the hearts of the enemies of the order, but that morning it served as a grim reminder of all that had been lost.

Each passenger's face bore a different expression, but their eyes all held the same weariness. In what felt like the blink of an eye, several totally different people from different walks of life found themselves thrown together by one common object, the Nimrod.

The Nimrod was not just a trident, but a thing of pure magic that was neither good nor evil and was empowered by the imprisoned spirit of a man known as the Bishop. During the Seven-Day Siege it was the Bishop whom the Nimrod had called master, until Titus the Betrayer slew him in an attempt to claim his weapon.

Because of the warped love affair between

weapon and master, the Bishop was denied the peace of the grave. The Bishop's displaced soul lay nestled in the bosom of the thing he had loved most in life, waiting for the moment when he would walk the earth again, cleansing it of its impurities. But to execute his plan the Bishop needed a willing vessel, which is where Gabriel came into the picture. The Bishop had expected the Nimrod to corrupt Gabriel as it had done with him centuries prior, but Gabriel's will was stronger than either of them had anticipated.

With his tattered clothes and mussed hair, you'd have hardly taken Gabriel Redfeather as someone who, only a few hours ago, had been living a bland life. He was a bookish-looking young man with pronounced Native American features and curious eyes, whose biggest thrills came from deciphering ancient languages and Thursday night chess club. He and his grandfather had lived a quiet life in a brownstone in Harlem until the day he met De Mona Sanchez and lost everything he had, including his free will.

To everyone's, especially Gabriel's, surprise, the Nimrod had responded to his touch and stirred the spirit within it. The Nimrod had bound itself to Gabriel's flesh while the Bishop invaded his heart, constantly tempting him with promises of power. For the most part Gabriel was still in control, but there was no denying the strength in the Bishop's words. Gabriel looked over at De Mona and cursed her for the hundredth time for coming into his life.

De Mona rested her head against the window and stared blankly out at the pinkish sky. The bubble-gum effect as the increasing light played on the clouds took her back to when her mother and father would buy her cotton candy at the carnival. That was before she found out that she was the real freak. De Mona walked in two worlds, those of men and demons. Her father had been a retired professor turned antique dealer who fell head over heels for a demon. Her mother, Mercy, was a Valkrin, a race of demons whose sole purpose was to wage war. Next to the goblins, the Valkrin were the most feared creatures in service to the dark lord, but that all changed shortly before De Mona was born.

Mercy had been the first of the Valkrin to cross over to the light, but she hadn't been the last. Soon others came seeking peace from the war that had been raging since the beginning of time. They found that peace within the walls of Sanctuary, but it wasn't to last. Not long before the anointed weapons began resurfacing, the Valkrin and some of the others began disappearing. No one knew what caused the withdrawal, but when a Valkrin was connected to the mass murder of the inhabitants of a missionary village in Guam, the reason had become clear. The dark lord had put out the call to arms and the Valkrin had answered.

De Mona ran her fingers through her hair and winced when she nicked her scalp. She held her hands in front of her face, almost expecting to see the smooth knuckles and frail digits she'd known for the first eleven years of her life, but she didn't. She hadn't called the change, but her fingers were gnarled and twisted with shiny black nails that looked like spearheads. Sucking in a deep breath, she tried to banish the demon that was inching toward the surface, but the best she could do was smooth out the skin on the back of her hands. Since coming in contact with the Nimrod she had been having difficulty controlling her changes. It was as if the demon inside her was becoming more pronounced and the woman less so. She didn't like it.

What felt like a soft whisper of wind touched her honey-colored cheek and she immediately knew what it was . . . *magic.* She turned her hooded brown eyes toward the rear of the transport, where the mage and the witch sat watching her intently, whispering together. When they noticed her watching them watch her, they averted their eyes. For this she was glad, because there was something about the starry flakes in the mage's eyes that made her uneasy.

"Why don't you take a picture or something?" De Mona snapped.

"Somebody woke up on the wrong side of the bed," Asha said with a crooked grin. Her familiar, Azuma, bristled on her lap, but he dared not go near the demon. While De Mona's form was hidden to human eyes, Azuma could see her for just what she was, and it frightened him.

"You'd be in a pissy mood too if you'd been

getting sucker punched by demons all night," De Mona said.

Asha rolled her eyes and folded her arms. "Try getting blown out of a third-story window. You ain't the only one who's had a trying night." The Blood witch replied. Asha represented a darker side of the coin than her sisters of the coven. Because of her mixed blood she was rejected and feared by her peers.

"I think we've all been through a lot over the last few hours, so why don't the both of you cool it?" Rogue interjected.

His ribs were still busted to hell, but at least he had gotten the bleeding to stop. He hadn't heard a peep from the demon he shared his soul with since he'd taken shadow-form. Normally the demon encouraged Rogue to tap further into his shadow magic, but never to attack one of its own species. Using his shadow-form, Rogue had managed to destroy Moses Shadow Master's host body, but the victory was a temporary one. You couldn't destroy a real shadow, only hold it back, especially one as powerful as Moses. The demon had been around since the early days, close to the time when the shadows first learned to think and move outside the collective.

"You're one to talk. I don't even know you well enough to be giving me orders, dude. So please tell me why your opinion should count for a damn thing?" De Mona asked defiantly. She hadn't known

Rogue more than a few hours and still wasn't sure where he fit into the mystery.

"Because if it hadn't been for him we would all be dead." Gabriel spoke up unexpectedly, drawing the attention of everyone in the Hummer. De Mona hadn't noticed it before but there was something different about him. He seemed somehow older than he had been when they'd first set out. "Rogue saved my life so I could be around to save yours, even though I don't know why I bothered since you caused all this."

"I don't think pointing fingers is going to help us much," Jackson said from the passenger seat. His leather jacket was ripped, but other than that he seemed in better shape than the rest of them. His incredible resilience was one of the upsides of surviving a vampire attack. The downsides hadn't shown themselves yet.

"Let me be the judge of what's helpful and what isn't, since I'm the one with a centuries-old relic bound to his arm." Gabriel flashed the tattoo on his arm, which was pulsing slightly.

"And how did you manage such a trick?" Morgan asked from behind the wheel. "My hammer has been with me since I was a boy and it's never done more than open the overripe skulls of demons and vampires. I fancy myself somewhat of an authority on these weapons, but I've never heard tales of the trident or any of the other anointed weapons merging with the wielder's flesh."

"As soon as I figure it out you'll be the first to know," Gabriel said sarcastically. He had been in a foul mood since being dragged onto the supernatural roller coaster.

But Morgan had asked the sixty-four thousand dollar question. Since he had come into possession of the Nimrod, Gabriel had learned a great many things, but its darkest secrets were still kept from him by its true master, the Bishop. When it suited him the Bishop allowed Gabriel to taste undreamed-of power, but the more powerful Gabriel became the more of himself he seemed to lose to the addictive properties of the magic he wielded. The rational side of him said that he should get rid of the trident and the vengeful spirit as soon as possible, but there was a little piece of him that craved the old magic, the same piece that seemed to be steadily growing. Knowing that he was his grandfather's only hope was the only thing that kept him from completely falling into the Bishop's thrall.

Azuma sat curled in Asha's lap, studying the lump of bound flesh in the shadowed corner of the Hummer between the door and rear seats. The creature did not move when Azuma ventured closer to him, but he kept his reptilian eyes glued on the monkey. Azuma reached his hand out cautiously and the creature snapped its razor sharp teeth, barely missing the monkey's fingers. Azuma shrieked and raked his nails down the side of the goblin's face before scuttling back into Asha's lap.

"Vermin!" Gilchrest hissed from the corner. He struggled against his invisible bonds, but even his heightened strength was no match for Asha's spell. He'd been taken hostage when his brother Orden and his troops had been forced back into the sewers by the blinding light of the trident during the battle at Sanctuary.

"I'd be quiet if I were you," Jackson snarled at the goblin. He'd wanted to kill the thing, but Jonas thought he might still be of some use to them.

"Be careful how you speak to me, I would," Gilchrest warned.

"You sure pop a lot of crap for something that's barely three feet tall," Gabriel mocked Gilchrest.

Gilchrest turned his hooded eyes to Gabriel and snickered. "Make sport if you will, but I have last laugh. You stink of magic, even for a mutation. The shadows of death follow you like second skin. Bound for the *Jihad* we all are for long as you stay."

Jackson snatched Gilchrest off the floor and pressed his face against the UV-resistant tinted window of the Hummer. Slowly he started to roll it down, sending a swift breeze through the vehicle. "Now, I've read a thing or two about what direct sunlight can do to you suckers, so unless you shut your damn mouth you're gonna get a real good view of this sunrise."

"Destroy me and risk wrath of entire goblin empire!" Gilchrest threatened nervously. He could see the pinkish sky beginning to turn blue.

Jackson flicked one of his blades out and pressed

it against Gilchrest's throat. To Gilchrest's surprise the blade pierced his rock-hard skin and drew a trickle of blood. "Bullshit. What would make me think that those nasty sons of bitches would give a rat's ass if a toad like you went missing?"

"Law say any who murder royal family meet slow death. Prince Orden not take kind if baby brother killed by man-things. Eat you I think he will, after boil you alive."

"That is a goblin prince?" Asha poked him mockingly, which caused Gilchrest to snap at her hand. "Keep that up and I'm gonna show you some of my nastier spells." Asha's eyes sparkled as the small gash on Gilchrest's neck began to bleed more freely.

"Filthy witch!" Gilchrest shook his head from side to side in an attempt to stop the pain spreading across his face.

Rogue placed a soothing hand on Asha's shoulder and the bleeding stopped. "If this thing is a goblin prince we may be able to use him as a bargaining chip to get Gabriel's grandfather back."

"Goblins never barter with topsiders, especially demons posing as humans." He glared from Rogue to De Mona. Something about the way the goblin looked at her made De Mona uncomfortable. "Why you hide your true face? Afraid they see you for what you really are—a whore of Belthon?"

"That's it, I'm offing this fucker!" In a flash, De Mona was across the Hummer with her claws fully extended. Even if Gilchrest hadn't been bound there was no way he could have moved faster than De Mona. Just before her claws tore into his pocked flesh, De Mona found herself wrapped from finger-tip to elbow in shadow.

"Enough," Rogue said evenly, holding the shadow restraint in place like a horse's reins. "He's worth more to us alive than dead, so why don't you cool it, or would you rather have to worry about every goblin within a hundred miles gunning for a piece of your hide?"

De Mona bared her fangs. "I can handle myself."

"That remains to be seen," Rogue told her. "You and Gabriel handled yourselves like real troopers earlier, but this is a whole different fight. No more limping dead men. They're gonna bring out the heavy guns."

"And they'll get dealt with too," she challenged.

Rogue shook his head in frustration. "I don't know if you noticed it or not, girlie, but we're in the *shit* here. This ain't about egos anymore, it's about survival and you can bet as sure as my ass is black that we're all on the short list of who Titus wants whacked. You're free to play the tough-ass loner if you want, but I'm thinking there's strength in numbers. We've gotta stick together if any of us plans to make it out of this alive."

"I agree." Lydia spoke up. She stroked Fin's head affectionately with one hand and ran her thumb over the runes on her spear with the other. Her long black hair was mussed and her face dark. "We are all that's left of the Great House and we must uphold what it stood for. Whether we are five hundred or five we must keep the darkness at bay." Lydia and Fin were both orphans who were taken in by the order so the fall of the Great House hit them harder than the others.

Jackson stared at Lydia quizzically. Even though she was blind she still displayed more courage than most when it came to tackling the dark forces. The gesture brought a smirk to his face. "Though I feel like a fool for saying so, I'm with the young lady. Look, each of us has been fighting his or her own battle, be it with the dark forces or our own souls"—he glanced at De Mona when he said this—"the point is that going at it solo ain't working, so maybe it's time we clique up and put an end to this."

Gilchrest scoffed. "Impossible to put an end to something older than you or I. This war go since first blood shed in Eden. This war go on forever, or until goblins rule all."

"Now that's a world I could do without," Asha said.

"Then we're all agreed. We regroup and put a plan together to get our people back," Rogue said.

Gilchrest laughed. It sounded like a sick wheezing when it belched from his chest. "Man-thing, no need plan for death, only hold on to prince and it come find you soon enough."

"Goddess, why don't you shut up already?" Asha waved her hand and an invisible strap clamped over Gilchrest's mouth.

"Plan? Why do we need a plan when we've got

this?" Gabriel pulled up his sleeve and exposed the pulsing tattoo. "If this thing is so powerful, why don't we just use it to find my grandfather and then go get him?"

"Didn't we just establish the fact that we don't wanna die?" Asha asked sarcastically.

Jackson placed a hand on Gabriel's forearm. "Dawg, I know you're hot right now, but we need a game plan before we go off into the Iron Mountains."

Gabriel slapped his hand away and manifested the trident. "I've got a game plan right here."

"Cool it with that thing before you give away our position," Rogue warned. Gabriel gave him a defiant look, but did as he was told. "Gabriel, you know no one wants to help you get Redfeather back more than me, but I have to agree with Jackson on this one. Even on holy ground we barely made it out with our skins, so charging into the bowels of Midland is suicide at best."

"What's Midland?" Asha asked curiously.

"The last place of true magic," Fin murmured and went back to staring blankly at the blacked-out window from Lydia's lap. Ever since Angelo had forced the spark into him he had been drifting in and out.

Seeing the confused expressions on their faces through the rearview mirror, Morgan chose to explain. "Keep in mind that what I am about to tell you is supposed to be a myth," he stroked his thick red beard, "But in light of some of the things my brothers and I have come across I have to believe the truth isn't too far off. Centuries ago, when magical things walked the earth, this was all Midland. When science forced the magic out, Midland began to die. To protect itself the land separated from this plane and retreated to a realm between the worlds of men and demons, where magic still flourishes. But like a tree, Midland's roots are still in this world. When the land separated, it caused small tears, called *rips*, in the fabric of the realities. These rips act as access points between this world and the forgotten."

"So you mean to say that both worlds occupy the same place, but on different levels?" De Mona asked. Her father had spoken of Midland, but he'd always made it seem like it no longer existed.

"In a way," Morgan confirmed. "The earth is one world of many, but it has different layers."

"Kinda like those Grams biscuits at the supermarket." Jackson offered.

Morgan shook his head. "Not quite, but my leather-clad friend isn't far off with his assessment. Midland is everywhere, yet nowhere at the same time. It hovers between the two planes like a layer of protective skin keeping the realms of science and magic from colliding. When I was a boy my father used to tell me tales of great magicians who could walk between both worlds as simply as walking through a door, but the days of magic that potent have long passed. The most conventional way to cross into Midland now is through the rips."

"So why don't we just roll up to one of these rips and cross into Midland?" De Mona asked.

"If only it were that simple," Morgan said. "With the passing of time and the evolution of technology there are fewer and fewer rips. The only ones that have withstood the changing of the world are those that lead to the last kingdoms of Midland, and even those are fraught with danger unless you are a member of that particular court. One such rip is the gateway to the Iron Mountains."

"Then why don't we have him lead us to the rip to find my grandfather?" Gabriel suggested, nodding at Gilchrest. The goblin tried to mumble something that sounded less than friendly.

"The little one would surely be helpful in gaining access to the Iron Mountains, but it's navigating the bloody place and the things that dwell there that chills my blood," Morgan said.

"What if we went in through one of the other pockets?" Rogue suggested.

"What are you getting at, Rogue?" Lydia asked. Until then she had just been listening and trying to comfort Finnious.

"We need to get to the Iron Mountains, but we may not have to use that pocket to cross into Midland. I've got a buddy I can reach out to who owes me a favor."

Asha tossed him her cell phone. "Be my guest." To her surprise, Rogue wrapped her phone in shadow and crushed it. "Hey! Do you know how much I paid for that thing?"

"It's a small price to pay for your life. Titus has everybody from street dealers to politicians on his payroll. If somebody's tracking the cell phone signal, using it is like painting a bull's-eye on your forehead," he said letting the phone's remains fall to the floor. "Besides, the person I plan to contact won't talk over the phone and I can't reach him until after sundown."

"Rogue, I know you ain't about to call in no vamps for help," Jackson said in disgust. He had a special hatred for vampires because of what they'd done to him.

Rogue smiled at him. "Vampires aren't the only things that go bump in the night."

Asha sucked her teeth. "You guys kill me with all this talk about the Iron Mountains as if they're some great house of horrors. How freaking bad could it be?"

CHAPTER TWO

"MERCY, PLEASE JUST LET ME DIE!" The scream echoed off the cavern walls and traveled throughout the Iron Mountains for all to hear, not that anyone cared. In the Iron Mountains the goblins ruled, and their only law was pain. The Iron Mountains had been around since the days before magic and men. It had once been a cornerstone of Midland, but now it was just a vast network of tunnels beneath the Bronx Zoo, hovering between the here and there like the rest of Midland.

"What do you mean, eat us? That's downright gross!" Lucy said in disgust.

Redfeather shook his head. "For a witch you know very little about the supernatural."

"And who said I was a witch?" Lucy stared at the old man defiantly with her knuckles resting on her hips. There was something about his aquiline features that tugged a cord of familiarity in her, but Lucy couldn't place him.

"When you've been dealing with the unexplained

for as long as I have, you tend to pick up on certain things. Besides, I saw you trying to work a spell on the bars."

Lucy tried to call her magic again but couldn't muster so much as a spark. "For all the good it did. What the hell are these things made of? Kryptonite?"

"They are made from pure iron and enchanted by dark magic." Redfeather knelt and inspected the runes on the bars. "I've read about them, but this is the first time I've actually seen one of these cages. Are you a refugee of Sanctuary?" Redfeather asked, wondering how many besides her had escaped the bloodbath and hoping his grandson was in that number.

"Hardly. I was supposed to assist with a healing and ended up getting caught up in this mess," she explained while conducting her own investigation of the bars.

Lucy's spell-casting abilities may have been hampered by the cage, but her senses were still intact. The markings on the bars were of no language she could read, but she recognized the distinct wards as belonging to the sorcerers, who were the long-time enemies of the witches and warlocks. Once they had been servants to the sorcerers, but a mystic holy war had earned them their independence. Still, the old hostilities lingered, and these bars were proof that the sorcerers had now thrown in their lot with the savage goblins, which did nothing to assuage Lucy's prejudices.

"The sorcerers enchanted those bars with holding witches in mind," Redfeather said, confirming her thoughts. "No spell may leave that cage. I'm afraid there's nothing that your young mind can conjure that will counteract such an old magic."

"Then you underestimate me." Lucy stepped back from the bars and focused. The air around her began to crackle faintly and even some of the hay beneath her feet stirred. "Tiki, be my strength!" No sooner had the command left Lucy's lips than the same power she expelled threatened to crush her body. Lucy collapsed on the dirty floor of the cage, clutching her tender ribs. She was in intense pain but was spared the sweet release of unconsciousness.

Redfeather waited until the young witch had caught her breath before speaking. "As I told you: no spell shall leave this cage, and summoning your familiar counts as a spell." He knelt, reaching between the bars to see if she was okay, which caused Lucy to recoil. "I was just trying to make sure you were okay."

"I'm just peachy." She staggered to her feet, still feeling the effects of the feedback. She studied Redfeather for a moment. There was something about him that she couldn't quite place, as if there was something hiding under the surface. "What are you hiding?"

"Excuse me?"

Lucy moved closer to the bars. "It's not a trick question. You look like a mortal, but there's something about your aura that's not quite right. You're too weak to be a warlock or sorcerer and you're breathing, so that rules out your being a vampire, yet your cage is enchanted too. I'm guessing you're some sort of magician, right?"

Redfeather chuckled. "Afraid not, child, though at this point I wish I were. Maybe if I had some sort of magical ability I could've done something more than get myself captured when they invaded. There was so much I could've done to prevent this, but I fear I will never have the chance."

"So you know what's going on?" Lucy asked.

Redfeather hesitated, then nodded. "I'm afraid I helped cause it." He went on to give her the short version of his tale.

Lucy's eyes flashed rage. "You called those things to this side of the dimensional plane?"

"Not me. My grandson and the thing that is trying to lay claim to his immortal soul, the Nimrod."

Without Redfeather having to elaborate, the pieces began falling into place. Lucy's supernatural history was rusty at best, but she knew enough to recognize the name of what the elders referred to as the Trident of Heaven. As it was told among the covens, the Nimrod was one of the greatest pieces of magic ever entrusted to the mortal realm. She now understood what the disturbance in the balance of magic had been, but she was still clueless as to what to do about it.

"So where are your grandson and this Nimrod now?" Lucy asked.

Redfeather shrugged. "I wish I could say. We

were attempting to find him when the goblins stormed Sanctuary." Redfeather closed his eyes as if he were living the battle again. "So many lives were lost."

Lucy thought of Sulin and how she had been viciously killed by the goblins. "We can't avenge our friends if we end up dead too. We've got to find a way to get outta here."

"Agreed, but I can't say that I have a clue how. I'm just an old man and your powers have been rendered useless by the bars."

Lucy rummaged around through her wild hair and produced a hairpin. "Even without my magic I'm never without my resources." Lucy knelt near the bars and began working on the lock. Even though her prison was enchanted, it was still just an old zoo cage on the surface. After nearly ten minutes of feverishly working at the lock, she finally heard the telltale clicks of progress. Just as she was about to try the cage door she heard heavy footfalls in the corridor.

"Someone's coming," Redfeather whispered.

"No shit." Lucy retreated to the corner of the cage and hugged her knees to her chest as if she were still traumatized by her plight.

A goblin that was almost skeletal in appearance came through the archway followed by a dwarf. He was a short, plump man with stringy brown hair and a clean-shaven face. He wasn't quite what Lucy had expected, since she had heard that all male dwarves wore beards as a sign of honor and respect. The little man kept his eyes fixed on the ground as he pushed a rickety cart. On the cart were two bowls full of something that Lucy sincerely hoped they didn't expect her to eat.

"Mealtime, meat sacks," the goblin mocked them. Yellow fangs jutted from behind mutilated lips in what passed for a smile.

"Wow, I didn't know you guys had room service at this fine establishment," Lucy said sarcastically.

When the goblin laughed it sounded like two pieces of metal being rubbed together. "That was rich. And here I thought witches weren't good for much other than lying on their backs and providing entertainment for their sorcerer masters."

"If I had my powers I'd wipe that smile off your face," Lucy warned.

"I'm sure you would, but since you don't that's something that I don't have to worry about, is it?" He addressed the dwarf. "You, hurry and feed the prisoners and get back to your duties. Nott needs your help in the kitchen."

"Yes, my lord," the dwarf said just above a whisper.

"Eat up, flesh sacks," the goblin told them.

"Aww, I didn't know you cared. Wouldn't want us to starve on your watch, would you?" Lucy said.

The goblin looked at her. "I couldn't care less if you choke on your own tongues and die, but Prince Orden wants to make sure that you're healthy for the banquet."

"Banquet?" Redfeather and Lucy asked at the same time.

"Yes, and you two are the main courses." The goblin snickered and disappeared back down the corridor.

The dwarf continued to stare at the floor until he was sure the goblin was out of earshot. When he looked up at Lucy, his big blue eyes seemed frightened. "It's not wise of you to taunt Brutus that way."

"Screw him and the rest of these freakish bastards. If I could cast my spells I'd show him a thing or two!" she shouted down the corridor.

"Please, miss, he may hear you. The goblins have ears all throughout these caverns." The dwarf was so frightened that he nearly spilled Redfeather's bowl as he knelt to slide it through the feeding slot at the base of the cage.

"If my memories serve me correctly these mountains were once the stronghold of the dwarves, weren't they?" Redfeather asked.

Shame crept across the dwarf's face as he lowered his head. "Yes, many seasons ago." The dwarf cast a cautionary glance down the corridor. "When the rightful kings of Midland still ruled, the dwarves held a place in the great court. We were praised as the greatest weapon smiths in all the lands. Even the first tribes of men came to us to craft their armor and blades. None could match us when it came to manipulating steel." His big blue eyes took on a faraway glint. "How proud we were in those days."

"What happened?" Redfeather wanted to know.

"The goblins," the dwarf said. "When Hades sought to overthrow Mica, king of the seventh level of hell, he tried to enlist the goblins to aid him in adding to his steadily growing kingdom. They refused, as at the time they were loyal subjects of Mica. Hades succeeded in overthrowing Mica anyhow, and when he claimed the seventh level of hell he forced the goblins topside as their punishment. Many of them fell to the sunlight or things fiercer than they that roamed Midland, and the ones who survived found temporary shelters where they could. If things had gone differently the goblin race would likely be extinct now and the dwarves would still rule the Iron Mountains."

Redfeather weighed what the dwarf was telling him against what he had read and some of the blanks began filling in, but the stories had always painted the dwarves as not only skilled blacksmiths, but battle-hardened warriors. From what he had seen during his unexpected stay in the Iron Mountains, these creatures were little more than slaves.

Redfeather measured his words carefully so as not to offend the dwarf. "The goblins are feared warriors, but so were the dwarves. If the goblins were as displaced and weakened as you say, then how could they take the impenetrable Iron Mountains?"

To everyone's surprise the dwarf smiled. It wasn't a pleasant smile, more like an insane thought had just floated into his brain. "That was the work of

Belthon and the fool King Isa of Themus. Themus was a small kingdom that sat at the mouth of the Iron Mountains, and only by crossing through Themus could you access the mountains directly. Our king proposed a bargain to King Isa, entrusting him to be our first line of defense against attack in exchange for us providing Themus with the finest weapons our fires could craft.

"The deal forged between our people was a boon that would have been gracefully accepted by any of the other kings of Midland, but not Isa. Themus was one of the smallest kingdoms in all of Midland, so Isa was always looking to expand his territory. Though he barely had enough troops to hold his own borders, Isa continuously went off on foolish crusades to assuage his ego. It was during one of these such times that Belthon offered him the fool's bargain. Isa would be the king of kings if he would provide refuge to a handful of refugees loyal to the dark lord. Belthon promised Isa warriors so fierce that all the kings of Midland would tremble in the face of his army, but what he gave him were the goblins." The dwarf leaned against the wall wearily. "King Krull and his people wasted no time in establishing who truly ruled Themus. They bled the people and the land before setting their sights on the Iron Mountains. Because we had become dependent on Themus to guard our main entrance we never even had a chance to prepare for the attack. It was the darkest day in our long history."

"One day the yoke will be lifted from the neck of the oxen," Redfeather said sincerely.

The dwarf mustered a weak smile. "It has been more seasons than even the oldest of us can remember, so I doubt if I will see this great miracle in my lifetime. My friend . . ." The dwarf's words were cut off when a lick of fire ran up his back, dropping him to one knee. Brutus stood in the archway sneering at the dwarf and holding a bloody whip.

Brutus stormed into the room, raining spittle as he cursed the dwarf. "Miserable worm, who gives you the right to talk?" he grabbed the dwarf and slammed him into Lucy's cage. "You speak of a history that not even your whore of a mother was here to see?"

"That's enough!" Redfeather shouted from his cage.

"Mind your business, human. Your blood will be spilled soon enough," Brutus warned. "Stinking dwarf." Brutus cracked the whip across his back again. "I'm going to beat the skin off you, then fry it!" Brutus drew back the whip, but when he tried to swing it he couldn't. He turned and saw Redfeather holding the end of the whip.

"I said enough!" Redfeather snarled, straining to hold the whip.

"Human, you are as stupid as you are ugly." Brutus yanked the whip, slamming Redfeather face first into the bars. Brutus opened the cage and snatched the dazed old man to his feet. Redfeather struggled as Brutus forced his hand up and examined his fingers. "Orden says that he wants to cook you alive, but he didn't say anything about bringing you in whole." Brutus's jaws opened incredibly wide, exposing his jagged teeth. He had come within inches of Redfeather's fingers when something sharp jabbed him in the back. The dwarf was standing there with a terrified expression on his face, holding a broken dagger. Brutus backhanded him across the room. "The cheap blade of a slave is no match for the skin of a goblin."

"How about a wooden heel?"

Brutus turned in time to receive the roundhouse kick Lucy sent his way. She dropped under his counterstrike and delivered a combination of quick blows to his gut. Hitting the goblin was like punching a brick wall. Brutus grabbed her by the throat and slammed her violently into the wall. "Where are your sharp words now?" Brutus spat as he tried to crush Lucy's windpipe.

"A little help here," Lucy croaked, trying to break Brutus's grip.

"I would if I could." Redfeather rattled the bars of his cage.

"Yes, be afraid, witch. Fear makes the blood sweeter." He drew a jagged nail over Lucy's collarbone, drawing blood. Brutus licked his finger and rolled his eyes back in his head in ecstasy. "Sweet indeed." Brutus eyed Lucy like a starved animal. "To blazes with Orden and his orders. The first taste of your flesh will go to me!" He clamped down on Lucy's collar and drank greedily as the blood flowed into his moth. Lucy was in such intense pain that she couldn't even think of a spell, much less cast it. She pressed both her feet against the goblin's gut and pushed with everything she had. Brutus flew backward and bounced against Redfeather's cage.

Redfeather reached through the bars, locking his arms around Brutus's throat and squeezing as hard as he could in the hopes that he could break Brutus's neck. He was incredibly strong, but the goblin's bones were like oak. "Child, if you have a plan I suggest you execute it!"

Still favoring her shoulder, Lucy rolled into a crouch in front of Brutus and placed the palm of her hand over his heart while chanting softly, but nothing happened. It was either her proximity to the enchanted bars or the lingering effects, but either way she needed to do something because Redfeather was losing his grip. "Come on," she urged. After a few seconds she could feel the power trying to build in her hand.

"Lucy!" Redfeather shouted as Brutus broke free.

There was a sound of air being released and Brutus's face suddenly took on a puzzled expression. A spot of gray appeared on the skin just above his heart. Lucy looked up at him with power sparkling in her eyes. "I told you I'd wipe that grin off your face," Lucy told him before putting her fist through his chest, shattering it and his heart. Piece by piece Brutus's body began to crumble away until there was nothing left but a pile of debris. Lucy collapsed to her knees and let out a breath. "That was too close."

"Are you okay?" The dwarf crouched next to Lucy and checked her wound.

Lucy shooed him away and checked the wound herself. The gash was a nasty one, but thankfully none of the muscles or nerves had been damaged. "Yeah, he just broke the skin."

"Luckily for you. A goblin bite can fester quite easily," the dwarf told her. He looked at Brutus's body and the realization of what they had done filled him with dread. "Orden will surely have us all killed for what has happened here."

"He'll have to catch us first." Lucy snatched the keys to the cages off Brutus's belt and tossed them to Redfeather. "Come on, we're getting out of here."

"That will be near impossible. The Iron Mountains are a maze of tunnels that stretch for miles in every direction. It'll take you hours to find your way out. And with that wound of yours, you will have every predator that hunts these mountains chasing the scent of your magical blood. The blood of a witch is a most precious thing down here."

"We should have no problem making it out before that happens with you to guide us," Lucy told him.

The dwarf shook his head in protest. "I cannot. Orden will have me killed it he finds out that I helped you escape the mountains."

"And what do you think that he will do to you

when he finds Brutus's corpse?" Redfeather asked. "I know you're afraid, as are we all, but you must help us. We have friends topside who may even be able to free your people from the goblins."

"No, we are doomed to suffer at the hands of our tormentors forever." The dwarf looked at the ground shamefully.

"Nothing is forever," Lucy said, thinking of how the sorcerers had once enslaved her people. "Help us and we'll see what we can do to help your people."

The dwarf weighed his options. It was better to let death catch him as opposed to sitting around and waiting for it. "Very well."

"Cristobel, what's keeping you? We have kitchen duty." Another dwarf entered the chamber. When he saw Lucy and Redfeather free of their cages his eyes went wide. "Are you insane? The goblins will punish us all for this!" the dwarf shouted.

"Please, keep your voice down!" Cristobel urged the other dwarf.

"No, I'll not have you seal all our fates because of your bleeding heart. Sound the alarm! The prisoners are escaping!" the dwarf shouted down the corridor. "Alarm, alarm—"

The dwarf's words died in his throat as what was left of Cristobel's dagger sailed across the room and planted itself in the dwarf's chest. Everyone turned and looked at Lucy, who had thrown the dagger.

"Sorry, but he was going to get us caught and I,

for one, don't relish the idea of being anyone's meal. Now, we can stand around and pray for the life of this little snitch or we can get outta here while we still can."

The sound of an alarm filled the halls outside the corridor. In the distance they could hear the scraping of feet across the floor and weapons being drawn as the guards closed on their position.

"We are too late," Cristobel said fearfully.

"The hell we are." Lucy yanked him by the arm and headed for the door with Redfeather on her heels.

As Redfeather followed Lucy and the dwarf through the archway and out to face God knew what, he couldn't help but wonder what had become of his grandson.

CHAPTER THREE

By the time they made it to Queens the sun was up and shining brightly. Though the sun's rays couldn't pierce the UV-resistant windows, Gilchrest still freaked out at the sight of it. The only way they were able to calm him was by putting him in one of the chests in the back that were used to transport weapons. It wasn't the most comfortable means of transport, but it would have to do.

All the other occupants of the van breathed a sigh of relief at the sight of the morning sun. Traffic had begun to thicken when they exited the 59th Street Bridge and the shops were just opening for business. New York was starting to look like New York again, instead of the war-torn freak show they'd lived through the night prior. For the time being they were safe from the threat of the flesh-craving Stalkers, but they weren't in the clear. Titus had agents everywhere, so they had to be constantly on guard.

Gabriel stared out the window, watching the

changing scenery. They were stopped at a traffic light when he noticed an old homeless man standing on the corner watching them. At first, Gabriel thought that the man was staring at the strange Hummer, but his eyes seemed to be fixed right on Gabriel, who should have been impossible to see through the heavily tinted glass. Testing his theory, Gabriel waved at the old man, and the old man waved back. A passing bus cut off his line of vision, and when the corner was visible again the old man was gone.

"Strange," Gabriel said to himself, absently stroking the area on his forearm where the trident had taken root. He could feel the waves of the tattoo rolling softly under his fingertips. When he looked at it he thought he could almost see the waves shifting beneath the malevolent trident, but it was only a trick of the shadows cast across his arm. Against his better judgment Gabriel let his guard down and tapped into the connection he shared with the magical relic. The magic answered in the form of the tattoo growing slightly brighter, but there was an emptiness to it that he couldn't place. Then it hit him. He couldn't hear the Bishop. Normally when he tapped into the magic he could feel the Bishop looming, but there was nothing. He wondered if it had had anything to do with the strange vision he had received earlier.

"How much farther to the Bat Cave, Morgan?" Rogue yawned.

"Not far at all," Morgan replied and turned his attention back to the road ahead.

"What's up with all this James Bond stuff? You're taking us to your hideout, but won't tell us where it is," Asha said.

"Because we still don't know how much we can trust you. For all we know any one of you could be a mole for the shitheads," Jackson told her.

Asha frowned. "Well, if that's the case, what would stop us from attacking you when we get to the secret location?"

Jackson smiled at the young witch. "Out here in the open you might have a chance, but not on our turf." He flicked his forearm blades out, then retracted them. "The fight would be over before it started."

"That one might be up for debate." De Mona raked her claws together and smirked.

Gabriel stared out the window, taking in the sights. He had passed through Queens a time or two, but had never bothered to give it much attention. The Hummer rumbled through a desolate area composed mostly of warehouses and lots. Above them loomed the gigantic letters that spelled out *Silvercup*. Seeing it brought back memories of *The Sopranos* reruns and other cheesy things that he had no business thinking about in light of his present crisis. He was possessed by a dead priest, bound to an ancient relic, and wanted by the police. His life had gone into a royal tailspin in the last twenty-four hours, but he no longer had the strength to care. All Gabriel could do was laugh and wonder how much further in the toilet his life would slip before it was all said and done.

"Share the joke. I wanna laugh too," Asha said.

"It's nothing," Gabriel lied.

Asha slid closer to him. "It doesn't seem like *nothing*. You've been slipping in and out for the whole ride. What gives?"

"I wish I knew." Gabriel rubbed his arm. "Lately I've been having trouble making heads or tails of stuff."

"It's the magic," Asha said. "Ever since I was a kid I was able to do stuff that most people couldn't, but it wasn't until I hit puberty that I really got a taste of what was coming. It can be hard when your powers mature faster than you do, and it can often be confusing. The thing that I've learned is that it's an easier transition if you stop fighting and let it in." Asha placed her hand on Gabriel's arm and immediately felt the power rush through her. "Own the magic, don't let it own you."

For a minute Gabriel allowed himself to find comfort in Asha's words, but the jolt from the transfer of magic brought him back to himself and he quickly snatched her arm away. "And what do you care? I find it hard to believe that you're just so god-awful concerned about me when you hardly know me. Just like everyone else I'm sure you've got an agenda too."

"Indeed I do," she said honestly. "The difference

between me and the rest of these jokers is that they're too chickenshit to just come out and say what's on their minds. I don't have those kinds of hang-ups. Wild magic, like what's running through you right now, is dangerous. It's gonna either cook you or cook us. Either way it isn't gonna end good if you don't show it who's boss, Gabriel." She leaned in close enough for him to feel the warmth of her breath on his cheek. From the slack look on his face he was unaware of the bit of magic she'd laced her words with. "I know some people, elders in the coven, who may be able to help you learn the control you're gonna need to carry that power around for the rest of your life."

"By making him a pawn of the Black King?" Rogue startled both of them. "Asha, we all know that every power monger close enough to have felt the Nimrod awaken is trying to figure out how to control it, including your king. I'm no big fan of Titus, but Dutch is running in a close second on my shit list. At least with the demons we know what to expect if they take control of the relic, but I'd hate to think what kind of trouble somebody as power hungry as Dutch would do with it."

"You don't know shit about Dutch, so watch your mouth," Asha snapped.

"I know more about your king than you do, little Blood witch. Dutch doesn't care about anything but power and gaining more of it. To him everybody is a pawn, including you."

Asha's jaw tightened and Azuma bared his fangs

at the mage. "You're wrong. Dutch took me in when everyone treated me like a leper."

"Yes, because you were powerful and vulnerable and he knew that he could take advantage of that. It's all shits and giggles now, but outlive your usefulness and see how far down the food chain you slide," Rogue warned. "Asha, I'm not gonna bother arguing with you about Dutch because there are more important things at stake here. We're going to help Gabriel, not turn him over to the greediest ruler. If you wanna help, that's fine. But if not I'll gladly kick that pretty ass of yours out at the next red light."

Magic flared in Asha's eyes. "Are you threatening me?"

"Not at all, love. I'm predicting the future." Rogue patted his guns and slid back into his seat.

"Let's cool it on the drama, kids. We're approaching the perimeter and any magical flare-ups will set off the security system. Trust me, you don't want that," Jackson said.

Asha almost caused Morgan to lose control of the car when she leaned over the front seat to get a better look and her hair gently brushed his shoulder. When she saw that there was nothing on the block but an old junkyard, she frowned. "Perimeter of what? There's nothing out here but trash!"

"Kick back and watch, shorty. You might learn something." Jackson winked before sliding out of the Hummer. When he got within ten feet of the tall fence the cameras mounted at their corners sprang to life and zeroed in on Jackson. He gave a sarcastic wave before beginning the numeric sequence that unlocked the gate. On the other side of the gate there was what looked like an old standing ashtray. Jackson flipped the lid back and fumbled with something, and the cameras went back into hibernation. Only when the flashing red lights had died did he wave the Hummer through.

"Figures they would make their base in a junkyard," Asha mumbled, watching the piles of debris they passed as Morgan drove deeper into the enclosure.

"If you'd prefer we could drop you on the street," Morgan said from behind the wheel.

"She was only joking. We're very grateful to have someplace safe to crash," De Mona said. She cut her eyes at Asha, who twisted her lips.

Jackson strode casually alongside the transport, fumbling with some kind of handheld device as he went. De Mona watched him curiously from the window of the Hummer. Jackson must have felt her eyes on him because he suddenly looked up and smiled. De Mona flipped him off and rolled the window up.

Along both sides of the narrow driveway were large mountains of trash and scrap metal. At the end of the driveway was a structure that resembled an airport hangar. It was almost half the size of the yard, with a domed roof and two gaping doors serving as the entrance. As the Hummer approached the doors they slid open to reveal what looked like a pit of darkness. Morgan spared a glance at the others through the rearview mirror and coasted into the hangar. When the doors closed behind them everything went dark. There was a brief humming before the hangar was illuminated by a faint red light. For all intents and purposes it looked no different than the interior of any other garage, but something about the place unnerved Fin.

Fin sat bolt upright and cast his terrified eyes out the window. "We shouldn't be here."

"Fin, what's wrong?" Lydia asked, startled by his sudden movement.

Finnious cupped Lydia's face and stared into her unseeing eyes. "Don't you feel it, Lydia? This place is bad."

Morgan tried to calm him. "My friend, I assure you that no harm will come to you here."

"No, no, this isn't right. Black magic clings to this place like dead skin." He unexpectedly grabbed Rogue by the arm. "You must make him take us away from here!"

"Calm down, son, everything is gonna be cool." Rogue scanned the hangar with his heightened vision. There were indeed dark threads of energy snaking around the place, but he could feel no immediate threat. On his second sweep of the hangar he spotted something: a robed man standing just in front of the Hummer who hadn't been there before. Rogue touched his gun for reassurance and glared at Morgan. "What's the deal, big man?"

Morgan put the Hummer in park. "Are all of you magicians so god-awful paranoid?"

"Only when it comes to snakes," Asha said. She too was clearly uneasy.

"Snakes? That was a good one." Jackson laughed as he held the back door open for them to get out of the Hummer.

"I'm not going out there," Finnious said.

"None of us are until we're sure what's going on." Lydia pulled Fin closer. She could not see the robed man, but she could feel the tension among the others.

Morgan turned and addressed his passengers. "You can all stay inside and debate theories or come out and be given a proper explanation. It makes no difference to me." He climbed from the vehicle and went to greet the robed man.

De Mona peered out the window at the exchange. She could see better in the dark than any of them, with the exception of Rogue, but for some reason she couldn't penetrate the darkness veiling the robed man's face. She turned to Gabriel, who seemed to be oblivious to their dilemma. "And what does our fearless leader say?"

"What?" Gabriel snapped out of his daze.

"How 'bout it, kid? You getting anything from the Bishop on this place?" Rogue asked.

Gabriel closed his eyes and tried to establish contact with the Bishop. The spirit was restless, but about what he either couldn't or wouldn't say. "I don't know," he said.

"That's reassuring," Asha mumbled. Azuma echoed her sentiment.

Jackson sighed. "Look, I know we've all been through some pretty weird crap, but now isn't the time to start getting all paranoid about each other. We risked our asses for you guys last night, so I think we've earned at least a little trust."

"Says you. For all we know this could be another ambush," De Mona accused.

"Right, we put ourselves on the shit list of every demon-worshiping sadist in the city just so we could lure you back here to kill you," Jackson said sarcastically. "If we wanted you dead then why didn't we just let Riel finish you off at the brownstone?"

"I don't know. Maybe you wanted to collect the bounty on our heads for yourself," De Mona shot back.

"Look, I'm getting a little tired of your mouth," Jackson told De Mona heatedly.

De Mona bared her fangs. "Then why don't you come close it for me?"

Jackson's blades appeared. "Gladly." He took a step toward the Hummer, but the sound of a gun being cocked gave him pause.

"Why don't you just calm down, son? No need to go getting yourself blasted," Rogue warned.

"*Blasting* him would only insure that you died here instead of out there fighting the real enemy."

Morgan approached the vehicle. His hammer was in his hand, but not in a threatening manner. "Now, we could all square off and leave it to fate or you could stop acting like a bunch of rattled children and come and meet your host. It was his decision for us to intervene so the least you could do is thank the man." Morgan hoisted his hammer onto his shoulder and walked away. Jackson followed a few paces behind.

An uncomfortable silence lingered in the truck. Everyone had their own opinion about how the situation should be handled, but because Rogue was holding the gun, Rogue was calling the shots. However, before he could make a decision Lydia spoke up.

"I trust him," she said. "They've bled for the order twice in a night. The least we could do is hear them out."

"Bad magic lives here," Fin said. He was trembling so badly that his form had begun fading in and out again. Lydia reached out to comfort him, but her hands passed through him.

"I'm with the little guy on this one. Rogue, there's definitely something lurking here," Asha said, glaring at the hooded man through the windshield. "We need to throw this baby in gear and haul ass outta here."

Rogue raised his eyebrow. "And go where? I don't know if you've noticed it or not, but there aren't many places we can go right now where Titus's people aren't looking for us," Rogue pointed out.

Gabriel's face twisted in frustration. "You guys can sit in here debating about it all you want, but if whoever this dude is can tell us how to save my grandfather then he's going to." Gabriel stepped defiantly from the truck.

"Gabriel!" Asha called after him, but the young man ignored her. She looked at Rogue, who just shrugged and got out as well. Asha sucked her teeth. "Out of the damn frying pan," she mumbled before following the mage.

Morgan, Jackson, and the hooded man were speaking among themselves when they noticed the young man approaching. The trident hadn't manifested, but Gabriel was giving off enough energy to illuminate the hangar. Morgan moved to step between Gabriel and the hooded man who waved him away.

"Let him pass," the hooded man said softly. "Welcome, Gabriel Redfeather. It is an honor to—"

"I wish I could say the same but I don't know you," Gabriel cut him off. "Who are you and where do you fit into all this?"

"Yes, where are my manners?" He pushed his hood back to reveal a face that was nothing like what any of them had expected. His skin was a moldy shade of green, with small sparkling scales slightly upraised about his cheeks and circling his rich brown eyes. Crowning his head were a half dozen snakes, which slithered about of their own accord. The robed man was no man at all, but a creature that looked like it had crawled out of Greek mythology. "I am Jonas."

De Mona was the first to snap out of the shock inflicted upon them by the sight of Jonas's face.

"I knew it was a freaking setup. I'm gonna waste you!" De Mona moved lightning quick, but Jackson was faster as he deflected her strike with one of his blades. She turned her rage on him, but it was an uncoordinated strike and before she could finish the motion he was behind her, holding the half-demon in a reverse choke hold.

Jackson slowly extended his blade and placed it against her throat. "As much as I want a taste of that sweet little ass of yours, this is hardly what I had in mind," he whispered. "Now why don't you relax?"

"You'd better let her go, or I'm gonna turn you into barbecue," Asha warned as she called her magic to her hands. The power crackled around her fists like water being dropped into hot grease.

Jackson moved De Mona to shield him. "Blast away, baby, and we'll see if her demon hide can take one of those souped-up bolts of magic you like to throw around."

"Last warning. Let her go or I'm going to let Azuma kick the shit outta you," Asha said, drawing a squawk of anticipation from the monkey.

Jackson gave the monkey an amused glance. "Sure, what's Cheetah gonna do? Claw my eyes out?" He laughed.

"I was thinking more along the lines of busting your skull open. Azuma"—Asha pointed a glowing hand at him—"attend your mistress!"

Azuma howled in pain as his body responded to his mistress's command. Sparks of magic leaped from his fur and he clawed at himself as if trying to fend off some internal enemy. They all watched in wide-eyed shock as the monkey's fur darkened and his body began to grow. When the transformation was complete Azuma was no longer a small monkey, but a salivating gorilla with bull horns jutting from its skull. Azuma looked down at Jackson and snarled.

"Oh, shit" was all Jackson had time to blurt out before everything went black.

CHAPTER FOUR

Azuma had palmed Jackson's face and thrown him across the room with the ease of a pebble, sending Jackson through the wall and out into the junkyard. Azuma let out a victorious roar so powerful that the walls of the hangar shook. The enraged primate locked Jonas in his sights and was charging in his direction when Morgan stepped between him with his hammer held firmly at his side. The gorilla snarled and slammed his fist against the ground, leaving two large holes at Morgan's feet, but the large man was unmoved by the performance.

With his hard eyes locked on the gorilla's, Morgan said, "Now that you've had your say, I'll have mine."

He hurled himself and the hammer at the gorilla's midsection with the speed of a bullet. The force knocked Azuma into the Hummer, stealing his breath, but it only slowed him for a moment before he was coming right back at Morgan. Jonas screamed for him to stop, but the battle rage made Morgan deaf to his pleas. He brought the hammer around in an arc and slammed it into the gorilla's chest before going back to his gut. The more he hit Azuma, the smaller the familiar seemed to get. By the time Azuma was back to his normal size he was hanging limply in Morgan's massive fist, breathing jaggedly. Still locked in the heat of battle, Morgan drew the hammer back for the death strike, but a bullet whistling past his ear drew his attention to the new threat.

"Enough," Rogue said, still pointing the smoking gun at Morgan. "Whenever I miss it's on purpose and never twice." He let the threat linger to make sure Morgan understood before turning back to Asha, who was lying on the ground unmoving. Blood ran from her nose and the corners of her eyes, but she was still alive. She moaned softly as Rogue and Lydia tried to sit her up.

When Morgan finally processed what he was seeing he took a worried step toward Asha, but De Mona cut him off. "I ain't going down as easy as that monkey did."

Morgan backed away to a respectable distance. Looking at Asha's battered form reminded him of how the demons had left him the night his wife and daughter were slaughtered. "But I never touched the girl. How did this happen?" he asked sadly.

"You didn't have to. It was her connection to the familiar." Jonas placed a reassuring hand on

Morgan's shoulder. Few knew of the connection between a witch and her familiar, but those who did knew that it was the lifeline of their power. Killing a bound familiar was as good as physically crippling the witch, or worse. "Gabriel"—Jonas turned to him—"we haven't brought you here to harm you. You have to believe me on that."

"And give us a good reason why we should?" Rogue stood and joined Gabriel, who was just studying Jonas curiously. "You walk us into a demon lair and nearly kill one of ours, and we should trust you? You and those snakes on your head must be hitting the pipe. We're getting out of here." Rogue pulled Gabriel toward Lydia and Asha, who was just getting to her feet.

"If you leave, you'll never solve the riddle of the trident or save Redfeather. I know the secret of the Bishop," Jonas called after him.

Rogue turned. "Oh yeah, and how did you come upon that information?" he asked.

"Because I was there when the Bishop was killed," Jonas admitted. This came as a shock to everyone, including Morgan. "It's a complicated story. If you'll all just please come inside, I will explain everything."

"And how are we to know you're not just bullshitting?" De Mona asked.

"You wouldn't, but he would." Jonas pointed at Gabriel.

"Me? Jonas, except for Rogue I don't know

anyone in this room from a can of paint. How am I supposed to know if you're telling the truth?" Gabriel asked.

The snakes on Jonas's head hissed to themselves as he glided closer to Gabriel. "Because of the magic." He nodded at the tattooed arm. "Magic that old can be lied to, but never fooled. If you call it, it will answer." Jonas extended his hand.

"Easy now." Rogue pointed his gun at Jonas.

"It's cool." Gabriel stepped forward. The Nimrod snaked from his arm like a wisp of smoke and materialized in his hand. When Gabriel looked up at Jonas it was with a young student's face, but he wore an expression Jonas hadn't seen in centuries.

"*Spin your lies, Medusan, but it changes nothing between us.*" The Bishop's words poured from Gabriel's lips, causing Jonas to step back.

Do not listen to the watcher. He will try and deceive you, the Bishop warned Gabriel.

"No more than you already have, I gather." Gabriel ignored the Bishop and reached for Jonas's hand. When their skin made contact Gabriel's mind was flooded with thousands of images that felt like they were ripping his brain to pieces. He saw Jonas whispering in the shadows with Titus and them casting some sort of spell. In the next image he saw the Bishop, bloodied and lying on a barren hill at the feet of Titus. That image melted away and he saw a city of glass being overrun by the hordes of Belthon with Titus leading the charge. Titus looked up, as if he could see Gabriel through the vision, and laughed. The image suddenly shattered, rocking Gabriel with pain and dropping him to one knee.

"The pain," Gabriel croaked.

There is no greater cleanser than the pain of the truth, boy. You'd do well to remember that, the Bishop told him. He said something else, but his voice trailed back to the distorted humming it had been earlier.

"I knew you were full of shit." De Mona extended her claws and stalked toward Jonas.

"No, it's okay." Gabriel raised his hand to stop her. With fire in his eyes he looked up at Jonas. "What happened?" he asked. When he tried to stand his legs were shaky, but Jonas helped to steady him.

"In due time, my friend. You've been through a great deal and need to rest. After you've had a chance to recover we'll speak more of what has passed and what will be."

"So what? We're just supposed to forget that he's a demon and that this jackass tried to kill Azuma?" Asha pointed at Jonas and Morgan respectively.

"Enough, Asha, they mean us no harm," Gabriel said.

Asha cut her eyes at Gabriel. "And what makes you such a good judge of character all of a sudden?"

"This." Gabriel tapped the Nimrod on the ground and sent a faint wave of magic through the room. "Asha, I'm just as leery about all of this as you guys, but I think Jonas may be able to help me better understand what this thing is and what it wants.

Once we figure that out we may actually stand a chance at stopping Titus."

"As much as I want to kick myself for saying so, he may have a point," Lydia said. "These guys have been at it a lot longer than we have so they may have some helpful insight as to the best way to stop the invasion."

"Or kill us when we let our guard down," Asha replied.

"Rogue, what do you think?" Lydia asked the mage.

"Like I said earlier, I think there's strength in numbers."

"A house divided," Finnious said.

Gabriel weighed the situation. "As much as I want to figure this Nimrod thing out I understand it's not just about me anymore. What happens from here on out affects all of us. If we move, then we move as a team."

Asha folded her arms. "So we're a team now?"

Gabriel looked around at the sea of faces, each waiting for him to reply. "Like it or not, destiny has forced us together to serve some greater purpose then feeling sorry for ourselves. I don't know about you guys, but I'm tired of running. It's time we took the fight to them."

"Then I guess it's settled." Rogue holstered his gun.

Jonas spread his arms and bowed from the waist. "Welcome and be recognized, Knights of Christ."

Just then the doors to the hangar flew open.

Jackson rushed into the room with both blades drawn. "Okay, you big-ass gorilla, let's see you try that . . ." His words trailed off when he noticed that the fighting had stopped and everyone was staring at him awkwardly. "What'd I miss?"

CHAPTER FIVE

After brokering an uneasy truce between Jackson and Azuma, Jonas led them to the back of the hangar. He knocked on the wall in a complex pattern and revealed a freight elevator behind the false wall. No one really trusted the pre-prohibition-looking thing, but it was the only way into the heart of the lair.

The elevator shook when it started its descent, throwing De Mona off balance and into Jackson's arms. When she looked up at his beaming face she quickly shrugged him off.

"You ain't the only chick to ever shrug me off and come to her senses after the fact," Jackson teased her.

De Mona rolled her eyes. "Please, I'd rather go down on a Stalker."

Morgan laughed. "That was a good one." He nudged Jackson playfully.

"Whose side are you on here, red?" Jackson asked him.

"Now, now, children, it's only a little while longer to the main level. The heart is just short of a mile below surface level," Jonas explained as the elevator came to an almost soundless stop.

"How can we have gone a mile when we've only been on the elevator for a few minutes?" Gabriel asked.

"Technology has come a long way over the years." Jonas placed his hand on the elevator door. "To someone to whom time means nothing, the possibilities are endless. Welcome to my workshop." Jonas slid the elevator door open and Gabriel's jaw dropped.

Stepping off the elevator was like stepping onto the bridge of the Starship *Enterprise*. The walls were all made from a smooth metal that looked like steel, but when you ran your hands along it, it felt more like solid rock. Whatever the material was, only Jonas knew. A tube ran the entire length of the walls and occasionally the group caught a glimpse of a ball of light that made its speedy rounds through the tubes. In the center of the room there was a high-backed black swivel chair with two complex control panels mounted on the arms. The northern wall was composed of dozens of small monitors, each showing real-time images of major intersections in New York City. The upper level of the lair was little more than the salvage yard it appeared to be, but the workshop was a marvel.

"You built all this?" Gabriel asked, examining one of the two stone gargoyles that sat on either side of the elevator door. To his surprise the stone was warm to the touch.

"Most of it. Some stuff had to be appropriated," Jonas admitted.

"Yeah, we had the five-finger discount," Jackson joked.

"Nice bling," Asha said, picking up a strange-looking necklace from one of the workstations only to have Jonas politely pluck it from her hands.

"That's no necklace, it's a restraint." Jonas pressed a button and a series of lights began flashing around the collar. He picked up a wristwatch that flashed in time with the lights on the collar. "We use these to control some of the nastier things we come across until we can figure ways of properly disposing of them."

"What the hell did you guys do, rob NASA or something?" De Mona asked, staring at the restraint.

"No, the Pentagon, but only for the hardware. The American government is by far one of the most advanced nations when it comes to weaponry, but they're still a few years behind compared to some of the other nations like Japan."

"I've never seen anything like it, not even in Sanctuary." Finnious marveled at all the equipment.

"And you probably never will, at least not in the near future. The technology itself was taken from many places, but the design is mine. Everything you see was built or modified by my hands," Jonas explained.

"I can't believe one person built all this," Gabriel said, still in awe of Jonas's workshop.

"I had a little help." Jonas nodded to Jackson and Morgan.

"So, what made you do all this?" De Mona asked. She was still trying to figure out what a creature as ancient as Jonas claimed to be would need or want with a computer, let alone a dozen of them.

"Because I realized that the battle between good and evil could no longer be fought with just wood and steel. As the times changed so did my methods of carrying out justice."

"How did this whole vigilante thing come about anyhow?" Rogue asked.

Jonas hesitated, searching for the right words. "It's a long story, but let's just say I was a victim of my own naiveté."

Asha shrugged. "Doesn't sound so bad to me."

"It is when your mistakes cost the lives of an entire species," Jonas said sadly. "When I watched my city and all its knowledge go up in flames, set burning by Titus and his lot, I wanted to do little more than lie down and die, but my rage fueled me to commit acts that I am none too proud of." The snakes on his head seemed to focus on De Mona when he said this. "I needed all who represented the evil that destroyed my people to suffer, and suffer they have at my hands. The vampires, Stalkers, demons, I'd track them to their resting places and destroy them. As I got better at it I would sometimes track down entire nests of the monsters and send them screaming back to hell."

"And you did all this by yourself?" Lydia asked. Her voice was heavy with sorrow.

"For the most part. From time to time I would come across others who felt as I did and wanted to aid me in my fight against the dark forces, but the relationships never lasted. They'd either fall victim to time and old age or the darkness while I remained, so I closed myself off and did my work alone. That was a lonely time for me, the first century or two on the path."

"So what made Morgan and Jackson so special that you stuck together?" De Mona asked.

Jonas smiled a bit. "You mean besides the fact that we were three souls who had lost everything? Much like me, Morgan is among the last of a dying race. We haven't been able to find out for sure, but there are said to be less than twenty of them left here or in Midland."

"Not that I'd care to be involved in their foolishness were we still a flourishing people," Morgan cut in. He didn't say it, but everyone could tell it was a sore spot for him.

"Morgan's people have been engaged in a very complicated civil war," Jonas explained.

"Why fight if there are so few of you left?" De Mona asked Morgan.

Morgan was about to tell her that it was none of her business, but when he looked into the girl's questioning eyes he couldn't help but to see flashes of himself. Who knew better than he what it was like to be abandoned by your own race and shunned by the one with whom you sought refuge? "For the same reason why jackals will still fight over the carcass of something that died more than a week ago: because that's what they're programmed to do. As far as I'm concerned it makes no difference whether Storm or Magma sits on the throne."

"What's Magma?" Finnious asked, but Lydia waved him silent so that Jonas could finish.

"I'll bet the fact that he's packing that hammer didn't hurt any either?" Asha chimed in.

Jonas chuckled. "No, the hammer has saved us more times than any of us care to recall. It has literally been the foundation of our crusade."

"And you, what do you bring to the table?" De Mona asked Jackson. There was no mistaking the challenge in her voice, but Jackson was never one to back down from a fight.

"Me." He stepped forward. "I do the stuff nobody else wants to." He flicked his blades and crisscrossed them.

"Jackson is somewhat of an oddity among us. I'm ashamed to say I haven't quite figured him out," Jonas said. "When you are infected with the vampire virus it ravages your body and devours your natural cells, which is why vampires must drink blood for the body to function. In Jackson it seems to have worked in reverse, with his cells feeding on the virus. Jackson possesses some extraordinary abilities, but we have yet to come up with a classification for him."

"But he has been infected, so doesn't that make him a vampire?" Lydia asked, a little more defensively than she intended to.

"I ain't no stinking vamp, so get that idea out of your head, little girl," Jackson snapped.

"I didn't mean to imply . . ."

"Nah, they never do. And let me make something clear to everybody right now." Jackson's eyes swept the room. His voice was heavy with emotion when he spoke. "Yeah, some vamps took a chunk outta my ass and left me to wake up a bloodsucker, but I didn't. Will the virus one day overrun my system and turn me?" He shrugged. "I don't know and honestly I'm not worried about it. Maybe I'll never completely turn or maybe I'll turn tomorrow, but it's not important. What is important is putting as many of these bastards to sleep as possible while I'm still here."

"And you'll be here for a long time to come, old friend," Morgan assured him. The big man hoisted the box holding Gilchrest and nodded at Jackson. "Why don't you come and help me stow this little bastard?"

Jackson gave one last look around the room to make sure he had made his point before following Morgan.

"I didn't mean to offend him, Jonas," Lydia said sincerely.

"Lydia, you didn't offend him. You just reminded him of the reality of his situation. None of us are without our shortcomings, but in time we will overcome, including Jackson," Jonas said. He looked at the large digital clock on the wall. "Come, we'll go into the next room and see what we can do about unraveling this mystery."

On the way into the next room Asha wandered over to the monitors and studied them. In a deserted alley somewhere in the Bronx was a shaggy-looking old man rummaging through some trash cans. He suddenly stopped his trash sifting and looked up. If Asha didn't know any better she would have sworn he was looking directly at the camera. The monitor went fuzzy for a second; when it cleared the old man was gone and the trash cans were undisturbed. Shaking off what she had just seen, she looked at the other monitors. She did a double take when she saw the one blinking in the top left corner. The camera was trained on the entrance of the Triple Six nightclub, which seemed to be unusually abuzz for that time of day considering it didn't open until after dark. Asha was trying to make heads or tails of what was going on when the Big Bad Witch herself came storming out. She didn't look happy.

Angelique's long fur coat blew in the morning breeze while two witches whom Asha didn't know by name tried to grovel and keep pace with her at the same time. Asha could see the last remnants of magic fading from Angelique's eyes, so she knew her presence at the Triple Six hadn't been social. The Triple Six was a SoHo club that catered to the supernatural, but it was also the haven of the Black Court.

"I wonder what could be wrong with her," a voice called behind Asha. She turned to see Rogue also watching the monitor over her shoulder, observing Angelique. She was the queen of the White Court and at times the consort of the Black King Dutch.

"I haven't the slightest idea," Asha said, and turned away from the monitor.

"Bullshit. Asha, what's Dutch's angle in all this, seriously?"

Asha frowned. "My king's business is his business."

Rogue shook his head. "That dude sent you on a suicide mission and you're still covering for him? I didn't know that the new followers of the Black Court were so naive these days."

Asha frowned at the insult. "Dutch trusts me to be his eyes and ears on the streets because I'm the most qualified witch for the job. Unlike Angelique's bunch, I don't shun the darkness. I command it." She raised the dagger she always carried. It was as black as night with a hilt carved from the bone of an infant. The cursed blade was the only thing she had left to remember her mother by.

"And who commands you?" Rogue took Asha by the arm and steered her toward the corner where they could speak privately. "Let's talk turkey, girlie, because my patience is sure gonna run thin soon. I know Dutch is either stupid or crazy enough to go after the Nimrod, but we both know that Angelique wouldn't touch magic that black with a ten-foot pole. From the look on her face when she came out of the Triple Six, Dutch has done something to piss her off, and nine times outta ten it has to do with the Nimrod. What's good?"

Asha glared up at him and sighed. "Everybody with a line to the inside knows the Nimrod's in New York, so it's only natural for the major players to make a bid for it. I was sent out to find out what had caused the disturbance and bring my findings back to Dutch. I didn't know anything about Gabriel or that fancy pig poker until he showed up at his buddy's apartment last night."

"And where does Angelique fit into this?" he pressed her.

"I told you I don't know."

"Is everything okay?" Jonas called. All eyes had suddenly turned to the whispering magicians.

"Right as rain," Asha replied. She went to rejoin the group but Rogue grabbed her by the arm.

"Asha, you know I can't let you take that thing back to Dutch."

She gave him a faint chuckle. "After what I saw it do, I'm not sure I even want to."

As Asha walked away from the screen two more familiar faces came into view and entered the Triple Six.

CHAPTER SIX

Dutch wore the expression of a worried man. For the last hundred years, under one name or another, he had been the undisputed ruler of the Black Court and one of the most powerful spell casters in the world. But that morning he felt like he had as a child when he would nervously wait for his father to come home and beat him for one thing or another. His normally immaculate office was in a state of disarray. Papers were strewn everywhere and there was glass all over the floor and embedded in his antique desk. Better his furniture than his flesh, he reasoned, because it could have just as easily played out that way. His greed had forced him to make a grave mistake, and now he was left with the puzzle of how to fix it.

Something very ancient and very powerful had been awakened in New York. All who were gifted enough in the blood felt the magic sweep across the city, a force so powerful that it made some of the most ancient inhabitants in New York take refuge elsewhere. The smart ones avoided the disturbance, but Dutch sought to control it . . . so he had called upon his prized pupil, Asha.

Dutch had dispatched the young Huntress on a secret mission to solve the mystery and claim the power for the Black Court. By the time the other three courts even realized what was happening, Dutch would control it all. But something had gone wrong.

Lucy Brisbane had thumbed her nose at her mother's legacy since she was old enough to form an opinion, but it still didn't change the fact that she was royalty at the White Court. Now she was dead and Asha was the suspect. The two girls had hated each other since their earliest days at court, and the rivalry only became more intense as they got older. Dutch found it hard to believe that it had become fatal, but Angelique wouldn't have made the accusation unless she was sure. Blood magic had been used at the scene of the crime and though there were a few blood witches left in the city, Asha was the only one skilled enough to kill with the craft. The only reason he didn't find himself under siege at the moment was because of Lucy's familiar. The agents of the White Court had found the thing alive at the scene of the crime. The ferret was in some sort of coma, so they hadn't learned anything from it. The fact that it still lived improved the odds that Lucy may still be alive, but didn't guarantee it. The bond between familiar and witch was a powerful one, but it was not unheard of for one to live after the other had passed.

Angelique demanded answers and so did Dutch, though he wasn't sure he wanted them aired in public. What he had planned could have been considered treason if it ever got out. The letting of one secret could very well have led to the letting of others and Dutch wasn't quite ready for that. He had to find Asha before Angelique's people did and silenced her.

"Goddess, what happened in here?" Lisa stepped through what was left of the enchanted mirror that had once been the entrance to Dutch's office. Her sister, Lane, followed closely behind her. Each had a wolf spider perched on her shoulder, one of an overcast gray and one almost transparent. The spiders were familiars, conduits between the witches and their magic.

Dutch dislodged a large piece of glass from his desk and pointed it at Lisa. "In case you hadn't noticed, I'm having a terrible morning and looking for someone to vent my frustrations on."

"Forgive my common sister, my king." Lane executed a half bow.

Dutch waved her off. "I'll let you kiss up later. Right now I need information. What did you find out?"

"It looks like Ground Zero down there," Lisa said with a tinge of sorrow in her voice. "Sanctuary was little more than a pile of rubble with wild magic flowing everywhere. Angelique's best people were out there to do damage control, but even they had a hard time keeping everything contained to the immediate area. Anyone with a nose could tell the pieces of rotted flesh that were strewn around belonged to Stalkers."

"And the rumors of the goblins coming topside?" he asked, not sure he really wanted the answer.

Lisa looked to her sister Lane, who picked up the tale. "Had to be, because there was barely anything left of the human and demon carcasses we found and most of them were missing their hearts. If those things have decided to come out of their caves and dance up here, then it's safe to say we've got a serious problem."

Dutch placed his head in his hands and cursed under his breath. Since he'd first arrived on the shores of New York, the tunnels below the city had been inhabited by goblins. They mostly kept to their mountains under the zoo, but once in a great while they would prey on the unfortunate who were foolish enough to take shelter in New York's vast tunnel system. They cared little for what went on topside and that suited everyone just fine. For them to come aboveground in full force and level the oldest building in the city, the situation must be graver than he'd thought. Dutch had seen firsthand the brutality of the goblins when they ravaged a kingdom, and if Orden had designs on the city then the End of Days was surely upon them.

"And Asha?" Dutch questioned.

Lane shrugged. "She was definitely there, because traces of her magic are all over the place, but there was no sign of her. Do you think the goblins got her?"

"I fear it's far worse than that," Dutch said, a wicked plan forming in his head. "What I am about to share with you must never leave this room, do you understand?"

"Of course, my king," they said in unison.

Dutch paused dramatically. "I have reason to believe that our sister has broken the circle."

"What?" Lisa asked in shock.

"No way, man. Asha is as loyal to the circle as any," Lane insisted.

"I felt the same way when the evidence was presented to me, but in light of what happened last night I can no longer turn a blind eye to the God's truth," Dutch said in a pained tone. "Last night, something powerful was handed over to the order, and they chose to safeguard it against the sorcerers, who had been planning to use it to conquer the world. Retrieving the item was the secret mission Asha was on last night."

Lisa's eyes watered, but no tears fell. "Not Asha. She's one of us."

Dutch came from around his desk and stood between the sisters. He placed a calming hand on Lisa's cheek, but spoke to Lane. "One of us, but not of the blood." Asha's mother had been a Voundon priestess who had murdered Asha's warlock father when he revealed that he wanted nothing to do with her or the child growing inside her. Asha's mixed blood and the crime her mother had committed had followed her like a dark shadow all her life. The coven had adopted her, but they had never really accepted her until Dutch welcomed her into the Black Court and made her part of the Hunt.

"For years we've all turned a blind eye to the impurity of her blood and I fear our love for our sister has come back to haunt us," Dutch continued. "We all know how powerful Asha is on her own, so I shudder to think of what she would be capable of if she possessed an item of such power and if she turned to the sorcerers to strengthen her position. It could very well mean the end of the entire circle of magicians, because we would surely all be slaves again if they come into power." Dutch let his eyes water up for effect.

"I'd die before becoming a slave," Lane said defiantly.

"As would we all, but I fear we won't have much of a choice if Asha takes the item to them. She must be dealt with," Dutch told the sisters.

"What are you saying?" Lisa looked at him in shock.

Dutch's eyes were cold. "I think you know what I'm saying. Asha must be brought to justice for her treachery."

"But it's Asha. She's part of the Hunt." Lisa said, disbelieving.

Dutch inhaled slowly and as he did Lisa felt the breath being sucked from her. "Traitors have no place in the circle and especially not in the Black Court."

"Enough!" Lane called her magic, but held off on attacking Dutch. She knew that she was no match for the Black King, but she wouldn't let him kill her sister. Thankfully Dutch released his hold on Lisa and she collapsed.

Dutch leaned against his desk and spoke sternly to the sisters. "Not even personal feelings must come before the well-being of the coven. Asha has betrayed us and must be punished. As members of the Hunt you are bound by duty and honor to dispatch justice when a crime against us is committed. To not uphold these responsibilities would mean to fall out of favor with your king. Is this your decision?"

Lisa and Lane exchanged knowing glances. Asha had been like a sister to them, but Dutch was their king. If they refused him then they would both be dead within seconds, if they were lucky. "No, my king," Lane answered for them.

"Good." He nodded. "I know it's a hard thing that I ask of you, but your loyalty will not go unrewarded. Destroy Asha and bring me the item she was sent for and I will make you my Mistresses of the Hunt."

This got both their attention. To be Mistress of the Hunt was one of the highest honors bestowed upon a witch or warlock. It was the king and queen who ruled the covens, but it was the Hunt that held the real power. As highly coveted as the Mistress of the Hunt position was, it was coming at a heavy price.

"Your will be done, my king," Lane finally said before helping her sister to her feet. "We'll find Asha and this thing you're looking for. What is it?"

Dutch smiled. "You'll know it when you see it."

As soon as Lisa and Lane had left his office, Dutch picked up the phone. He knew that the two girls were very skilled at what they did, but there were no guarantees that they could pull off what he'd asked of them and Dutch couldn't leave anything to chance. The Nimrod resurfacing right in his back-yard was both a blessing and a curse. Dutch had tasted the power of the relic many years ago, but it had come at a price, a price that he had avoided paying for many years. It might be time for him to pay that debt. If he wanted to guard his secrets, he had to make sure he had plans within plans.

The phone rang four times before a female voice finally came on the line. "M.T.C., how may I direct your call?"

Angelique sat in the high chair in her personal study pinching the bridge of her nose in frustration. For hours she had been watching closed-circuit video, poring over reports of the last few nights' events, and she was still no closer to finding out what had happened to her students.

At the request of the high brothers of Sanctuary she had sent her most skilled healer, Sulin, to deal with some unknown injury to a high-ranking member of their order. It should have been a simple assignment, but something had gone wrong. The Great House was attacked and her students were caught in the crossfire. Now Sulin and most likely Lucy were dead, and Angelique had no one to blame but herself.

She had felt the disturbance when it first hit the city, but she'd ignored it as some passing anomaly. In a city like New York there was always one catastrophe or another plaguing its inhabitants, and she didn't see any reason to pay this one any more attention than she did the others. To Angelique, matters outside of coven business were no concern of hers. Unlike Dutch, Angelique had no desire to engage in the petty power struggles of the supernatural. It was her separatist thinking that caused her to miss the writing on the wall and because of it two of her students had been made to suffer.

Thinking of her counterpart, the Black King, made her blood boil. She couldn't yet prove it, but she knew that if she dug deep enough she would find Dutch's prints all over the mystery of her missing students. She knew that Dutch sometimes operated outside the laws that governed the covens, but she'd never expected him to stoop to order the assassination of one of her students. Still, she couldn't deny the fact that there were heavy traces of blood magic all over the crime scene and Asha was the only one skilled and powerful enough at it to leave such heavy traces. If Asha was found to have had a hand in the murder of her students, she would die and her king would follow her into the afterlife shortly thereafter.

Sulin's death represented a great loss to the coven, but it was Lucy's misfortune that struck a personal chord with Angelique. Lucy was by far the most rebellious and troublesome of her students, but also the most promising. Lucy's natural ability for spell casting was remarkable and with the proper training she would have one day made an excellent successor to Angelique. Angelique had promised Lucy's mother, Wanda, as much before she died. She had promised the former queen that she would watch over her daughter if anything ever happened to her, a promise she had failed to keep. The thought of her girls being gone brought tears to Angelique's eyes.

"Sister, forgive me," Angelique said, running her finger over the photo of her and Wanda as teenagers that she kept on her desk.

"Is everything all right, Mistress?" Marsha asked, startling Angelique. She was a thin, pale girl with mouse-brown hair that she kept cut in a bob. She wasn't much in the way of a spell-caster, but she was a gifted scientist and fanatically loyal to Angelique.

Angelique wiped the tears away with the back of her white robe. "I told you that I wasn't to be disturbed!" She shot to her feet.

Marsha shrank back. "I'm sorry, Mistress, but you said that I should let you know if there was a change in the familiar's condition."

"Is he awake?" Angelique asked in anticipation of finally getting some answers as to the whereabouts or conditions of her students.

"No, but he's started bleeding off magic." By this she meant excess magic was rolling off the rodent like heat waves.

Angelique's eyes registered shock. "What?"

"It started about fifteen minutes ago and has been slowly draining ever since," Marsha explained.

"You keep that familiar alive until we can find out if Lucy still lives or not," Angelique ordered.

"I'll do what I can," Marsha assured her.

"You'll do more than that if you value your life. Now go back to your work." Angelique sat down and went back to her reading, but Marsha didn't move. "Is there something else?"

"Yes, Mistress. As you instructed I had some people watch the Triple Six. The two Huntresses, Lisa and Lane, took a meeting with Dutch and then rushed off somewhere. We had a tail on them, but she lost them on the Cross Bronx."

This got Angelique thinking. "Now why would Dutch be meeting with his Hunt at this hour of the morning, unless he's trying to hide something?"

"Or silence *someone*," Marsha offered.

Lisa and Lane didn't say a word until they were out of the Triple Six and several blocks away. They knew that Dutch had eyes and ears everywhere and they didn't need anyone eavesdropping on what they were about to discuss.

"I don't like this," Lisa said, breaking the silence.

"Me neither," Lane agreed. "I can't believe Asha has turned on us."

Lisa looked at Lane in shock. "You're buying that cow dung Dutch was shoveling in there?"

Lane thought about it. "Don't you? Come on, Lisa, you've seen how Asha has been acting lately."

"She's not the only one that's been acting strange. For the last few nights it seems like everyone in the city has been on edge about something. It's obviously tied into whatever Dutch is busting his brain trying to find," Lisa replied.

"Listen, I don't care if it's a mystic disturbance, drug-induced rage, or swine flu; if you break the laws of the coven, then the Hunt is sent for you. It's our job, remember?"

"Some freaking job," Lisa mumbled.

"Look, if you want you can go in there and tell Dutch to piss off, but I'm inclined to live a little longer. I know your feelings are all caught up in this, but look at the bigger picture, sis. If we bring in Asha, then we command the Hunt. Most witches don't get that kind of power until they're at least twice our ages, if ever. I say it's too big to pass on."

"But she's one of us," Lisa said weakly.

Lane took her by the shoulders and turned her so that they were eye to eye. "But not of the blood. I can't do this without you, sister. Are you in or out?"

Lisa kept her eyes glued to the floor. "I'm in," she said shamefully.

"Good. Now let's get started. We've got a lot of ground to cover if we wanna catch up with Asha before she realizes we're on to her and fries us."

"Could you spare some change, young ladies?" an old man asked as he came stumbling out of the alley. His clothes were tattered and he smelled like stale urine on a summer day.

"Get a job, degenerate." Lane pushed past the old man.

Lisa reached into her pocket and handed him some crumpled bills. "Don't spend it all at the liquor store."

"Thank you kindly, ma'am." The old man waved as the witch walked away.

He stared at the bills in his hand and closed his fist around them. When he opened his hand again several butterflies fluttered from it. "Soon the ugly duckling will discover the swan hiding beneath," he said before disappearing back into the alley.

CHAPTER SEVEN

"The prisoner has been secured," Morgan said as he entered the workshop, where everyone was gathered around the table. Jackson followed closely behind. He was no longer scowling, but the pain was still in his eyes.

They had locked Gilchrest in one of the cells they had on the lower levels for the rare occasions that they took captives. Morgan looked over at Asha, who was tending to Azuma. The familiar kept giving him dirty looks. He wanted to say something to the girl, but thought better of it and joined the rest of the group around the worktable.

"It has been almost four hundred years since I last saw this thing, and never like this," Jonas said, examining the tattoo on Gabriel's forearm, careful not to touch it. Even without making contact he could feel the malevolent energy pulsating from the tattoo.

An icy finger of power slithered up Gabriel's arm. He rubbed it, but couldn't seem to generate any heat. "The Bishop doesn't seem to like you very much."

"I wouldn't expect him to, since he blames what happened on me."

Rogue gave him a quizzical look. "What gives with that, Jonas? We all know the story of the Seven-Day Siege, and the legends say it was Titus who betrayed the Bishop."

"Yes, but it was me who opened the window of opportunity." Jonas walked over to the corner and retrieved a lead box. He placed the box on the table and motioned for everyone to gather around. "If we are going to trust each other, there can be no secrets among us," he said, wiping away a film of dust. Along the edges and on the lid of the box there was an inscription in a language that was familiar to none of them except Jonas, as it was the language of his people.

Gabriel moved closer to inspect the box. As with the Nimrod, the letters swelled and became legible to him. *"Only the worthy shall ever behold the strands of fate and not be driven to madness.* What does that mean?" He looked to Jonas.

"It was a saying among my people, when I still had a people." With a wave of his hand Jonas undid the lock and the lid sprang open. From it he pulled a small spindle that was crisscrossed with threads of every shade, from richest gold to darkest night.

Rogue's eyes widened as his heightened sight showed him the truth of what he was seeing. "The Strands of Time."

"Not quite. Only an interpretation." Jonas ran his finger delicately down one of the stands. The movement caused flakes of stardust to fall to the table. "These strands represent what has passed, what is, and sometimes what may be, though I have no control over any. They were the responsibility of my order until Belthon's soldiers wiped us out and destroyed the magic. This," he said, cradling the spindle tenderly, "is all that is left."

To everyone's surprise, Finnious walked over to Jonas and touched his arm. "What happened?"

"Foolish pride." Jonas strummed the strands, sending a mist of sparkling dust into the air. As they looked on, images began to form in the mist. "I am the last surviving member of the Medusan, a race of creatures who were chosen by the fates to accurately record the passage of time." Jonas picked up a screwdriver off the work bench and tossed it into the air. The screwdriver flipped end over end before eventually slowing to a crawl, guided by Jonas's outstretched hand.

"You can control time?" Rogue asked curiously.

Jonas waited until the screwdriver had almost reached the bench before releasing his hold and allowing it to embed itself in the table near the spindle. "No, but I can manipulate small fragments of it when I tap the power of the spindles. If my race could control time or fate, we may have been able to stop our own destruction."

Jonas blew the dust softly and the image shifted. "Belthon's men petitioned the Medusan to aid them in their conquest of humanity, but we refused. As is decreed by the fates, we are never to interfere with the affairs of man or demon, only record them. When we refused they began hunting the Medusan and butchering them. We petitioned the Knights to help us, but the Bishop was too consumed with eradicating the demons to think of anything else. There were even whispers among some of his Knights about the man's obsession. It was Titus who came to me and said that he had a way to end the war and save all our people. He claimed that he could get the support of the church to broker a truce, but he could not execute his plan while the Bishop still wielded the Nimrod."

"So you used your powers over time to help him steal it." Gabriel recalled the image he had seen of Jonas near the Bishop's tent.

Jonas nodded. "At the time I knew nothing of the Bishop's bargain with Belthon, or Titus's plans of betrayal. As you all know, it was Titus who slew the Bishop and it was Redfeather who turned the tide of the battle, but what you do not know is the aftermath of my foolishness. My people were wiped out and the magic of the spindles consumed by the darkness. All I wanted to do was stop innocent people from being slaughtered, but instead the Medusan ended up on the chopping block. Titus let me live as a walking reminder of what I had caused, but sparing my life is a mistake I vowed to make him regret." There was fire in Jonas's eyes when he said this.

"Sounds like you've got as much reason as any of us to want to get at Titus," De Mona said. She had been standing in the corner, quietly listening to the tale.

"Which is what we've been trying to tell you," Morgan spoke up. "If Titus seizes the day then every living thing will suffer the fate of the Medusan."

"That's not going to happen while I still have a say in it," Gabriel declared.

Spoken like a true Knight of the cross, young Hunter. Your foolish heart may even be bigger than that of your meddling ancestors, the Bishop whispered.

"Yes, but unlike my ancestors I'm going to finish this thing for good."

"You feeling okay, kid?" Rogue asked, seeing Gabriel seemingly talking to himself.

"The Bishop mocks him," Jonas answered for Gabriel. Gabriel gave Jonas a puzzled look, since he thought no one but he could hear the spirit. "No, I cannot hear him, nor am I reading your mind, but the spindle has shown me certain things in order to better aid you in stopping the Bishop and Titus in their insane quests. I know the Nimrod better than even the Bishop thinks."

"Then you know a whole lot more than I do, and I'm sharing my body with this warped dude," Gabriel said. "Jonas, do you think you and the spindle could help me figure out what this thing wants? Maybe if I know that we'll have a better idea of how to stop the invasion."

The snakes on Jonas's head hissed softly as his face darkened. "You are but a vessel for the Bishop and his twisted mistress, the Nimrod."

"I'm nobody's pawn," Gabriel's voice was sharp.

"Aren't you? We all are pawns in the Bishop and Titus's sick games. The spindle has shown me a great many things, but I fear the best course of action in stopping what is coming wasn't one of them."

"So, what are we supposed to do? Fly in blind and hope Titus doesn't mop the floor with us?" Asha asked, cradling Azuma like a child. The monkey was conscious again but still suffering from the beating Morgan had given him.

"Of course not. You are all gifted with great powers, but it is Gabriel who will be the glue that binds them together. As the leader of the Knights, it is he who must lead you into battle against your enemies."

"Me? I've been getting pushed around since I was a kid. What do I know about being a leader?" Gabriel sounded disheartened.

Morgan placed a reassuring hand on his shoulder. "The man I saw strike down our attackers hardly seemed like a pushover. There is a little hero hiding in us all, Gabriel. It's just a matter of finding him."

Gabriel chuckled. "I wouldn't even know where to start looking."

"And that's why you have been led here. I believe that the spindle can answer a great deal about what we have been chosen to do. But to truly understand who you are becoming, you must understand who you were."

"That's easy, a nobody. Until all this stuff started I had never been a blip on anybody's radar," Gabriel said.

"Even Jesus started out as just a carpenter," Jackson reminded him.

Rogue looked at Jackson oddly. "You know, as twisted as it sounds coming from him, it actually makes sense."

"The wisdom of fools," De Mona mumbled, to which Jackson flipped her off.

Gabriel cut his eyes at De Mona. "You're awful opinionated all of a sudden, considering you brought this on our heads."

"Gabriel, that's not fair," De Mona said.

"Isn't it? De Mona, you knew what that thing was before you brought it to me. You let me walk blindly into a shit storm that took everything I had: my life, my home, my grandfather. Jesus, you might as well have just walked into that library and killed me instead of dragging it out." He hadn't meant to be so harsh but his feelings of hopelessness had him frustrated.

De Mona turned her moonlit eyes on him. "You know, I'm about sick of you trying to heap this pile of shit on me like I intended any of it to happen." De Mona raked her claws along the table as she moved closer to Gabriel. Hostility came off her in waves. "The only reason I even brought the Nimrod to you was because your grandfather's name was on my father's lips when he died. I was scared shitless, angry, and alone, so *please* excuse me for coming to the one person whom my father felt would make everything okay. I know you blame me for all this and I can't say that I disagree with you, but placing blame ain't gonna bring my dad back or do jack shit for your grandfather. I don't even care who's to blame anymore. What I *do* care about is taking it to these fools and making sure that our people didn't go out for nothing." De Mona extended her hand. Her face was hard from the change that always seemed to loom near the surface, but her eyes said she was tired of arguing. Gabriel hesitated, but accepted her truce and shook her hand.

"Jonas, you said that the spindle can give us some insight. How?" Gabriel asked.

Jonas patted Gabriel on the back. "It has its ways, but the process will take some time. In the meantime you need to rest, all of you. We've prepared the bunkers for you to use while you're with us."

"They ain't the Ritz, but you don't have to worry about nobody trying to kill you in your sleep," Jackson offered.

"I can't go to sleep while the goblins have my grandfather. Even now they could be torturing him while we're in here mapping strategies," Gabriel said heatedly.

"As greedy for flesh as the goblins are, Titus knows your grandfather is their only lead to the Nimrod. His life is safe, but for how long I can't say," Jonas told him.

"Then we need to come up with a plan of attack sooner rather than later," Rogue said, tucking in his shirt. He still looked a hot mess, but the gesture was more out of habit than anything else. "I've got some leads I need to follow up on."

"I'll go with you," Gabriel offered.

"No. Like Jonas said, you need to rest."

"C'mon, Rogue. If those things come at you again you might need the Nimrod. You've seen what it can do."

"Yes, I've seen what it can do, and it also attracts a lot of unwanted attention," Rogue reminded him. "I need to move quickly and quietly and I can't do that worrying about you getting hurt or drawing Titus's people to us like flies to shit." Rogue saw the look of hurt on Gabriel's face. He hadn't meant to bruise the young man's ego. "Gabe"—he placed a hand on his shoulder—"no matter what anyone says about all this, you are our leader and we gotta keep you safe. If the Nimrod falls, we don't stand a chance at saving the world. You'd serve us better by staying here and working with Jonas and the spindle to understand your role in all this."

Gabriel nodded that he understood, but clearly didn't like it.

"Don't worry, G. I'll make sure he stays outta

trouble," Asha spoke up. Though everyone seemed to be warming to Jonas's hospitality, she still didn't trust him and was reluctant to stay closed up in their base.

Rogue scowled at her. "Didn't you hear what I just told the kid? It's bad enough that I gotta watch my own ass out there. I can't afford to be responsible for someone else too."

"Then let's be the eyes in the back of each other's heads. Regardless of how you feel about me, you can't deny the fact that I kick ass in a fight. We've both got contacts out there that might be able to give us a leg up on Titus, so why not work together?" It was clear Asha was not likely to be swayed from her stance.

"She's got a point, Rogue," Gabriel said.

Rogue glared at him. "Oh, so *now* you're interested in calling the shots?"

"I'm not calling the shots; I'm just doing the math. If something does happen to get the drop on you, it'd be best if you weren't alone. I need you to stay alive long enough to help me rescue my grandfather," Gabriel said.

"All right, you win," Rogue said, still not looking happy. He turned to Asha. "Before we head out let me make something very clear to you. You stay close to me, and if I tell you to do something you do it without a moment's hesitation, you understand?"

"Yes, daddy." Asha blew him a playful kiss.

"You can take Jackson too," Jonas offered.

Jackson's head snapped up at the mention of his name. "Hold on, I didn't say anything about wanting to join in on this remake of *Cannonball Run*."

"You didn't have to. I know you'd like nothing more than to honor your oath, which is to protect humanity," Jonas said in a flat tone.

"Ain't neither of them human!" Jackson pointed out.

Asha stuck her middle finger up, but Rogue ignored the remark.

"And who of us are?" Morgan stepped up. "I know better than any of us that all blood runs the same at the mercy of our enemies." He cut his eyes at Jackson when he said this. "Rogue, Asha, I'm with you if you'll have me."

Rogue just nodded before heading for the door. Asha took a minute to examine the jeweled hammer in Morgan's thick fist. "You might prove useful."

"Gabriel, stay at the compound while we're gone. I don't have to tell you what's waiting for you out there, do I?" Rogue asked.

Gabriel laughed. "Hardly, Rogue. The police want me locked away, the forces of hell want me dead, and the Bishop wants me to be a vegetable. I think I've run out of people to piss off."

Jonas nodded in approval. "Then it's settled. Morgan will accompany Rogue and Asha while we try and devise a plan of attack. Jackson, would you please escort our guests to the bunker? I'll be in my study; there is much to do and little time in which to do it."

"Right this way, kids." Jackson led them back to the elevators.

Gabriel followed Jackson, but he did so reluctantly. He felt like a coward for hiding in the underground bunker while his grandfather was suffering in the Iron Mountains, and it left a bad taste in his mouth. Since he had lost his parents he had watched his grandfather make sacrifices for him, and it was time that he returned the favor. Nothing would stop him from rescuing his grandfather, even if he had to face the horrors of the Iron Mountains alone.

CHAPTER EIGHT

"This way!" Cristobel shouted, hanging a hard left at the end of the corridor they were sprinting down. As they rounded the corner an arrow pierced the wall just above Lucy's head.

In the blink of an eye the situation for Lucy, Redfeather, and their guide/hostage went from bad to worse. Before the little dwarf could be silenced, he had successfully thwarted their quiet escape. Brutus had been a frightening opponent, but the creatures on their heels were much worse.

"Do these things ever tire?" Redfeather spared a glance over his shoulder and saw at least half a dozen goblins hot on their heels.

"No." Cristobel barely dodged the arrow aimed at his heart. "The servants' entrance isn't much farther. If we make it there we can escape into the woods. This way." He motioned but stopped in his tracks when he saw the goblin blocking their path. He was a hulking creature with an enormous head and four arms, each holding a weapon.

"Come, little vermin, come to Vez." the monster waved them on.

"We're trapped!" Redfeather stopped in his tracks.

"We're all doomed." Cristobel shook his head sadly.

"The hell we are," Lucy said, picking up speed. "Come on, baby, I need you," she called to her magic. Lucy leaped into the air, waving her hands in a complex pattern as she sailed over Vez's head and landed on the other side. When he turned toward her his head rolled off his shoulders and onto the ground, followed by two of his limbs. "Thank you, Goddess."

"Don't be so quick to offer up your thanks." Cristobel pointed down the hall, where a second group of goblins were joining in the chase. They were now trapped.

"Then we fight." Redfeather pried a broadsword from Vez's dead hand and motioned for Cristobel to take up the ax.

"There're too many of them. This way." Lucy yanked Redfeather and Cristobel down another hallway. She had no idea where she was going, but she felt wind coming from the corridor she chose and wind usually meant *outside*. She could see an archway that opened up outside and her heart swelled with hope, knowing that her guess had been correct. The hope soon died when she realized her error. The steps that had once led to the small exit were broken and it was at least a fifty-foot drop into what looked like a river of raw sewage.

Redfeather peered over the ledge. "I don't suppose you could conjure a spell to help us get out of this, could you?"

Lucy flexed her hands but didn't feel much more than a slight vibration. "My magic is still shorting in and out, but even if I did have my full powers I wouldn't be able to levitate all of us to safety."

"We're going to have to jump," Cristobel said, adjusting his grip on the ax.

"Then go. I'll hold them off until you two clear the river and make it to shore." Redfeather took a defensive stance as the first of the goblins became visible at the mouth of the corridor.

"No dice. We're not leaving you here to face them. We all jump at the same time or we don't do it," Lucy said. Though she hardly knew the old man, circumstances had bound them. Her conscience would never rest if she left him to the mercy of the goblins.

"We can't. One of us has to hold them off just long enough for you to get to shore or we'll be sitting ducks for their archers. Now, stop arguing with your elder and go." Redfeather pushed Lucy through the archway. She hit the sludge below awkwardly, but she composed herself quickly and made for the shore.

"Your turn, my friend," Redfeather told Cristobel.

The dwarf stared up at him with a look of both curiosity and sadness. "I've only heard of this level of bravery in the stories of what we once were."

"Then let my example kindle the spark of what

you can be again. Now, go. Lucy may need your help." Cristobel nodded, but he was hesitant. "I'll be right behind you," Redfeather assured him. Before Cristobel made his jump, Redfeather had another thought. "If by chance I don't make it, protect the girl and help her to escape these mountains and find my grandson. He and his friends have the means to help."

Cristobel nodded. "We will wait for you on the banks," he promised, and leaped.

With his friends safely away, Redfeather turned to face his enemies. The first goblin to come within striking distance lost his hand and the lower half of his face in two strokes. Redfeather hadn't handled a sword in years, and even back then it was only ceremonial, but his reflexes came alive as if he had combat experience. The second goblin found himself speared by the tip of Redfeather's sword. Using his foot, Redfeather pushed the goblin off the sword and turned to make his escape. His leap was awkward and slow and he paid for it when a goblin grabbed him by the pants leg. Redfeather's chin smashed against the ground, knocking him out and leaving him at the mercy of the goblins.

"This is probably gonna be infected." Lucy tried to clean as much of the sludge from the wound at her collar as she could. It had began to swell up and was starting to look nasty. "And don't even get me started on this smell." Both she and Cristobel were covered with a foul-smelling brown substance that she wasn't sure if she wanted to identify.

"The elders can tend your wound when we reach my village, and as for the stink, be thankful it was the waste and not the rocks." Cristobel directed her gaze to the jagged rocks that surrounded Orden's fort.

"Not a pleasant thought." Lucy scanned the side of the fort for Redfeather but didn't see him. "Where the hell is he?"

"There." Cristobel pointed up at the exit they'd jumped through. They saw Redfeather go airborne, but he was immediately snatched back by goblin hands. "Oh no."

"We've got to go back!" Lucy took a step, but Cristobel grabbed her by the arm. He was surprisingly strong for someone his size.

"To escape the Iron Mountains was a blessing, but it would be impossible for us to do it twice. We'll do him no good if we're dead. We'll find another way, I swear it." From the entrance of the fort, goblins of all sizes spilled out, screaming for blood . . . their blood. "We must go." He tugged Lucy and she finally allowed him to lead her away.

Lucy had heard a few ghost stories about the Iron Mountains, but the stories paled in comparison to the reality of what she saw before her. Under the mountains nothing grew. The vegetation had all died, leaving only the withered remains of trees and bushes. The riverbeds that had once cooled some of the greatest weapons created by the dwarfs had long since dried out and now streams of lava flowed freely. Orden's fort, as well as most of the structures around it, was carved directly into the rock faces of the mountains. The land was so vast that it seemed impossible to fit it beneath New York City, but where the kingdoms of Midland were concerned time and space meant nothing.

"This way." Cristobel continued pulling her.

"Slow down, will ya? These heels are killing me." Lucy stumbled.

"Then get rid of them!" he urged, leading Lucy down a rocky path that was littered with dead and dying vegetation. "If we make it to the woods we may still have a chance."

The path led them across an open field and to the mouth of the woods, which were as black as night. Lucy cupped her hands into them and blew, building a ball of light that was slightly larger than a tennis ball. With a nudge she sent the ball floating, illuminating what had once been a forest. The leaves had died off long ago, but the trunks of the trees still stood like great crippled giants. The pathways through the woods were overgrown with wilted bushes bearing sharp thorns.

"At least my magic's coming back." She shrugged. "How are we gonna get through this and into the woods?"

"I'll make a way." Cristobel hefted the battle ax and began wading through the thorns. The ax was almost the same height as he was, but Cristobel handled it with great ease. Within minutes he had carved a path to the main road that went through the woods.

"You're pretty handy with that thing," Lucy told him.

Cristobel simply shrugged. An arrow whistled between them and struck one of the dead trees. A few yards behind them Lucy could see the goblins closing in. "Do these guys ever quit?"

"Not until their prey is dead."

"Release the Slovs!" one of the goblins shouted.

"No!" Cristobel's heart was gripped with fear. "Come on!" He grabbed Lucy with so much force that he almost ripped her arm out of its socket.

"What the hell is a Slov?" she asked, running behind him.

"Just keep running and don't look back," he warned her.

Of course Lucy's curiosity got the best of her. When she did look over her shoulder, her heart almost stopped in her chest. There were at least a dozen of them, creatures that had been mutated from living in the Iron Mountains. Their green, hairless bodies were shaped like wolves, but their faces appeared more reptilian, with large, scaled heads and loose sacks of flesh hanging under the jaws. The largest of them, which had to be the leader of the pack, unhinged its jaws like a snake and opened its mouth wide enough to swallow a beach ball as it hissed at them in rage. The creatures moved as swiftly as gazelles as they navigated the rough terrain of the woods. Some even took to the trees in an attempt to cut the fugitives off. Lucy had never seen anything like them and never wanted to again.

Lucy tried to keep up with Cristobel but the heels were making it difficult and there was no time to take them off. She stumbled on a rock that was hidden under some dead leaves and fell flat on her face. Lucy rolled over on her back just in time to see one of the creatures closing in on her. The creature leaped into the air and came at Lucy with its fangs bared, but before it could close the distance its head went sailing into the bushes. Lucy looked up and saw Cristobel standing over her holding a bloodied ax.

"Come." He extended his hand. Lucy nodded in thanks and allowed him to help her up, then they were off again.

"What are those things?" Lucy asked as Cristobel led her along.

"Slovs—pack animals that hunt by overpowering their prey," he called over his shoulder. One of the Slovs dropped down onto the path and cut them off. Without missing a beat, Cristobel swung the ax and cut off the creature's front quarters. Two more of the Slovs dropped from the trees and blocked their escape.

"These are mine." Lucy stepped forward. She

scooped up a handful of dirt and rubbed it between her palms while casting a spell. The bushes on either side of the Slovs came to life and snared the creatures. The growth wasn't strong enough to kill them, but it slowed them down.

"This way." Cristobel pulled her to the left. A Slov leaped from the bushes and Cristobel split it from throat to privates. Two more lunged from the darkness but before they could do any damage Lucy telekinetically slammed them violently into a tree. "There're too many to fight; we must keep moving!"

"Tell that to them," Lucy said, raising a magical barrier. A charging Slov slammed into the invisible wall, breaking its neck. Lucy tried to raise a barrier to cut off the second charging beast, but her magic was weakening. It broke through and knocked her to the ground. Lucy quickly grabbed the creature by the throat to keep it from biting her face, but with only one arm it was a losing battle for her. When Lucy looked into the creature's gaping jaws, she could see it producing some kind of mucus in the back of its throat. It reared back to spit the fluid in Lucy's face, but Cristobel's ax piercing its skull denied it the chance.

Lucy quickly rolled from under the creature's corpse, got to her feet, and blurted out the first spell that popped into her head. The woods lit up in a beautiful burst of rainbow-colored fireworks. It was a spell she had learned from a warlock her mother had hired as entertainment at her eighth birthday party. It wasn't at all a powerful spell, but the lights made the Slovs back off and gave her and Cristobel a minute to breathe.

"They're coming from everywhere," Cristobel said. In the shadows around them he could see the Slovs' reptilian eyes watching. The fireworks had scared them off, but it was only a matter of time before they mounted another attack or the goblins caught up with them. Neither was a promising possibility. From behind him, Cristobel heard a coughing sound and then a gust of wind. He spun around in time to split the ball of mucus in half with his ax. With a second motion he threw the ax, pinning the Slov by its skull to a nearby tree. When he retrieved the ax he found a ball of the same mucus the Slov had tried to spit into Lucy's face.

"What the hell is that?" Lucy asked, examining the mucus. She reached for the ax, but Cristobel snatched it out of her reach.

"Are you mad?"

"I was just curious, man. Chill out," Lucy said.

"And your curiosity would've been your undoing, my friend." Cristobel held the ax out for them to get a closer look at the goo. It looked like a scoop of jelly, but when Lucy examined it closely she could see dozens of tiny spines floating inside it.

"What is it?" Lucy asked.

"Slow death," Cristobel said. "When the Slovs hunt larger prey, they poison it with the needles in their venom and wait for them to die before feeding."

A collective hissing rolled through the pack of Slovs, causing Lucy's head to whip back and forth between their attackers, but there was none. "Sounds like they're moving in from all sides." Lucy backed toward Cristobel. "Cristobel, I don't know about you but I think I'd rather take my chances with these Slovs than the goblins."

"We may end up having to defeat them both." He motioned toward the goblin torches, which were coming closer. "If I am to die, I will take as many of them as I can into the hereafter with me." Cristobel tightened his grip on the ax. He feared death, but he feared the agony of what the goblins would do to him more.

"Maybe neither of us has to die." Lucy knelt and began tracing symbols in the dirt. "I have a spell that may help, but I'll need time to work it."

"Do what you must and I'll hold them off," he told her.

Lucy worked feverishly in the dirt, etching symbols only to erase them and start over because she wasn't sure the glyphs were correct. She closed her eyes and tried to go back to the day her mother had first showed her the very rare spell. Drowning out the hissing sounds of the Slov and her mounting fear, Lucy managed to relax and let her hands work on their own. When she closed the circle she heard the telltale click letting her know she had drawn the symbols correctly. Now all she had to do was empower it.

When she raised her hands to cast the spell something slammed into her. She was caught off guard and didn't even have a chance to slow her momentum before she crashed into a thick tree. Pain shot from her injured collarbone and down to the tips of her fingers upon impact, and she slid limply to the floor with her vision blurred from the pain. She regained her focus just as one of the Slovs was making a mad dash for her. She managed to jam her forearm into its throat to keep it from ripping her face off, but with only one arm she wouldn't be able to hold it off for long. She tried to raise her bad arm to cast the spell, but it was useless to her.

Cristobel appeared like a guardian angel and yanked the thing off Lucy. He and the monster crashed to the ground in a tussle. Lucy scrambled over and yanked the Slov off Cristobel by its tail, turning its attention to her long enough for Cristobel to get back on his feet. With a swing of his ax he split the creature in two. When Lucy looked up to thank him, a horrified expression crossed his face. Lucy saw the shadow on the ground, felt the wind and smelled the stink of death as it soared toward her. She promised herself she wouldn't look, but curiosity got the best of her. She wanted to know what her parents had seen in their final moments, so she turned around. The Slov hurled itself at her with its teeth bared.

Lucy raised her good arm heavenward. "Goddess, protect me." She empowered her spell just seconds before the pain came.

The blade struck silently. Not even the tearing of skin or severing of bone made a sound. Blood that was an off shade of orange sprayed in a high arc and decorated the trees and dried bushes. The creature's eyes were wide with shock and its mouth frozen as if trapped in a moment of time. Blood and a noxious fluid squirted from its mouth as the lower and upper halves of its face slid in two different directions.

A few feet away Cristobel knelt on one knee, resting on the ax that was dripping blood onto the dry earth. He turned slowly and there was an unnatural glint in his eyes, the same glint you might see in the eyes of a wolf or some other predatory animal stalking the night. Wisps of loose magic rose from his body and dissipated in the air, lingering effects of whatever Lucy had done to him. Cristobel turned to the slowly advancing Slovs and raised his ax in challenge. The Slovs quickly answered.

The creatures descended on Cristobel in force, only to have three of them lose their heads in one stroke. In the same fluid motion he cleaved the legs from another Slov and planted the ax in its skull. He commanded the ax like it was an extension of his arm, lopping off pieces of whatever was foolish enough to veer close to him. Cristobel managed to drive the Slovs back into the woods, long enough to buy the fugitives a few precious moments.

"What sort of enchantment have you cast on me?" Cristobel looked at his hands in amazement. They still trembled and glowed faintly from the spell.

"An old one that my mother taught me as a girl," she explained.

"I feel like I could take on the entire goblin horde." Cristobel tossed his ax in the air and caught it in his other hand.

"Don't get too cocky, because it's only temporary. Now, I suggest we get out of these woods and someplace safe before the goblins reach us."

"Agreed." Cristobel helped Lucy to her feet. "We've only a few more yards until the edge of the woods. Once we clear them we'll be safe."

"It's about time," Lucy said, rubbing her arms. She had a scratch from one of the thorn bushes that was starting to burn like it had become infected.

"Are you well?" Cristobel asked, noticing the film of sweat on Lucy's brow.

"Yeah, but those thorn bushes did a number on me. I hope you guys have some peroxide in your village."

"Peroxide?" Cristobel asked with a confused expression on his face.

Lucy just shook her head. "Never mind. Let's just get out of here."

When Lucy and Cristobel finally cleared the woods, it seemed like they had shook the goblins and Slovs . . . but for how long she had no idea.

"My village is just over this hill. We'll be given shelter and food once we arrive. Even now I can see the cook fires burning." Cristobel pointed to the rising smoke visible just beyond the valley walls. "Come." He pulled her along by the hand as they crossed the last hill overlooking the village. When it finally came into sight, a horrified expression crossed Cristobel's face.

"No" was all he could say before he dropped to his knees and began to weep. All that remained of the village were the charred husks of the huts Cristobel had once called home.

CHAPTER NINE

The taxi jerked to a stop on the corner of Seventy-ninth Street and West End Avenue. The portly driver had been suspicious of the odd-looking trio, but when Rogue placed a hundred dollar bill in his hand and told him to keep the change it quieted his rumbling. Asha received more than a few curious glances from the residents and she couldn't say that she blamed them. Her leather outfit was ripped across the thigh and the dried blood made her hair sit at a funny angle. That and the fact that she was carrying a monkey made her quite the spectacle.

"I swear I haven't been stared at this much since my first day of grade school." Asha hugged Azuma to her chest.

"Don't worry. You look fine," Morgan said with a slight smile. Asha didn't return the gesture.

They entered Rogue's building just as an elderly couple was coming out. The old man stepped out in front of the wife defensively, but he relaxed when he saw Rogue. "Mr. Rogue," the elderly man greeted him in a less than welcoming tone.

"Good afternoon, Mr. Harmon, Mrs. Harmon." Rogue nodded to each of them and mustered his phoniest smile. The Harmons were notorious troublemakers who had been the most vocal in blocking Rogue's bid to purchase his apartment in the building. Even without reading their auras he knew there had to be a reason they were speaking to him other than courtesy.

"So how's the investigation coming along? I hope the police catch those three before they can do any more damage," Mrs. Harmon said.

Rogue raised his eyebrow. "Excuse me?"

Mr. Harmon gave his wife a look that said *Mind your business*, but she ignored him and continued her prying. "You know, that murdering Indian family that they've been talking about on the news all night. I hear that after they killed those people uptown, they burned a church in Brooklyn, even killed some of the priests who lived there."

Rogue, Asha, and Morgan exchanged nervous glances. "I'm afraid I haven't heard anything about it."

"Is that right?" Mrs. Harmon looked at Rogue over the top of her glasses. "Funny, because we saw that rolling ball of noise you like to drive at the crime scene."

Rogue felt ice form in his stomach. If the Harmons could place him at the scene of the crime, there was no telling who else was connecting the dots. "Well, officially I'm not working the case. I'm just advising the police on the matter."

"You see, I told you," Mrs. Harmon said to her husband.

"Well, we'll leave you people to it." Mr. Harmon grabbed his wife by the arm and ushered her down the walkway. "Have a good one."

"You too." Rogue nodded. He was glad to be rid of the Harmons and their snooping. He had made it into the lobby when he heard Mrs. Harmon call after him.

"Oh, some of your police friends came by looking for you this morning," Mrs. Harmon told him before her husband snatched her down the block.

Rogue, Asha, and Morgan looked at each other. One name flashed in all their heads at the same time. "Titus," Rogue said before bounding up the stairs with Asha and Morgan on his heels.

Rogue hit every other step on his way up the stairs. He cleared the landing on his floor with his gun drawn, sweeping the hallway for trouble. Morgan was at his side with his hammer raised, prepared to strike down anything that moved. Asha was still taking her time making her way up the stairs. Rogue heard footsteps to his left and spun with his gun drawn, scaring the blazes out of his neighbor. He was an older man with a mane of white hair that he never seemed to comb. He had been living down the hall from Rogue for six months, but for some reason the mage couldn't think of his name.

"Don't shoot!" The old man threw his hands up.

"Ah, sorry about that," Rogue said awkwardly and lowered his gun.

"Is there some sort of trouble?" the old man asked.

"Nothing to worry yourself about. We've got it under control," Rogue told him.

"That's a relief. Enjoy your day, Officer Rogue," the man said and continued down the hall. He stopped in front of Morgan and looked the big man up and down. "Nice hammer." He smiled and headed down the stairs.

"What are you guys doing just standing around?" Asha asked as she rounded the landing.

"I was talking to the old man you just passed," Rogue told her.

"What old man?" Asha asked.

Morgan and Rogue exchanged curious glances. They cautiously made their way down the hall until they reached Rogue's apartment door. He checked the wards that had been cast around his door and none seemed broken, but he knew that not all of their enemies had need of doors. With a wave of his hand he undid the locks and the door creaked open.

"Wait here for a sec," Rogue instructed them, then went inside. The room was dark and still, save for the curtain fluttering in the breeze of the air conditioner. Using his demon sight he checked the house for magical residue or any unwanted guests. When he was confident that the apartment was secure he waved his guests inside. "Someone has been here, but they couldn't get past the wards."

Rogue muttered something under his breath and the living room lights winked on. His apartment was modestly decorated with a sofa, a love seat, and a small television that was covered in a film of dust. Covering the shelves built into the wall and every table in the place were books on everything from spells to American history.

Asha stared around the room and nodded in approval. "Not quite what I expected from my first time at a mage's pad."

"And what's that supposed to mean?" Rogue slipped off his jacket and tossed it on the floor.

Asha shrugged. "I don't know. I guess I expected something a little creepier, like heads in jars and the moaning of the restless dead. I mean, death magic is what you guys do, right?"

Rogue's eyes drank Asha in, sending a chill through her. "Some of us, but I've never been one to follow trends. Kinda like you, kid. The witches of the coven are all flowers and nature, but that isn't quite your bag." He touched her bloodstained cheek, creating a tiny spark of magic between them. Asha gasped and backed away.

"Guess it isn't." She looked at the floor in embarrassment.

Something darted across the floor and Azuma immediately sprang into motion. He knocked over a table and two chairs before he finally got hold of the blur, which turned out to be a black kitten.

"Get off him." Rogue formed a thin thread of shadow and cracked it like a whip. Azuma yelped and scrambled behind Asha's legs. Rogue knelt and picked the kitten up. "You okay, Mr. Jynx?" The kitten purred in his arms. Its jade green eyes sparkled as it stared menacingly at Asha and Azuma.

"Mr. Jynx?" Asha looked at him in amusement.

"Yeah, what's wrong with that?" Rogue asked defensively.

"Nothing at all." Asha smothered her laughter. "I thought witches were the only ones who used familiars?"

"Mr. Jynx isn't a familiar. I got him to keep the mice away. These old buildings are rank with rodents."

Asha looked at the cat a little more closely. The traces were faint, but she could see the magical residue clinging to the animal. "Rogue, this is no normal house cat."

"I never said he was." Rogue placed the cat on the floor and watched him dart into the bedroom. Azuma looked like he wanted to follow, but he was in no rush to catch another lash of shadow. "I'm gonna grab a few things and then we can leave."

"While you two are up here I'm going to check the perimeter just in case anyone or anything is still lurking about," Morgan said.

"That might not be such a bad idea. If you run into trouble don't try to go at it alone, Morgan.

Titus's agents could come in any shape at this point and we've got to be on our toes," Rogue said.

Morgan tested the weight of his hammer before hooking it to his belt beneath his jacket. "I think I'll be okay," he said before excusing himself.

"Hey, do you mind if I use your bathroom to try to wash some of this blood out of my hair before I end up having to cut it?" Asha tugged at the mess. It had already started to harden at the roots.

"Sure, you can use the guest bathroom." Rogue pointed at a door on the far side of the living room. "There should be clean towels and soap in the closet."

"Thank the Goddess." Asha set Azuma down. "Behave yourself," she told the monkey before heading off to the bathroom.

"Looks like it's just you and me," Rogue told Azuma, making his way to the dining room table near the window. Carefully he pulled off his shirt and undershirt and took stock of his injuries. Everything that could hurt did, and his smooth chocolate skin was bruised all over, but at least the wound on his shoulder was almost completely healed. He couldn't say the same thing about his side. The bleeding had stopped, but the gash was still raw and looked to be infected. Unlike the bullet hole, wounds inflicted by magic would need a little help healing.

"I don't suppose you could keep a secret?" Rogue asked the monkey. Azuma just stared at the mage quizzically. "Figured as much." Rogue sat cross-legged in the center of the living room and relaxed.

Rogue knew what he was about to attempt was extremely dangerous, but he didn't have time to see a healer or fumble around with his own spells. It would be nightfall soon and the Hunt would begin. He relaxed and let his mind wander. The room around him fell away piece by piece, leaving him in a place of total darkness. He had crossed over into the shadows. He heard the murmurs of the shadows like the buzzing of bees in his ears. In the shadow realm there was no individuality, only the perfection of the collective. Reaching out with his mind, Rogue pulled pieces of shadows to him, wrapping them around his broken form. The blackness nestled against him like a protective mother, exploring every pore of his body.

"Stay with us," the shadows whispered.

"Yes," Rogue whispered back. The oblivion was sweeter than any drug and twice as addictive. The deeper he sank, the more natural it felt. Somewhere far away there was disharmony in the shadows, like someone disturbing the collective uninvited, but Rogue paid no attention to it as the shadows pulled him further into their protective embrace. Rogue wanted to let himself slip away, but something held him between the two worlds, something important that he needed to do. He couldn't bring himself to care at that moment. Suddenly there was a sharp pain in his hand and Rogue found himself violently jerked from his trance and plunged back into the world. He blinked, looked around his apartment, and found Azuma with his teeth sunk into his hand.

"Ouch." Rogue swatted the monkey away. As the fog lifted from his mind Rogue realized where he was and what he had almost allowed to happen. "Thanks for bringing me back," he told Azuma and patted the monkey's head tenderly.

"I felt your black magic all the way in the other room. What are you doing to him?" Asha came rushing out of the bathroom. "I swear you better not have been out here trying to steal my familiar's soul!"

"I was just . . ." Rogue's words got stuck in his throat when he saw Asha standing there wrapped only in a towel. Washed free of the blood and dirt, her mocha skin was flawless. Asha's locks were soaked, sending droplets of water down her neck and pooling in the crease of her breasts. He must have been staring for quite some time, because she cleared her throat to get his attention.

"You know, the easiest way to offend a lady is by talking to her breasts instead of her face," she told him. "Come." She beckoned the monkey, who rushed to her side.

Rogue finally managed to find his tongue. "Sorry, I was just . . . ah. Look, I wasn't trying to do anything to your monkey. He actually saved me from a ritual that almost went horribly wrong."

"Is that right?" Asha glared down at Azuma. The monkey backed away from his mistress, cringing.

"Don't worry. I wasn't trying to tap into your magic through your pet," Rogue told her.

"Had you been trying to tap my magic, mine wouldn't have been the head in trouble," she assured him.

"Whatever." Rogue got up from the table and checked himself in the mirror. His skin was still bruised but all of the wounds had closed. With his back to her, Asha could admire the well-defined curves of his back and shoulders.

"Nice," she said.

Rogue turned and flexed his chest muscles a bit. "So I've been told."

Asha rolled her eyes. "Not your body, you egomaniac, I was talking about the job you did patching yourself up. I didn't know that mages were good for much other than stealing souls and raping them for their secrets."

"What is your problem with mages? Did one of us break your heart and cause you to hate the entire race, or are you just a bitch in general?" he asked heatedly.

Asha laughed. "You're right about me being a general bitch, but is has nothing to do with getting my heart broken by a mage. As if I would ever let one of you into my pants. Give me some kind of credit."

"So what's your problem?"

"My problem is that I see everything and everyone for what they really are. You know just as well as I do that you guys are like lepers among the spell casters, even more shunned than the sorcerers. And that's saying a lot considering that those godless bastards are the scum of the earth."

Rogue had finally tired of Asha's mouth. "You're one to talk, blood witch." He moved closer to her. "Ever since you came around you've been pointing the finger at everyone else and picking them apart for their shortcomings, but I think it's just to hide your own insecurities."

"What are you babbling about?"

"I'm talking about the scared little outcast who has to throw stones at everyone else because she's still not comfortable in the skin she's in. You do work for Dutch that nobody else will because you're still trying to make up for your mother's mistakes. Get over it already!"

"Watch it," Asha warned him.

Rogue just smiled, knowing he had hit a nerve. "What? You can dish it out but can't take it? You think I care what you or anybody else says about the mages? Hell no, because I'm not the *mages*, I'm just Jonathan Rogue. You can't judge me as a person based on what my people have done. I refuse to wear that shame. You, on the other hand, sport it like a new wristwatch you want everybody to see. As tough as you act, Asha, you ain't no badass Huntress. You're just a scared-ass little punk still looking for Daddy to pat her on the head and say good job."

When Rogue turned to walk away, Asha struck. She punched him in the back of the head with so much force that it felt like she had cracked her knuckle along with his skull. Rogue turned around and she cracked him in the jaw, knocking him off balance. She tried to follow up with a spinning kick, but he was ready for her. Rogue grabbed her leg and waggled his finger at her. Grabbing her by the ankle, he spun her around twice and sent her flying into the bookshelf.

"Now, cut it out before somebody gets hurt," he huffed.

Asha's towel had abandoned her and she was now nude, but it didn't deter her. Screaming, she came back at him with her hands raised and power building in them. She tried to touch Rogue, but he was able to spin out of the way and grab her wrist. When she tried the other hand he did the same thing. They stood eye to eye with their arms crossed over each other, both breathing heavily.

Rogue looked down at her perfect breasts and flat stomach and smiled. "You had enough yet?"

Asha headbutted him right between the eyes. She managed to free one of her hands and pressed the palm on the shoulder he had healed down to a small nick. Fire shot through his shoulder as the wound reopened and blood sprayed the room. Asha tried to sweep his leg, but he blocked with his shin. The two of them spilled to the ground with Asha landing on top. Asha looked down into his eyes and didn't see the ugliness of the demon he inherited them from, but beautiful stars dancing across the night sky. Before either of them knew it their scrape turned into a bout of passionate kissing. Their bodies seemed almost weightless as their magics explored each other. The two magicians were so caught up in each other that they didn't even hear Morgan's heavy footfalls when he came back into the apartment.

"I could come back later, if you like." Morgan's voice startled them, but he seemed to be the most embarrassed of the three.

"It's not what it looks like," Rogue said, still lying on his back.

"It's none of my business, really." Morgan raised his hands in surrender.

"Yeah, we were just having a conversation about respect and understanding," Asha told Morgan. Unexpectedly she punched Rogue in the mouth. "Do we understand each other?"

Rogue massaged his tender jaw. "You got it, lady."

CHAPTER TEN

As promised the bunker wasn't the Ritz, but the mattresses were soft and the sheets were clean. Jackson took Lydia and Finnious off to find something to eat and tour the vast library, while Jonas retired to his chambers to consult the spindle about their problems. This left Gabriel and De Mona in the sleeping quarters. It was the first time they had been alone together since that night at the library. He wanted to hate the girl for what had happened, but he couldn't. In his heart he knew that she was little more than a child in search of answers, as he had been at that point. The mystery of the Nimrod was unraveling far too slowly for his taste.

The Nimrod was made of far more complex magic than any of them could comprehend. Even Gabriel, the chosen vessel, didn't fully understand what drove the thing, but the Bishop did and he was taking his time with telling. If Gabriel could somehow exorcise the vengeful spirit, maybe he could gain control over the trident, but its former master didn't seem to be in a rush to leave. As long as the Bishop remained, Gabriel would be little more than a tool for the fallen Knight and whatever evil designs he had on the world. If he wanted his life back, he would have to get rid of the Bishop and eventually the Nimrod.

Foolish boy, there are no secrets between us. We are bound, you and I. Your heart says what your mouth will not, the Bishop taunted him.

"Do you ever get tired of hearing yourself talk?" Gabriel waved the voice away and when he did so his hand left a faint trail of electricity in the air. Curious, Gabriel cupped his hands and tried to produce another spark. To his surprise the power answered him, creating a web of lightning between his palms.

"That's a neat new trick. Do you do birthday parties too?" De Mona startled him and the lightning disappeared. "Sorry, I didn't mean to intrude."

"It's cool. I've been meaning to talk to you anyhow." Gabriel motioned for her to take a seat next to him on the bed. When De Mona sat, Gabriel immediately felt the butterflies in his stomach that he always got when he was too close to a girl. If she noticed his discomfort she gave no sign of it. "Listen," Gabriel said, "I want to apologize for giving you a hard time about all this. I know it's not your fault that my grandfather was taken prisoner."

De Mona nodded in approval. "And I apologize for getting you guys caught up in this mess. Gabriel, I swear I didn't know any of this was gonna happen. I just wanted answers and I thought coming to the Redfeathers was my best chance at getting them."

"I can understand that. When my parents were killed I wanted answers too. I just had no idea what those answers would yield until recently. I guess we're all victims in this."

"Which is what's pissing me off," De Mona said. "I'm a fighter. Sitting around on my hands while somebody does the dirty work isn't my style. Even though your grandfather didn't completely trust me, he opened his home to me to keep me safe, and I couldn't stop the goblins from taking him." Tears danced in De Mona's eyes, but she wouldn't let them fall. "It ain't right, man. It just ain't right."

"De Mona, you fought harder than anyone out there when they attacked, but we were overrun. Even with the Nimrod we barely made it out of that situation alive. I'm just as much a fuck-up as you are in this." He hung his head.

De Mona lifted Gabriel's chin so that he was looking at her. He couldn't hold back his tears. "You're not a fuck-up, Gabe. You're just a kid who's trying to get used to his new gifts."

"You call this a gift?" He raised his arm. "For all its magnificence it couldn't do jack to save my grandfather. If you ask me it's a fraud. Do you hear me talking to you," he spoke to his arm. "If you're such a badass, why don't you tell me how I can rescue my grandfather?"

The Bishop snickered. *Blame not the Nimrod*

for the work of the Medusan, for it is he who keeps you hidden away like a scared lamb while your grandfather remains at the mercy of the goblins. All you have to do is embrace the power presented to you.

"More lies," Gabriel snapped.

"Dude, who are you talking to?" De Mona asked.

"Never mind. Have you heard anything from Jonas or the others?"

"Nothing yet. I asked Jackson about it and all he would say was that Jonas will address our concerns when he's done with his meditation, however long that might be. He's been gone for hours and still hasn't presented us with anything useful."

"Damn it, I hate all this waiting around." Gabriel threw a phantom punch at the wall and to his surprise a bolt of lightning snaked from his hand and scorched the paint.

You're getting better. Focus your rage, Hunter, and taste the power of the Nimrod.

Gabriel raised his hand and watched as the sparks of lightning jumped from his fingertips. When he raised his other hand, the two rows of sparks connected in the middle and leaped back and forth. He could feel the power building in his stomach and spreading through his body. The more power he called, the more he reveled in the wave of euphoria that washed over him. Gabriel pushed a little harder, making the sparks dance. He could see the tattoo on his arm writhing back and forth.

Yes, let your anger fuel your vengeance. Cleanse your enemies of their sins.

Gabriel raised his hands to the heavens and it started to rain over his bed. He could feel the power pushing harder and harder against his spirit, and he invited it. Just as he felt himself about to explode, the storm abruptly stopped. He blinked. De Mona stood in front of him, holding him by the wrist.

"What the hell is with you?" she asked in a panicked tone.

Gabriel looked around at the mess he had created. The bedsheets were charred and there was about an inch of water pooled at his feet. "What happened?"

"I was hoping you could tell me. One minute we're sitting here having a heart-to-heart conversation and the next you go all white-eyed on me and this freak shows up. I've been trying to get your attention for almost ten minutes. It was as if your mind was somewhere else."

Gabriel looked down at his tattoo. It was now still and calm, but he could hear the Bishop's mocking laughter in his ears. "It's this trident. De Mona, I feel like I'm gonna go crazy if I stay here. I can't wait for Jonas anymore. I'm going after my grandfather." He got up off the bed and headed for the door, but De Mona cut him off. "Don't try to stop me."

"I'm not trying to stop you, I'm just making sure you don't go off half-cocked and get yourself killed. If you're going to tackle the Iron Mountains, you're gonna need some backup and a plan."

"De Mona, I don't have time to wait for Jonas to come out of his meditations. I need to get to my grandfather."

"Who said anything about Jonas? Look, I'm part of the reason that Redfeather isn't here, so rescuing him falls on me too. I just happen to have the perfect plan to get us into the Iron Mountains."

"Well, spill it already," he said anxiously.

"I can show you better than I can tell you. Come on." She led him toward the exit.

"Wait, what about Rogue and the others?"

"Gabriel, there's no telling how long they're gonna be and we still don't know what kind of time your grandfather has left. Do you really wanna risk us getting there too late?"

Gabriel thought about it for a second. "No."

"Good, then move your ass. It'll be sunset in a little while and we gotta get moving."

It took some doing, but Gabriel and De Mona finally figured out how to work the elevators and headed to the lower levels of the compound. Gabriel felt guilty for going behind Jonas's back and stealing from his workshop, but De Mona assured him that it was for the greater good. They visited six different levels before they finally found the one they were looking for, the one that housed the holding cells. It was an underground chamber with a half dozen small cells carved into the stone walls. This served as the rarely used, but highly secure dungeon.

"Smells like piss down here," Gabriel said when he stepped off the elevator.

"I'll be sure to voice your complaints to the cleaning staff," De Mona said sarcastically. She sniffed the air, trying to find a particular scent. When she located it, she followed her nose to the cell at the far end where Gilchrest was being kept.

"Rise and shine, asshole," she said, banging on the bars.

Gilchrest snarled and lunged at the cage. Asha's binding spell had worn off, but he was still a captive and not happy about it.

Gabriel smiled a little. Somehow it pleased him to know that.

"Let me out and I tear that smile from your face, Redskin," Gilchrest threatened.

Gabriel released a small spark from his hand, making Gilchrest back up. "Keep running your mouth and I'll see how much power it takes to bake that thick skin you goblins are so proud of."

"Come here to taunt me more, you have?" Gilchrest eyed them.

"No, we've actually come to take you for a little walk." Gabriel held up the collar Jonas had showed them earlier.

"Come in, if you dare. Rend you I will," Gilchrest threatened, backing away from the bars.

"Oh, I'm sure those nasty little claws of yours would do quite a number on me, which is why I'm not coming in." Gabriel looked to De Mona, who was grinning from ear to ear. He waved his hand over the digital lock on the cage door, shorting it out. "Ms. Sanchez, would you be so kind as to help me put this on our little friend?"

De Mona's face changed and her claws extended. "Gladly." She stepped into the cage. True to his word, Gilchrest attacked. He was incredibly quick, but hardly a match for De Mona in her demon form. She plucked the goblin up by his arms and began pulling them apart until she could hear the bones cracking.

"Vile demon, break my arms you will!" Gilchrest howled in pain.

"I sure will, unless you calm down and act like you've got some sense," she told him.

"Agreed, agreed, no problems from Gilchrest," the goblin whimpered.

"He's all yours, Gabriel."

"Thank you." He stepped into the cage and placed the collar around Gilchrest's neck. Once it was secured he clicked a device that was strapped to his wrist and the flashing green lights of the collar became solid red. "You can let him go now."

De Mona looked at him. "But what if he tries to attack again?"

"Let him. I figured out how to work this thing on the way down here and if he attacks it's gonna hurt him more than it hurts me," Gabriel said, playing with the controls.

No sooner had De Mona released Gilchrest than he charged at Gabriel. The goblin launched himself into the air with his claws poised to take out Gabriel's eyes. Gabriel shook his head and hit the switch on his wrist. Gilchrest dropped like a stone. He rolled around the floor feverishly clutching at the collar, which was sending electric currents through his nervous system. Gabriel kept it up for a few seconds to make sure the goblin got the point and shut off the charge.

"Witchcraft," Gilchrest croaked when he was able to speak again.

"Not witchcraft. Good old-fashioned technology," Gabriel told him. "Grabbing the collar was a great idea, De Mona."

"I told you I had it all worked out," she said proudly. "Now let's get moving." She grabbed Gilchrest by the collar and shoved him out of the cage.

"Where are you taking me?" Gilchrest asked timidly as he made his way out of the cell.

"We're not taking you anywhere, but you're gonna take us someplace. We need to find the entrance to the Iron Mountains," Gabriel said.

Gilchrest looked at him and fell over laughing. "Just as foolish as ugly you are, human. If death is what you look for, remove the collar and I will give it to you." Gabriel sent another charge through the collar and silenced the goblin's laughing.

Gabriel grabbed Gilchrest by the collar and lifted him off the ground. "I've been hitting you with the low setting, but if you keep trying my patience I'm gonna crank this baby up and see how tough the body of a goblin really is. We've got something Orden wants and he has something we want. We can do this clean and everybody is happy, or we can do this messy"—Gabriel called the lightning to his hand—"and everybody loses. But with or without your help we're going into the Iron Mountains to find my grandfather."

"Can I shock him this time?" De Mona asked, reaching for the control.

"No more, no more. I lead you," Gilchrest conceded.

"Good, now let's get moving." Gabriel dropped him to the ground. "Do you really think we can trust him?" he whispered to De Mona.

"Not really, but he's our best shot at getting into the mountains and the only thing we have to barter with. Let's get topside so we can do this as quickly as possible. It's dark outside and there's no telling what we may run into on the way."

"Hold on, De Mona, how are we supposed to get to the Iron Mountains?" Gabriel asked.

De Mona smirked. "I told you I had a plan."

"This is your plan?" Gabriel asked in shock. They were back on the main level in the hangar, looking at a Mini Cooper that had seen better days. One of the front tires was sitting on a doughnut while the other was patched with layers of duct tape.

De Mona shrugged. "Hey, all I can do is work with what I have. We can either jack this or the Hummer, but I think the Mini will draw a lot less attention."

"No way for a goblin prince to travel," Gilchrest mumbled.

"We could be delivering you in a body bag, so if I were you I'd shut my hole," De Mona snapped at the goblin.

"This is too damn crazy." Gabriel shook his head. "We don't even have the keys."

"You don't need a key when you're rolling with De Mona Sanchez." She climbed under the dashboard and began playing with the wires. Within a few seconds the car coughed to life. "We gonna do this or what?"

Gabriel sighed. "Okay, let's go." He got in on the passenger side and placed Gilchrest between them in case he tried something funny. De Mona revved the engine and threw the car in gear, but then something dawned on Gabriel. "How are we gonna get the hangar door open?"

"I appropriated the car and the collar. This one is on you," she told him.

"Great," Gabriel said and leaned out the window. He focused, channeling his emotions until he could feel the familiar tingle of power in his gut. With a grunt, he released a bolt of lightning that smashed a hole in the hangar door. Alarms sounded all through the complex. "I sure hope Jonas doesn't get too pissed about this."

"He'll thank us for it when we save the world." She threw the car in gear and peeled out of the hangar en route to the Iron Mountains.

CHAPTER ELEVEN

The fog was slow to lift from Redfeather's head. He found himself strapped to a wooden cross that was suspended from rusty chains over a large wooden table in a room full of goblins and Flagg the mage who had been with them during the battle at Sanctuary. Sitting at the head of the table was Orden and he did not look happy.

"Glad you could join us, little rabbit." Orden slapped the cross, spinning Redfeather until he was dizzy. "You murdered several of my brothers, old man."

"And I would've slain more if I had the chance," Redfeather said defiantly. This got a hostile roar from the goblins assembled. One of them even hit him in the face with a piece of rotten meat.

"Silence!" Orden slammed his fist against the table, spilling ale all over everyone. The room got deathly quiet except for the soft squeak of the chain as Redfeather swung back and forth. Orden eventually stopped his swinging when he grabbed

Redfeather by the face. "The price for an outsider slaying a goblin is death."

When Redfeather saw the hungry look in Orden's eyes, his entire life flashed before him. As much as he wanted to plead for his life he wouldn't give the goblins, or the onlooking mage, the satisfaction. "Do what you will, goblin. I'll see the lot of you in hell."

"Indeed you will, flesh sack. Let the punishment fit the crime!" Orden bellowed and opened his jaws impossibly wide to bite Redfeather's head off.

"Wait," Flagg spoke up, surprising everyone, especially Redfeather. All eyes in the room turned to the mage. He was Rogue's magician and Titus's closest advisor. Flagg's face was a mask of calm, but the icy sweat running down his forehead betrayed his fear. He only hoped that his hosts couldn't smell it. "The old man may be of use to us."

"Bah, what use could this mortal possibly serve other than sating the hunger of our prince?" Illini, asked, drawing a murmur from the crowd.

Flagg swallowed, knowing he was about to take one hell of a gamble. "Because it is the progeny of this human who wielded the weapon that defeated your goblins on the field of combat. Using him to lure in the grandson is the only way you will have your revenge and restore honor to this great court."

Orden's eyes flashed with rage as he sped toward Flagg, knocking over chairs and goblins as he passed. "And what do you know of honor, mage?

What do any of you topsiders know of dying on the battlefield with the blood of your enemies staining your lips? The goblins threw in our lot with the demons because we were promised power and flesh, but so far all we have been dealt is death for the fool's mission Titus sent us to perform. The so-called whelp you sent us after turned day into night before our very eyes. This is a feat that not even your most powerful sorcerers could accomplish, yet this *boy* as you called him did so with ease!" He kicked over a table.

"I have only heard stories about the kind of powers the boy turned against us topside. It was old magic, older than even us, I fear," Illini offered softly. He was Titus's most trusted aide and executioner. Illini was a fierce warrior and his hand of fire made him deadly in a fight. He had stolen the arm of an elemental and taken it for his own, giving him command over fire.

Orden turned on his friend and most trusted captain and slapped him across the room. Blood rage seized Illini, but as powerful as he was, he knew better than to rebel against the prince unless he was ready to battle to the death.

"Before the goblins, savages infested the world like ticks on a dog. Before the goblins, there was nothing. None is greater than the empire." Orden snatched Illini to his feet. "NONE!"

Illini kept his eyes locked on his feet, which were hovering off the ground. "None, my prince."

For a second Orden's eyes became sane again

and he placed his friend down gently, but as quickly as the sanity came, it faded. His rage needed a new target. When his eyes landed on Flagg, the mage flinched. "You brought this on us." He pointed an accusatory finger at Flagg.

"Me?" Flagg took a step back as the goblin prince approached him. The honor guard closed ranks behind him, more than willing to sacrifice the mage to assuage their prince's rage. "Great prince, I assure you I have no idea what you mean."

"Oh, but you do." Orden drew a blade from his belt. "You and your bootlicking master called on us to help you capture the weapon from a helpless human child, but what you did was lead us into the fires of a god. That was no boy we faced—it was the Bishop made flesh again!"

Flagg knew that even if he had the chance to call up a spell powerful enough to strike Orden down, the others would maul him before he could reach the door, so he tried a different approach.

"Great and wise prince . . ." Flagg dropped to his knees at Orden's feet. "On the honor of my house and my children I swear that we did not know the power had awakened in the boy. We would never be so foolish as to make a false offering of flesh to the almighty goblin empire."

A low grumbling escaped from Orden. Everyone in the room prayed it was a laugh. "Flagg, you have no honor and whatever bastards you may lay claim to were no doubt sold into slavery long ago to further your master's gains. Do not try to make a fool of me twice, mage." Orden began pacing the room. "Not only did the order defeat my soldiers, but they have captured my brother. All goblins are protected by the sword of their prince and to touch one of the royal families is to die a thousand deaths. There will be a reckoning and Titus will help see to it."

Before Flagg could respond, there was a soft knock on the door. One of the honor guards stepped out into the hall and came back a few seconds later with a dwarf in tow. He was an elderly man with wild hair and a clean-shaven face. When he looked into the fiery eyes of Orden, a wet spot appeared at the center of his dingy pants.

"Are you miserable dwarves deaf as well as dumb? The prince left orders that he was not to be disturbed while we were in council," Illini snapped.

"Please forgive me, but I thought you would want to hear this right away," the dwarf stammered.

"What could be important enough for you to risk punishment for interrupting us?" Orden towered over the dwarf.

The dwarf was so nervous that his mouth had gone completely dry. "The dwarf and the witch have escaped our hunting parties. The Slovs—"

Orden grabbed the dwarf by the throat and lifted him high above his head. Orden's roar of anger was almost deafening, but everyone in the room heard the sound of the dwarf's neck being broken when Orden's bit his head clean off. He tossed the headless corpse into the corner and turned his bloody face to Illini. "I want the witch and that ungrateful dwarf found. I don't care if you have to level their whole village to make it so, but you will bring me their hides or I will have yours!"

"Your will be done." Illini bowed before leading the honor guard from the room.

Flagg tried to slip from the room with the honor guard, but Orden's hand around his throat stopped him.

The goblin prince lifted Flagg off his feet and turned him around so they were eye to eye. "Hear me and hear me well, vessel of the betrayer. Tell your master that the goblin empire will tolerate no more of his games. Goblin blood has been spilled and so blood will run in rivers when the sun sets. Whether it is that of my enemies or allies matters little at this point, as long as my thirst in quenched." He threw Flagg roughly to the ground, where he landed in the dwarf's blood.

"As you command, Prince Orden," Flagg croaked before rushing from the room. Only when he was on the other side of the thick door did he dare to take a breath. Titus wasn't going to like what he had to report, but at the moment Flagg didn't care. Orden's whims were the only thing keeping him alive at the moment and he intended to do whatever it took to stay on his good side, at least until he was free of the Iron Mountains. It had been foolish for Titus to leave Flagg in the company of the goblins, and even more foolish on his part to accept the task. Pulling a small mirror from his pocket, he prepared to deliver the news.

Redfeather breathed a sigh of relief at the news of Lucy and Cristobel's successful escape. If he was lucky they would be able to make it topside and bring word to Gabriel and whatever was left of the order. The prospect of knowing that help could soon be on the way made him smile, but it was quickly wiped away by a brutal backhand from Orden.

Orden stepped onto the table. Even though Redfeather was suspended on the cross, the goblin still towered over him. "Just because Titus's pet asswiper has bought you some time doesn't mean you will not suffer the horrors of the mighty goblin empire," he snarled before biting off Redfeather's left hand.

CHAPTER TWELVE

Titus stood in the center of the hall of mirrors surrounded by a half dozen spell-casters. The seams of his tailored black blazer seemed to loosen a little more with every breath he took, but the irritation was still there, lying under the surface of his already dark mood. The transmission had ended ten minutes prior, but still he stared at the mirror in front of him. Flagg had made his fear-laden report about Orden's displeasure and his demand for an audience, but Titus didn't feel moved to accommodate him until he was ready. Titus realized full well that it was in his best interest to keep the peace with the goblins, but he would not be summoned like a common soldier. He was still commander of the Dark Father's army and the goblins would do well to remember it.

The goblins were some of the fiercest and most bloodthirsty warriors in all the land, and Titus had felt that they were the ideal choice to aid him in retrieving the Nimrod from the boy. He had been wrong. With the help of his new companions, the descendant of the Hunter had not only made life-long enemies of the goblins, but he had taught Titus something very important: he was getting stronger. Still, Gabriel was just a boy stumbling around in the dark while Titus could see quite clearly the power that was up for grabs. He had tasted the fruit from the forbidden tree and would not be denied a second helping.

Circling overhead was a flock of ravens darting in and out of the pulsating mirrors as the spell-casters empowered the teleportation spells. The ritual put a great strain on the casters and it was doubtful that the weaker ones would survive the ordeal, but their lives mattered little at that point. He needed to get word to his allies and he needed to do it quickly.

"The last of the couriers have been dispatched," Alex told him. He looked worn and haggard, but he was still standing, which was more than could be said for two of his fellow casters. The young warlock was showing great promise and Titus made a note to himself to thank Dutch for sending him.

"Thank you, Alex." Titus patted his broad shoulder.

"Will there be anything further?" Alex wiped a trickle of blood from his nose with the back of his hand.

Titus looked over just in time to see another one

of the spell-casters keel over. "Yes, bring me fresh vessels to cast a teleportation spell."

Judy couldn't believe her luck when the security firm she worked for had informed her that she would be getting a transfer to Titus Corp, one of downtown Ontario's most prestigious companies. Maxwell Titus was one of the most powerful men in the country and known to pay his employees far more than the average salary. When she'd accepted the transfer she expected to be assigned to one of the bigwigs who worked for Titus Corp, but for the last three days she'd been little more than a babysitter for Titus's niece, Leah.

Even though she had been briefed beforehand she still wasn't prepared for what she saw. Leah was a beautiful girl barely into her teens with soft pink hair and eyes of molten gold. Her skin was white, but not like the color, more like looking at the moon on a clear night. It was obvious that she was not human, but her origin wasn't in the brief and Judy dared not ask. The one thing that had been made clear to her before taking the job with Titus Corp was that she was not to ask questions.

Judy stretched and looked at her watch. She had another five hours to go before her shift was over and watching the paint dry in the girl's room didn't help the time to pass any quicker. Judy gave a cautious glance around before slipping the pocket-size book from the pocket of her fatigue pants. She had been warned by her superiors about bringing any kind of foreign material into the room, but it's not like she was bringing in drugs. There was no way that a copy of Kris Greene's *Pretty in Black* could cause any harm.

"What've you got there?" Leah called from the bed, scaring Judy. In the three days she had been looking after Leah, she couldn't recall ever having heard the girl speak. Her voice was almost musical in pitch, but there was something about the power in her words that made the hairs on Judy's arms stand up.

"Nothing," Judy lied and went back to her post near the door.

"Come now, I won't tell my uncle. Let me see." Leah's lips curled into a hint of a smile. It tugged at Judy's heart.

After giving a cautious look around, she leaned her rifle against the door and walked over to the edge of the bed. In the light she could really see Leah, and the child was almost too beautiful to turn away from. Without even realizing that she was doing it she held up the small paperback novel for Leah to see.

"Oh, a Kris Greene novel. I absolutely love her." Leah's eyes lit up. "My uncle Titus doesn't let me read much, as you can see."

"Yeah, I noticed that your uncle is pretty protective of you," Judy said.

"He's more like my jailer than my uncle with all his rules. Of all the things I've been denied since coming to stay with him, reading has been the hardest to live without." Leah pouted. Her eyes suddenly lit up as if she had an idea. "Do you think I could read a few passages?"

"No, I'm not supposed to," Judy told her.

"Please, please, please, I pinky swear that I won't tell anyone." Leah held her pinky up.

Judy beamed at the girl as if she were the sister she never had and locked pinkies. "Okay, but keep your mouth shut. I can lose my job for this," she whispered.

Leah's face lit up as if Christmas had come early. "Don't worry, I won't tell a soul." Leah extended her hands for the book hoping that the woman didn't see them trembling in nervous anticipation. The illustrated cover was barely an inch from Leah's reach when Judy and the book were snatched away. Standing a few feet away were Titus and his vampire consorts, Helena and Raven.

Helena glared up at the frightened woman with her lips pulled back into a snarl. Judy could see razor-sharp fangs slip down from behind her gums. "Do you know what you almost did, human?" Helena snarled.

"I was just—"

"Giving our sneaky little guest exactly what she wanted," Titus said as he strode into the room. Trailing him were Raven and the two female security officers who had been standing guard outside the room. Titus knelt and picked up the discarded book that Leah had been reaching for. He flipped through the pages briefly before incinerating the book in his hands. He turned to Judy, who was still in Helena's grip. "Had you been foolish enough to give her the book, I can only imagine what kinds of catastrophes our little goddess might've cooked up. She may even have managed to escape."

"I would've done more than escape, Titus. I would've shown you the true meaning of pain," Leah threatened. She tried to muster up even a fraction of her stolen powers, but could do little more than flutter the net of her canopy bed. Leah was a powerful sprite who had once been worshiped as a goddess. Decades prior, she had been tricked by Belthon and fallen victim to an ancient spell. Leah had been trapped inside the body of a teenage girl. Her powers could not reach maturity and therefore she could not break the spell. She had inhabited several hosts' bodies over the years, but with each it was the same. Just before the girl reached maturity she would be murdered and Leah cast into another host. She had been leapfrogging through time that way for almost one hundred years, waiting for an opportunity to reclaim her powers and seek revenge against Belthon and Titus for her imprisonment.

"Leah, why do you strain yourself when you know you cannot break the spell binding you to this room? I must say I'm surprised you were even able to manipulate this human the way you did."

Leah folded her arms. "It wasn't hard. Anyone working for you, mortal or supernatural, can't boast of having good sense." She looked at Raven when she said this. The vampire took a menacing step toward Leah, who smiled. "Do my words anger you, demon? I'll bet nothing would please you more than to rip my throat out. Have you ever tasted the blood of a goddess?" Leah held out her wrist invitingly. "They say it is sweeter than the blood of ten witches."

Raven's eyes were fixed on the small blue veins under Leah's white skin. She could smell the rich fey blood in the young girl so strongly that it left a sweet taste on the back of her tongue. A low growl escaped Raven and before she could stop herself she was moving forward. Only the firm grip Titus had on her shoulder stopped her from swooping down on the young girl.

"Control yourself, Raven," he whispered to her. Raven nodded in understanding, but kept her hungry eyes locked on Leah. Titus was warning Raven against touching the girl more for her own safety than that of the sprite. Raven was an old and very strong vampire and if the sprite were to gain access to her it would end disastrously. "Leah, it would be wise for you to stop taunting my aides."

"Why, when the gods taunt me every day that they allow you to live? You disgust me, Titus!"

"Of this I am sure, but it does not change the fact that you are here to serve me and only the death of one of us will change that."

"Good, because I see your death coming sooner than expected, which I'm sure is why you've come." Leah folded her legs under her and glared up at Titus. "How many of your forces has the Hunter slain already? Ten, maybe ten thousand? Either way, the results will be the same. As long as you chase the Nimrod, you will be undone."

Titus's eyes flashed with anger. "Taunt me all you want, sprite. Even your once great powers cannot manipulate the strands of fate, but I can and you will help me. Helena." He turned to the vampire.

Helena smiled and punched a hole in Judy's chest. She turned her hand left and right inside the girl's ribcage and pulled out her still-beating heart. Slowly she sank her teeth into the organ and drank deeply. She reluctantly pulled her fangs loose and offered the heart to Raven, who bit down and drank her fill, all the while keeping her eyes on Leah. The blood had slowed to a trickle when the heart was finally passed to Titus. His powerful hands flattened the heart, spilling blood over his knuckles and onto the floor. Titus turned, hands dripping blood, and stalked over to the bed.

There was madness dancing under the surface of Titus's words when he spoke. "I see that all these years as my slave have done nothing to dull that sharp tongue of yours, but I will break your spirit yet, sprite. Blood and bone is the dowry for what I need."

Leah screamed and backpedaled, knocking

over her nightstand and the plate that had been on it. She quickly grabbed the plate and broke it against the ground, threatening Titus with a jagged piece. "There will be blood here today, demon, but it will be yours!" Leah charged Titus with the shard of porcelain, intent on carving his eyes out. Before she could complete her lunge, however, Raven had her, hanging helplessly in the air. From the look in Raven's eyes you could tell that her control had finally slipped. Her fangs flashed and she was on Leah, but before she could break the skin Titus grabbed her head. With a snap he wrenched the vampire's head to the side and broke her neck.

"NO!" Helena shouted and rushed toward Titus. He grabbed a fistful of her golden hair and jerked her head back so that her throat was exposed to him.

"Have you all taken leave of your senses?" Titus threw Helena across the room and into a wall. The impact wasn't severe enough to do any real damage but it certainly brought her back to her senses. "If you want to fight over flesh like dogs then I will be more than happy to drop you back off in the swamps where I found you, whoring and feeding on tourists and animals to sustain yourselves." Titus turned to the door guards. "If either of these jackals moves without my say-so shoot them through the head."

"Yes, sir," both guards answered.

"And you." Titus snatched Leah by the front of her nightgown. She cringed in his grip as the blood on his hands stained the soft silk, threatening to seep through. "I believe you have a story to tell." Titus smeared the blood across Leah's face and stepped back.

Leah's body jerked and seized as the blood on her skin began to boil. She howled in pain, sending a beam of light from her mouth to bounce on the ceiling. As the blood cooled, it sank into her skin and the pain seemed to subside as a glow began to develop around Leah. Her body snapped upright and when she slowly turned to Titus her eyes burned like the morning sun. When Leah spoke, the power of her voice humbled all in the room. "Ask and receive the goddess's truth."

Titus got right to the point. "Why does the Nimrod still elude me?"

"Of course, your fool's mission." A soft breeze swept through the room, blowing Leah's hair back from her face and showing the hard lines around her eyes and mouth. She always looked older in the thrall of her power. "The Nimrod eludes you because it is not meant for you to have. It has chosen the Hunter as its new mate. Even the Bishop struggles to maintain his influence over the Hunter as the bond between weapon and host grows increasingly stronger."

"Yes, but the Hunter is still just a man. He does not yet understand the power bestowed upon him," Titus pointed out.

"A temporary setback. The Knights of Christ are reborn and will soon come into their own. Though the Hunter is still a novice, he learns a bit more every day. Under the tutelage of the Medusan, the Hunter will awaken and lead the Knights against the dark forces," Leah told him.

"You are wrong, goddess. The Medusan are extinct. I saw to that personally," Titus corrected her.

Leah hovered closer to the foot of the bed, but Titus did not back away. "Four hundred years ago, your treachery destroyed the sacred order of the Time Keepers, but your ego saw to it that there would be one to watch you fail."

"Jonas." Titus recalled the young scholar he had betrayed and left to die.

Leah nodded. "The Medusan has seen all that has passed and all that will be. It is this knowledge that will help consummate the marriage between the Hunter and the relic. For now the Hunter is still blind, but the light of Sanctuary will soon show him the way."

"With all due respect, goddess, your vision is flawed. Sanctuary was burned to the ground and its leader murdered."

Leah slowly descended to the ground and stood before Titus. He was a foot taller than the girl but still felt small in her presence. She looked at him not with her usual scorn, but with pity. "The Great House has indeed fallen, but what do wood and stone matter when the magic still lives?"

"But Angelo . . ." Titus started.

". . . is dead. You've said as much already. The High Brother's spirit has ascended, but his power remains on Earth, tucked quietly in another and waiting to be discovered."

This was something Titus hadn't expected. Each Spark was the very life force and source of its house's power. Each was powerful in its own right, but together they empowered the order. When Riel slew Angelo it was a great boon for the dark order, not just because one of their greatest adversaries was no more, but because the destruction of Angelo's Spark meant that the circle of power had been broken, leaving the order vulnerable for the first time in almost a millennium. Had Angelo passed it to another of the High Brothers, the house wouldn't have burned—which meant he'd entrusted it to someone or something outside the order. As long as someone carried the Spark, there was always the threat that the Great House in New York could be resurrected. Titus couldn't allow that.

"Where is the Spark?" Titus asked.

Leah smirked. "Neither here nor there, but in between."

"I've not time nor the patience for your riddles, sprite," he warned.

"It is no riddle, Lord Titus, but a truth. One that your ignorance blinds you to, but in time you will learn."

"Time means nothing to the immortal," Titus told her.

"But you are no immortal, Titus of Athens. It is magic that sustains your wretched life, the same magic that prevents your master from bestowing true demonhood upon you."

Titus absently rubbed the scar on his chest. During his botched coup of the Seven-Day Siege, the Hunter had buried the trident in Titus's chest. For reasons unknown to any of them the blow didn't kill Titus, but the center point of the trident had snapped off and four hundred years later remained lodged in his chest. The broken piece was both a gift and a curse: it made Titus more powerful, but it also rejected Belthon's attempts at making Titus a full demon. The piece of the Nimrod that remained in Titus's chest was a constant reminder of what he had lost and what continued to elude him.

"No, but the Nimrod will change that. Four centuries ago I was denied my chance at godhood, but I will have my reward. If I have to level New York City to make it so, I will have my prize."

Leah hovered a few feet off the ground and looked Titus in the eyes. "And do you think the aristocrats who rule will sit by and allow your personal vendetta to spill into the mortal world and risk exposure? You will call your gathering and spread your lies. Some will listen, but others will see you for the serpent you are."

"And it will matter not when I am master of all. I will usher in a new age for supernatural beings as well as mortals."

"What you will usher in is war, Titus. Not all of Midland's refugees will be receptive to falling under the rule of Belthon and the dark order. They will not follow you."

"Then they will die!" Titus said heatedly.

"Or you will," she shot back. Leah sat on the bed and curled her legs beneath her. The light in her eyes was beginning to fade, but she had a parting warning. "Beware, Titus, for the mouse has become the cat. You won't have to chase the Nimrod much longer because it will come to you." With that the goddess's light faded and Leah was a child again. She lay on the bed, curled snugly under her blankets, and drifted off to sleep.

"Damn you," Titus cursed the sleeping girl. He stormed toward the door when suddenly he remembered Helena and Raven. "Take her to your quarters," he said to Helena, pointing at Raven. "She'll be fine in a few nights."

"I will attend her personally," Helena assured him, scooping Raven in her arms. The girl's body was completely limp, but her eyes were wide and staring at Titus with contempt.

"No, you have more pressing duties. Help the sorcerers bind Leah for transport and then join me in the Hall of Mirrors."

This surprised Helena. In all the years she had been with Titus, Leah had never been moved from her room—and for good reason. The body she was trapped inside and the wards binding the room were the only things keeping her from reclaiming her power. If she were able to unlock even a fraction of her magic, she would surely destroy Titus and all who served him.

"My lord, I don't think we should move her from the room. If she happens to get loose . . ."

"I know full well what could happen if Leah is freed, which is why I'm bringing her with us. With Flagg gone there is no one here I can trust to make sure our little guest is kept secure. Once all is ready we will be leaving Ontario for a time."

"And where are we going?"

"To New York City," he said, much to Helena's surprise. "We have a gathering to attend and then we'll see to the youngest of the Redfeather clan and my weapon!"

CHAPTER THIRTEEN

"This is it?" Gabriel looked at the sign in front of them quizzically.

"According to our little friend here it is," De Mona said, covering her nose with her hand. The overwhelming stench of the various animals seemed to invade every one of her senses. They had crossed three boroughs before finally winding up in the Bronx, where the rips closest to the Iron Mountains were hidden. According to Gilchrest the main entrance to the goblin court was located somewhere within the Botanical Gardens, but De Mona had been apprehensive about dropping into Midland so close to the goblin stronghold and the unknown. Gilchrest had reluctantly told them about a second entrance that was located inside the Bronx Zoo.

"I don't know, I expected something a little more . . . magical, I guess," Gabriel said.

"Rips here open to marketplace, where slaves and commoners mingle to sing sob stories." Gilchrest spat on the ground. "From here many miles we walk to reach goblin kingdom. Told you I did we should use main rip, but not trust Gilchrest," the small goblin said.

"We sure don't. Walking through the main entrance to get ambushed by a bunch of your buddies is the last thing we need. Nah, the servants' entrance is fine by us. Now, lead on." De Mona shoved the goblin through the tiny hole in the fence.

The sun had set and the zoo was closed for the day, but the staff still roamed the grounds, so they had to move carefully to avoid discovery. Most of the humans who serviced the zoo at night were supporters of Titus who would like nothing more than to discover the fugitives and turn them in to gain Titus's favor. Between De Mona and Gabriel they could surely handle whatever the humans could dish out, but fighting them would blow the element of surprise and they knew they only had one shot at penetrating the mountains.

"I don't like this, De Mona," Gabriel whispered.

"Me either. Following a goblin into the heart of his kingdom doesn't sit well with me, but what choice do we have?"

"Not just that. I mean leaving the others. Jonas and the others have as much stake in this as we do. It seems kind of wrong that we left them behind."

"No more wrong than leaving your grandfather in the hands of the goblins while Jonas looks for spiritual enlightenment," De Mona shot back. "Gabriel, I feel you on not wanting to leave them behind, but they didn't leave us a choice. I've already lost someone close to me because of this business with the Nimrod and I'm trying to spare you the heartache."

"And I appreciate that, but at the same time I have to wonder if maybe Rogue and Jonas were right about not rushing into this headlong without a plan."

"Oh, I've got a plan. We go in quietly if possible and rescue your grandfather. If not"—she extended her claws—"we make shredded beef out of everyone standing between us and Redfeather. Now let's go." She stalked off.

Gilchrest led them through several winding paths that snaked between and behind some of the animal cages. The growls and other sounds emitting from the cages they passed said that their presence there rattled the animals. As they passed the gorilla cages the primates became very agitated. One of them actually threw himself violently against the bars when it spotted the goblin.

"He doesn't seem to like you much. I can't say that I blame him," De Mona told Gilchrest, to which he just snickered.

"Goblins use beasts for training warriors, eaten they are when can no longer fight. No fight, no purpose, so become food you do."

Gabriel looked at the raging gorillas with pity. "That's just sick. You goblins are nothing more than cannibals!"

Gilchrest laughed. "More civilized humans are

you think, but I say not! You eat the flesh as we do, just not your own. Goblins devour all to survive. It natural order of things under the mountains," Gilchrest explained.

It was no easy task, but the trio managed to make it to the heart of the zoo undetected. When they reached the pit housing the crocodiles, Gilchrest stopped and peered over the side. Below them several large crocodiles floated about in the murky waters or rested lazily on rocks. They seemed almost docile, but when one larger crocodile took a chunk out of a smaller one who had swum too close it brought them back to the reality of what they were dealing with.

"I'd hate to meet one of those guys in a dark alley," De Mona said, watching the reptiles.

"Yeah, those things are creepy," Gabriel agreed.

"Too bad for you humans, because within their lair lies the entrance." Gilchrest pointed to the far end of the pit. Gabriel couldn't see it in the dark, but De Mona could. Behind one of the man-made islands was a tiny hole in the rock face. It was too small for one of the crocodiles to swim through, but it was big enough for a man . . . barely.

"You can't be serious." De Mona looked down at Gilchrest.

"Indeed, indeed. You say no to main rip so this only other way," Gilchrest said with a smirk.

"No dice, creep. Come on, Gabriel, we can head over to the Botanical Gardens and go in through there." De Mona tugged at his arm, but Gabriel continued to stare into the crocodile pit.

"There's no time." He removed his overcoat and tossed it to the ground. "I'll distract them while you guys make for the hole." He braced himself against the railing to jump over, but De Mona stopped him.

"You're way too slow and your human flesh wouldn't stand a chance against those things. Get to the hole as quickly as you can, then get the hell out of my way. I don't plan on dancing with these things any longer than I have to. Now, let's do this." De Mona leaped over the side and into the pit. No sooner had she hit the water than the crocodiles were on her.

De Mona broke the surface of the water with a gasp. It only took a few seconds for her eyes to adjust to the near pitch-dark and take stock of her surroundings. What she saw wasn't good. Two of the crocodiles that had been lounging on the rocks had slipped into the water and were heading straight for her.

"Crap," De Mona spat and began swimming toward dry land. She was an excellent swimmer, but no match for the predators in their element.

Something that felt like solid rock slammed into her legs under the water, knocking her off balance. A pair of massive jaws tried to capitalize on her temporary disorientation, but missed by a hair when De Mona dipped under the water. As the attacking crocodile passed overhead, she gutted it with her claws. She'd managed to get rid of one opponent, but the blood that now filled the water not only made it hard for her too see, it also attracted more crocodiles. A sleek reptile closed in on her from behind with its massive jaws barreling at her midsection. De Mona tried to maneuver out of the way, but the crocodile still managed to grab hold of her leg. The force from the crocodile's jaws was so intense that she screamed out, taking in a mouthful of water when she did. The crocodile held tight to De Mona's leg, going into its death roll, steadily sinking into the depths of the pit. Though the croc's teeth weren't strong enough to pierce her Valkrin skin, she couldn't break its lock, and with all the twisting and turning it was impossible for her to use her claws. If the crocodile got her to the bottom of the pit she knew she was as good as dead.

De Mona could feel herself panicking when she saw the other crocodiles coming to join in on the meal. The air in her lungs was becoming thin and she knew she'd black out soon. As her eyes drifted up she saw a beautiful white light just above the surface of the water. She smiled because she knew it was an angel coming to whisk her spirit away to heaven. She wondered if her mother's demon blood would prevent her from getting into heaven, where her father was surely waiting for her. The angel's magnificent glow expanded and then crashed into the pit, burning the crocodile to a crisp and freeing her. The water rose in great waves that hung in the air above De Mona. Thankfully her ankle was only bruised, so she was able to scramble out of reach of the roiling water and the crocodiles. When she looked up, it wasn't an angel that she saw but a Redfeather.

"Hurry up. I don't know how long I can hold this," he grunted. The Nimrod was held high over his head, bursting with power.

De Mona leaped onto the wall, using her razor-sharp claws to scale the damp rocks to freedom. When she reached Gabriel she was so happy that she wanted to kiss him, but the studied expression on his face gave her pause. "How are you doing that?"

"Does it matter? Get to the hole. When I let this thing go the pit is gonna flood and we already know you're not the best swimmer."

De Mona grabbed Gilchrest, who had been cowering behind a rock, and leaped to the small island where the hole was. She could hear the snap of thunder followed by a great splashing. When she looked over her shoulder, she saw a massive wave rolling in their direction. De Mona barely had time to secure the goblin when the water swept them both into the hole. The three-by-three hole carved in the rock went on for several yards before finally depositing them inside a small chamber.

De Mona shifted to her night vision and scanned the room for further dangers. It was a high-roofed cavern hidden within the crocodile pit that only had one way in and one way out. The air was heavy with the stink of death and the floor was littered with bones. Most appeared to be animal bones, but she could make out a few human ones in the pile as well as some she couldn't identify. Remembering that Gabriel had yet to come out of the tunnel took her mind off the bones momentarily. She was beginning to think he hadn't made it when she heard a high shriek, followed by a last belch of water that spat Gabriel onto the ground at her feet.

Gabriel rolled over onto his hands and knees and began coughing water onto the earth. "That is not something I would want to do again." He looked around at the dark chamber and felt a chill. "Where the hell are we?"

"On border of Midland," Gilchrest told him. "Gateway we seek at end of corridor." He pointed a gnarled finger into the dark tunnel and stepped back, waiting for one of his captors to take the lead.

De Mona could smell the fear coming off the goblin in waves. "Okay, what gives? You've already led us through a crocodile pit. What's next? We gotta wrestle bears?"

"All rips to Midland fraught with danger, but none more than goblins. Only strong fit enough to set foot on our lands. Tell me, human"—he looked up at Gabriel—"how much willing to risk you are for old man's life?"

"Everything," Gabriel said, and stepped into the darkness.

"Hold on, Gabe." De Mona caught up with him, dragging Gilchrest behind her. "I don't like the stink coming outta this place."

"Relax, De Mona. We just kicked the asses of six hungry crocodiles. I think we can handle whatever is lurking down here." Gabriel tapped the Nimrod's shaft on the ground twice and sent a flash of lightning into the air to illuminate the tunnel. When the bolt exploded, lighting up the tunnel like mid-afternoon, Gabriel saw what could only be described as a school bus with teeth coming right at him.

CHAPTER FOURTEEN

It was a crocodile—or it least it had been at one point. Its body was nearly the length of a subway car, with shiny scales that covered it like armor. The whiplike tail thrashed back and forth, knocking stones free from the chamber walls. The reptile's head and muzzle were long and sloped with two rows of chainsawlike teeth jutting out from its jaws. The only parts of the beast that hadn't been mutated were the cold reptilian eyes that had Gabriel locked in their sights.

Gabriel was rooted to the spot with fear as the creature charged him, but thankfully De Mona wasn't. She knocked him out of the way seconds before the creature's teeth cut through the space where he had been standing. "Shake it off, Gabriel!" De Mona slapped him across the face to snap him out of it.

Gabriel finally came around and gasped when he saw the creature coming toward them again. "Look out," he warned, but it was too late. The creature's tail whipped around like a length of iron coil and crashed into De Mona, sending her sailing across the room and into a wall. The creature turned its attention to Gabriel and bared its fangs.

Gabriel rolled out of the way as the thing's teeth carved a gash in the cave wall behind him. It was surprisingly quick for its size, so it didn't take long for it to mount another strike. The creature whipped its tail over its head like a scorpion and tried to spear Gabriel, but the Nimrod, which had manifested itself in Gabriel's hand, deflected the blow. Calling the lightning to the points of the trident, Gabriel sent a bolt at the creature—but to his surprise, the bolt bounced off and tore a chunk out of the ceiling. The enraged creature stumbled forward with its head bowed to ram Gabriel, who had backed himself into a corner. At the last possible second Gabriel leaped out of the way and the creature's head crashed into the stone wall. Firing on the run, Gabriel unleashed bolt after bolt into the creature's hide, but they seemed to do little more than agitate it.

There was a cry of rage from somewhere behind the creature seconds before De Mona, who had called up her full change, came soaring out of the darkness and landed on its back. She tore into the back of the creature's neck and the top of its head with her claws. Sparks jumped from the creature's body as she struck it over and over, trying to penetrate the armor with only slightly better results than Gabriel had had with the lightning.

"How do we stop that thing?" Gabriel asked Gilchrest.

"You die. That only way to stop the guardian," Gilchrest snickered. "Promise to get you to Midland I did, but to get you inside alive I did not. Die well, human scum!" The goblin scampered off down the corridor.

"You little bastard." Gabriel reached for the remote on his wrist, but the creature's tail knocked him to the ground. It launched a second strike to crush him, but the Nimrod erected a barrier around him that the beast could not break. Gabriel rolled back to his feet and charged the creature with the trident bared. He delivered a powerful strike to the side of the creature's head, igniting a backlash of power that sent them both reeling.

De Mona continued the assault on the creature's body with her claws, trying to find a chink in the armor. One of her hands got caught between the creature's scales and she could feel its soft flesh beneath. This gave her an idea. "Gabriel, on my mark go for the head and lay this big bastard down!" she called to him while trying to wedge her fingers between the scales on top of the creature's skull. Once she had a good grip, she began to pull with everything she had. Scales began to bend and then there was a ripping noise as she pulled a bare spot in the center of its skull, drawing a roar from the beast. "Now!" She leaped off the creature.

Gabriel ran toward the creature at top speed

with the Nimrod held like a javelin. As he closed the distance, he thought about his parents' murders, his grandfather's abduction, and Katy and Carter.

That's right, feed it, the Bishop urged. The trident glowed brilliantly as he forced everything he had into it and let go. The relic cut across the darkened chamber like a shooting star and dug into the creature's skull with a burst of blinding white light that knocked Gabriel to the ground. When he finally regained his composure he saw the creature lying in a heap with half its skull sizzled to a crisp.

"You okay?" De Mona asked while helping him to his feet.

"Thanks to you, yes." Gabriel smiled. "Good job exposing the soft spot on that thing's head."

"Better job hitting the mark in one shot," she countered. "Hey, we gotta look out for each other, right? I gotta admit, I wasn't totally sure that you'd be able to stop that thing."

"Neither was I, but the Bishop was." Gabriel looked at the tattoo that had reappeared on his forearm.

"Where'd our little friend get off to?" De Mona scanned the cave. She heard faint moaning coming from the far end of the tunnel that the creature had been guarding. When she and Gabriel went to investigate, they found Gilchrest curled up into a ball on the floor in pain. His little tunic was singed and the collar around his neck beeped frantically.

"I guess this thing only allows you to get so far from the remote," Gabriel observed. He reset the controls and snatched Gilchrest roughly off the ground. "I should cook your little ass for the stunt you pulled, but we still need to get into Midland. But if you try another trick like that . . ." Gabriel raised his arm and showed Gilchrest the remote. "I guess I don't have to tell you what'll happen."

"No more, no more. I lead you now," Gilchrest croaked.

"You damn well better, and if we run into any more surprises that remote is going to be the least of your concerns." De Mona jabbed him with one of her talons.

A few yards down the tunnel dipped, taking them farther beneath the zoo. Down that way the air was less stale and they could feel a cool breeze coming from up ahead. A thin mist rolled along the ground and began to thicken the farther they went.

"Close we are," Gilchrest explained.

Just ahead of them was set of wooden doors with brass rings hanging from them. Carved into the wood of the doors were the images of two squat men with shaggy beards dressed in battle armor. Both men were holding shields and twin battle axes. Gabriel approached the doors and studied them in fascination.

"Magnificent," he said, running his hands along the doors. The Nimrod stirred within him and he could feel the magic coming from the doors. "Are they enchanted?"

"Bah, the magic here died long ago with the spirit of the dwarfs," Gilchrest spat. "Through these doors lies the place you seek, Midland."

"Then what are we waiting for?" Gabriel pressed his hands against the doors.

"Careful, there may be another surprise waiting for us on the other side," De Mona warned.

"Paranoid you are, demon," Gilchrest mocked her. "No more tricks. Step through and arrive in Midland we will."

De Mona looked hesitant but she finally gave in. "Okay, let's make it happen." She pressed her hands against the door opposite Gabriel's. "On the count of three. One, two, three," she grunted and pushed the door. It took all of her demonic strength before the doors began to give. When they finally opened, more fog poured from the entrance and surrounded them. De Mona looked at Gilchrest suspiciously, but he motioned for them to go on. She still didn't trust the goblin, so she shoved him through first. When she didn't hear him screaming she decided it was probably safe and looked over at Gabriel.

"If you've got any reservations, now is the time to voice them," she told him.

"We've come too far to turn back now, De Mona. Let's do it." He extended his hand.

De Mona shrugged. "Who wants to live forever anyway?" She took his hand and together they stepped into the unknown.

For at least ten minutes Gabriel was speechless. He had read about some truly mythical places but nothing prepared him for the view he beheld from what Gilchrest called the Black Hills. The night sky was a lovely shade of lavender with twin blush-colored moons illuminating the valley directly below them, which was decorated with dozens of tiny lights from the shops that were still open for business.

"I've never seen anything like this. It's beauti-ful," Gabriel said in awe.

"Do not be fooled, human. The cities of Midland all filled with danger, but none more than where we go, the Iron Mountains." Gilchrest pointed to the east. Looming in the distance were massive mist-capped mountains that loomed over the villages like a shadow of death. Lightning crashed somewhere in the distance and De Mona visibly trembled. "Lost your heart for the fight, have you, demon?"

"I'll show you just how much heart I have when we reach the Iron Mountains," she assured him. "Now lead the way."

"Anxious to meet death you are, and more anx-ious I am to make the introduction, but not yet," Gilchrest told her.

"What do you mean not yet?" Gabriel snatched Gilchrest up by the collar. "We came to rescue my grandfather from the Iron Mountains and you're going to take us there!" Gabriel's hands crackled with power and threatened to incinerate the little goblin.

"If you kill me then you'll never get into mountains," Gilchrest said, shying away from the sparks. Gabriel hesitated, but eventually dropped the goblin back to the ground. "Wise choice. Enter the mountains we will, but make a stop in the market first we must."

"Dude, we didn't come down here to shop," De Mona told him.

"Stupid topsider, never make it through Midland without detection in human rags." He pointed at their clothes.

Gabriel looked from his worn sweatshirt to De Mona's dirty jeans. "He does have a point. I guess we're going to the market."

"Hold on." De Mona sized the goblin up. "Why do you care if we're spotted or not? If anything I'd have thought you'd be banking on someone ratting us out to the goblins so you can get away from us."

Gilchrest laughed at the statement. "My freedom come soon enough, demon. Need you to get into Iron Mountains so that my brother, Orden, will have the honor of taking your life, not goblin soldiers. Now come." Gilchrest started down the hills toward the village.

"Now that's reassuring," De Mona said, before following Gilchrest.

Gabriel lingered behind for a while, staring at the Iron Mountains off in the distance and thinking of his grandfather and what he must be going through in the goblin dungeons. To say that he wasn't afraid of what lay ahead of him would have been a lie, but Gabriel had come to a point where it was time to lock his fear away in a box with no key. The dark forces had already stolen his parents and he refused to lose the only person left in the world who loved him. If it was a war Titus wanted, Gabriel would give him one that would be remembered for all time.

My will be done? the Bishop whispered softly. There was a pleading note in his tone this time.

Gabriel took one last look at the Iron Mountains and closed his fist tightly. "Yes, it will."

CHAPTER FIFTEEN

Lucy could not hide the horror on her face when she saw what the goblins had done to the dwarfs of Cristobel's village. The streets were littered with bodies that had been either burned or gutted. Birdlike creatures sat perched on rooftops, occasionally swooping down to peck at the flesh of one of the victims. In the shadows of a doorway two dogs fought over the remains of a small boy who had been speared through the heart. It was the worst massacre she had ever seen.

"Cassy!" Cristobel shouted, checking bodies and the wreckage of the buildings.

"Cristobel, if you don't stop yelling you'll attract the goblins, or whatever the hell else is skulking around here," Lucy warned him. The birds must have smelled her blood because they had inched closer. Lucy tossed a ball of magic at the birds, scattering them, but within seconds they were back to stalking her. "Can we get out of here?"

"No, I must find my sister. Cassy!" he shouted.

"Cristobel?" a small voice called from a doorway down the street. From it stepped a female dwarf with blond hair and clear blue eyes. When she saw her brother she ran to him and they shared a tight hug.

"Thank goodness, I thought they had gotten you too." He checked her for injuries, but thankfully she was unharmed. "What happened?"

She looked up at him with tear-filled eyes. "It was the goblins. They accused us of harboring enemies of the empire and demanded that we give them up. When we told them that we knew nothing about it they began the slaughter." She shook her head, trying to rid herself of the memories. "Cristobel, they said that you caused this by killing one of Orden's men and helping the topsiders escape."

"I'm afraid I'm to blame for that." Lucy stepped forward. She tried to muster a smile but couldn't quite manage. Her skin had gone pale and she was now sweating heavily.

"Who are you?" Cassy eyed Lucy suspiciously.

"She is a friend. She saved me and killed one of the goblins in the dungeon," Cristobel told his sister.

"Good riddance." Cassy spat on the ground. "I hate them for what they have done to us, brother. I wish she'd killed them *all* instead of just one."

"Cassy, do not say such things. Your heart is too pure to be tainted by hate. Are there any more survivors?" Cristobel asked.

"Yes, some of us managed to escape the raid and make it to the tunnels beneath the temple."

"Good. We should get under cover too. The goblins will surely be back. The temple is this way." Cristobel motioned for Lucy to follow.

"You'll get no arguments from me." Lucy took a step, then staggered.

"Are you okay?" Cristobel asked with a concerned look on his face.

"Yeah, I'm just not feeling too hot. Damned thorns," she said before passing out in his arms.

"Is she okay?" Cassy asked, peering down at Lucy. The witch's eyes were now rolling into her head.

"I don't know." Cristobel knelt beside her. He touched her forehead and she was burning with fever. Frantically he checked Lucy's body for signs of a wound. He flipped her over and ran his hands up the length of her legs and back. When he got to her arm his face darkened.

"What's wrong, brother?" Cassy asked, now kneeling beside Lucy also.

"Cassy, give me your dagger." He extended his hand, and Cassy placed her dagger in it while watching her brother closely. Carefully he sliced the skin on the back of Lucy's left bicep and pulled off a loose piece. Holding it to the light, he could see the tiny spines sticking out from it. "She must've been hit in the battle with the Slovs."

"Poison." Cassy recoiled as if the skin could infect her too.

"Yes." Cristobel sat Lucy up and checked her for a pulse. "She's very weak. We must get her to the healers."

"The healers were the first ones to fall under the goblin blades. Most of them are no more, and the few who survive have fled," Cassy explained.

"Then you must attend to her, sister."

"Me? Cristobel, I'm no healer. Mother taught me a few potions but I'm hardly skilled enough to treat the venom of a Slov."

"You must at least try, Cassy. I owe it to her and Redfeather." He thought back to the old man who had sacrificed himself so that they could escape.

"Very well," Cassy finally agreed. "Let's get her below."

Marsha had been on duty for so many hours that she could barely keep her eyes open. She so wanted to delegate her responsibilities to someone else while she got just a few moments of sleep, but Angelique had demanded that she conducted the tests personally.

In all her years studying the link between witches and familiars she had never encountered anything like what had come over Tiki. He had fallen into some sort of coma and no spell they had tried was able to bring him out of it. Marsha reasoned that the coma had to have been caused by some traumatic experience his mistress had gone through, but what that experience was remained an unanswered question. Lucy could very well be dead, but if so, why hadn't her familiar passed on also? It wasn't unheard of for a witch or familiar to live after the death of her partner, but those instances were one in ten thousand. There had to be an explanation.

A shriek snapped Marsha out of her daydream. She rushed over to the glass enclosure where Tiki slept and the ferret seemed to be having some sort of seizure. Black blood was oozing from the creature's mouth and rectum. Marsha managed to stabilize the ferret and collected a sample of his blood to examine under the microscope. What she saw puzzled her.

"What's wrong?" the lab tech who had been assigned to assist Marsha asked.

"Who has had access to this familiar besides you and me?" Marsha asked sharply.

"No one, ma'am. Why?"

Marsha looked at the tech seriously. "Because he's been poisoned."

Lucy felt like she had been hit in the back of the head with a small hammer when she finally regained consciousness. She tried to open her eyes, but the light made her feel like needles were being shoved into them. She gave herself a minute to let them adjust and then tried again to open them.

Things were blurry at first but she was gradually able to focus on what had looked like shadows shifting about her. Lucy found herself surrounded by six sets of large blue eyes. Startled, she tried to sit up and the room swam.

"Don't try to move, child." The female dwarf pushed her gently back down on the pile of straw she had been resting on. The dwarf had a pleasant face with thin worry lines in the corners of her eyes. Her mousy brown hair hung down around her face in two pigtails.

"Who . . ." Lucy croaked. Her mouth was as dry as a desert wind and she could feel her lips crack when she moved them.

"Water, fetch me some water," the female dwarf ordered. After a few moments a small boy came through the crowd of onlookers carrying a bowl filled with water, which he handed to the female attending Lucy. Gently, she lifted Lucy's head and poured a little of the water into her mouth. The cool water was so soothing to her dry throat that she tried to gulp it down and ended up choking. "You don't have to swallow it all in one gulp, child, we have plenty more."

"Until the goblins decide to poison our supplies." This came from a young dwarf who had been standing in the doorway. He had cropped red hair and the first signs of a beard on his chin. From the way he was staring at Lucy it was clear that he was not happy about having the witch as a guest.

"You mind your manners, Alec," the female dwarf warned him.

"Come now, Mavis, I am only speaking the truth. It is because of Cristobel and his friends that the goblins have forced us to live underground like gophers. It is only a matter of time before we are unearthed and they finish what they started. If it were up to me I would give the murderers over to the goblins so that we can be at peace."

"Peace?" Cristobel stepped into the room. He was still carrying the bloodstained battle ax. "Living as slaves while the goblins play gods with the lives of our women and children, is that what you call peace, Alec?"

Alec looked at the ground, shamefaced. "I only meant that helping the strangers can only bring more trouble to us."

Mavis twisted her thin lips. "As long as the goblins inhabit these mountains, there will be trouble with them in one form or another. Helping this girl won't change that for better or worse."

"Listen, I'm nobody's charity case, so I'll just get out of your way." Lucy managed to sit up, but no sooner had she she done so than she almost fell on her face. Mavis and Cristobel caught her and laid her back on the haystack.

"You won't get very far on those shaky legs," Mavis told Lucy while dabbing her forehead with a damp cloth. "You pay Alec no mind, child. You are our guest and welcome to stay as long as need be."

Numbness ran from the fingertips of Lucy's left hand to her shoulder. She tried to flex her hand but her fingers did little more than tingle. "What's wrong with me?" she asked, trying to keep her eyes focused on the swirling faces of the dwarfs.

"You were hit by some of the Slov's spines. The poison is trying to kill off the nerves in your arm," Cristobel explained.

Lucy turned her head and for the first time noticed the bandage covering her left bicep. "How bad is it, doc?" she asked Mavis in a weak attempt at humor.

Mavis's eyes welled up with tears. "Young Cassy did the best she could with the wound and slowed the poison from reaching your heart, but I fear that it's only a temporary solution. The magic in your blood seems to be feeding the poison. I've tried every herb at my disposal, but I'm afraid I just don't have much to work with down here. Someone will have to brave the journey to the marketplace outside the mountains to fetch the things we need to treat this properly."

"Then I will go," Cristobel said.

"Please don't, brother." Cassy tugged at his arm. "You are already a fugitive and if the goblins find you out there they will surely kill you and I will truly be alone."

"Cassy, I must. Had it not been for Lucy and her friend Redfeather I would be dead right now. If it is within my power to help then I will do so. I'll leave for the market immediately.

"No," Lucy wheezed. "I won't let you put your-self at risk for me."

"If your wounds aren't treated, you will die," Mavis told her.

"Then maybe death is better," Lucy said de-liriously. "Yes, just let me sleep so I can see my parents."

Mavis pried one of Lucy's eyes open and checked her pupils. "She's getting worse."

"Then I must hurry," Cristobel said.

"Brother, please, there will be goblins at the market. You must rethink this!" Cassy pleaded.

"Enough, Cassy. Tonight I saw more courage mustered in an old man and girl than I have ever been able to claim in my entire life. Their kind-ness must be repaid. I will go to the market and get what is needed, goblins be damned! Will any of you come with me?" Cristobel looked around at the dwarfs assembled in the room. Most avoided his gaze but one brave soul stepped up.

"I am with you," the dark-haired dwarf pledged.

A blond dwarf stepped up. "As am I."

Cristobel smiled and placed his hands on the shoulders of the dwarfs. "Then let's gather what we need and set out."

"I'll pray for you, brother," Cassy told him.

Cristobel smiled. "Do not pray for me, sister. Pray for the goblins that will loose their heads if they try and stop me." He retrieved the goblin ax and hoisted it onto his shoulder.

"Well, if you insist upon going on this mission

you at least need a weapon that will give you a better chance then that crudely crafted thing." Mavis nodded at the ax.

"This ax served me well against the Slovs in the forest," Cristobel said defensively.

"Yes, but these are no scavengers, these are hell's enforcers." Mavis walked over to the large anvil in the corner and began to push. "Help me," she urged. Cristobel helped her move the anvil, revealing a trapdoor hiding under it. Brushing away the dirt and cobwebs, Mavis pulled open the door and hauled out a large sack from the cubbyhole. "If you are going to take goblins' heads, you will do it with dwarfish blades." She opened the sack and revealed a beautiful golden ax.

"It's stunning." Cristobel ran his hand over the blades lovingly. "Mavis, where in the name of the gods did you get this?"

The old maid winked at him. "My family was among the finest weapon smiths in all of Midland when we still counted for something. The blade you are holding was crafted by my late husband for my son when he came to manhood. My son died with it in his hand during the goblin wars," she said emotionally.

Cristobel touched her shoulder. "I will return it to you, I promise."

"And it is a promise I will hold you to, Cristobel. But there is something I would ask of you before you go."

"Anything."

Mavis cupped his face in her hands and looked at him very seriously. "When you return the blade to me, make sure that it is stained with the blood of our tormentors."

"Done," he agreed. "We'd better be going."

Mavis and what was left of the villagers followed them to the mouth of the tunnels. "Travel safely, young warriors, and show no mercy. The goblins will surely have none to show to you." After seeing Cristobel off, Mavis and Cassy returned to Lucy's side. She tossed and turned restlessly on the straw, moaning feverishly as the venom racked her system.

"She doesn't have much time," Cassy said, running a cool cloth over Lucy's face.

"Then let's hope our warriors travel with the speed of the gods. Alec, could you fetch me some water," she called to the bitter young dwarf, but when she turned around to see if he was complying he was nowhere in sight. "Where did that fool boy get off to?"

Alec was out of breath by the time he crossed the final hill. As soon as he had lain eyes on the witch, he had known she was the source of their troubles. Cristobel had been a fool to rise up against the goblins and help the strangers, and now he had brought their wrath down upon the heads of the entire village.

Looming in the distance ahead was the stronghold of the goblins. Just seeing the rocky structure filled Alec with such dread that he was worried he would get cold feet and turn around. A thundering sound coming from somewhere beyond the hills to his left drew his attention. Alec hid behind a rock just as three great, hulking, horseless carriages barreled down the road en route to the fort. Through the glass windows of one carriage he could see a human and a demon. Something very important was going on inside the fort.

Alec waited for almost an hour before scuttling out from behind the rock and making his way toward the fort. The two guards at the front gate were too busy arguing over the carcass of some small animal to notice Alec when he slipped in. He ran down a winding hallway, completely unsure of where he was going and what he would do when he got there. When he slammed into a pair of stone legs the choice was taken from him. A stream of urine ran down Alec's leg as he stared into the terrifying eyes of Illini, Orden's executioner.

"What have we here?" Illini regarded the dwarf. Alec's face said that he was about to bolt, so Illini gave him something to think about. He raised his blackened hand, which was beginning to smoke as it heated. "Tell me, little dwarf, do you think you can make it back down the hall before I incinerate you?"

Alec trembled. "Please don't kill me."

"And why shouldn't I?" Illini placed his hand close enough to the dwarf's face for him to feel the intense heat.

"Because I can tell you where to find the witch."

CHAPTER SIXTEEN

After about a half hour of trying to convince Morgan that what he had seen wasn't what it looked like, with both of them wrestling naked, they were back on the road again. Rogue had retrieved his black Suburban from a nearby parking garage. He normally only drove the bulky SUV when he was doing surveillance but since his Viper was totaled, it was either that or catch a taxi. Rogue was not about to let himself be crammed in the back of a taxi with Morgan again.

It was after six. Though the rush-hour traffic had began to thin, the West Side Highway was still teeming with cars, which only irritated the impatient mage. Rogue pulled a bogus police light from under his seat, placed it on the dashboard, and turned it on, parting the cars before him like the Red Sea. Rogue whipped the big truck in and out of traffic as if it were a VW Beetle, almost clipping a Mercedes. Morgan was gripping the armrest so tight that Rogue was afraid he might break it. Asha, on the other hand, looked like she was having the time of her life.

"Man, I didn't know these things could move so fast," Asha said, watching the passing scenery.

"They can't, unless you have a friend of a friend who knows a little something about jet engines," Rogue told her, steering with one hand and typing on his portable laptop with the other. He wasn't worried about Titus's agents picking up on his wireless signal and finding them, because it ran through a series of routers that changed every ten minutes. It made for poor connection speed, but it was better than dying.

Asha leaned forward on the backrest of Rogue's seat. She was so close he could feel her warm breath on his neck when she spoke. "So, are you going to tell us where we're going or do we have to guess?"

"All we're gonna end up doing is crashing if you don't cut that out," Rogue said. "We're gonna see a friend of mine and see if he can't help us with gaining access to Midland."

"So you've said, but you still haven't told us who this friend is," Asha pointed out.

"You wouldn't know him even if I did. This friend of mine likes to keep a very low profile," Rogue said, and left it at that.

They exited the West Side Highway at Canal Street and headed east. The smell of fish permeated the air from the many markets that lined the streets. People roamed up and down the sidewalks buying, selling, or plotting. In the back alleys of Chinatown you could get a knockoff of a thousand dollar handbag for a few hundred bucks, or something more sinister if that was your pleasure. Not only was Chinatown a popular attraction for tourists, it was also the center for much of the supernatural activity in New York City.

"I don't like it down here." Asha ran her hands up and down her arms. Azuma bristled uncomfortably in the seat beside her. There was heavy magic in the air, and she could feel it on her skin like an army of ants.

"I feel it too," Morgan told her. "Jackson and I have had our fair share of skirmishes in this part of town. Jonas calls it the Devil's Playground."

"Well put, considering the amount of demon activity that goes on in this place. Over the last few centuries the Dragon Lords have turned this into quite a hot spot," Rogue told them.

"Dragon Lords? What are they? Some type of Asian street gang?" Asha asked.

Morgan had to laugh. "No, child, they are a thousand times worse. The Dragon Lords is an ancient society of supernatural beings that dates back further than most civilizations. For the most part they keep to themselves, but have been known to make nasty examples of those who are foolish enough to run afoul of them. Rogue, if it's a member of the Dragons you've come down to barter with, we'd best come up with another plan. I've seen the price they extract for their services," Morgan said, thinking of the budding young mobster they had come across a few years prior.

The mobster had allied himself with the Lords in order to conquer the territories of his enemies, and once he was in power he crossed them out of the agreement. The Dragon Lords wiped out the mobster's whole crew as well as their families. The children were spared, but only to be sold into slavery or kept as lab rats for their twisted rituals. The mobster, however, was allowed to live, if living is what you can call what they had reduced him to. They took his eyes, tongue, and privates before putting him on display in a glass case in one of their gambling halls. The mobster served as a warning to those who would seek to cross the undisputed rulers of Chinatown.

"Don't worry, Morgan, I'm not that desperate. At least not yet," Rogue said with a chuckle. He turned the SUV up a small side street and pulled up next to a fire hydrant in front of an herb shop. "Hang tight, I'll be out in a few."

"What? Are we supposed to just sit here twiddling our thumbs until you come back?" Asha asked, clearly not happy with the prospect of being left behind and missing out on whatever Rogue was up to.

"No, you can make sure I don't get a ticket while I'm gone. These New York cops are like Nazis when it comes to parking," Rogue said, and disappeared into the herb shop.

The bell hanging over the door announced Rogue as he entered the shop. His nose tingled from the smells of all the different spices that hung in the air. Vegetation grew from pots, the ceiling, and everywhere else it could take root. Along the walls were shelves lined with jars of herbs and powders for everything from treating the common cold to satisfying darker fetishes. Rogue made a note to himself to stop back at the store another day to replenish some of the items he needed for his spells.

Behind the counter a withered old woman sat trimming the stems off a strange yellow flower. She spat a mouthful of tobacco into a cup near the register and peered at Rogue over the rim of her thick glasses. "What you want here?" she asked in a heavy Chinese accent.

"Hello to you too, Mrs. Chang." Rogue gave her his winning smile.

Mrs. Chang stopped her trimming and waggled the shears at Rogue. "Don't come here give me smiley, you trouble. Every time show your face trouble follow. We pay fifteen hundred dollars for last windows you break!"

"Mrs. Chang, I didn't start that fight and I paid for the window," Rogue reminded her.

"No care, no care. I tell my husband, 'No let

Johnny in shop, but he no listen and what happen? You fight, you break. Cause us much trouble. Police ask questions and I tell my husband, 'Tell them truth,' but the idiot lie for you." Mrs. Chang squinted at Rogue. "I tell you all the time about wild ways, but you no listen. Look at your face, look like someone kick your ass, yeah? Good for them. Maybe few more beatings keep you calm and away from trouble."

"What's all the noise up here?" An elderly man came in from the back room. He was dressed in a smock and had on a pair of thick gardening gloves. When he saw Rogue a broad smile crossed his lips. "Johnny!" He embraced the taller man.

"What's up, Uncle Chang? Man, it seems like every time I see you, you look younger," Rogue greeted him warmly.

"Clean living." Uncle Chang patted his slight potbelly.

"More like dirty magic," Mrs. Chang added.

"Wife, where are your manners? We have a guest."

Mrs. Chang rolled her eyes. "You call him guest, I call him something else that not so nice."

Uncle Chang shook his head. "Please excuse my wife. Sometimes she can hold a grudge longer than she needs to."

"You know I know, Uncle Chang. We busted that window two years ago and she still hasn't let me forget it."

"And I never will," Mrs. Chang assured him.

Uncle Chang barked something at her in Chinese that seemed to calm her, then turned his attention back to Rogue. "So, what brings you here tonight, Rogue? Do you need herbs or have you come to partake of something a little more exotic?" Uncle Chang leaned in to whisper to Rouge so that his wife wouldn't overhear. "We got some new girls in last week from Burma. I tried two of them myself, *very* sweet." He winked.

"Nah, Uncle Chang. You know I like my women to be at least of legal drinking age. I actually came to speak to Mesh. Is he around?"

The smile faded from Uncle Chang's face and he gave Rogue a suspicious look. "What do you want with him, Johnny?"

"Nothing, I just need to speak with him about something," Rogue said innocently.

"Ha," Mrs. Chang laughed from behind the counter.

"Seriously, Uncle Chang, I'm working on a case and I just need some information from Mesh."

Uncle Chang shook his head. "I don't think so. He's meeting with some important people and doesn't want to be disturbed."

"No problem, I don't mind waiting until he's done."

Uncle Chang stared at Rogue for a long moment. "Okay, go downstairs and wait at the bar. When he's done I'll let him know that you're waiting to see him." Uncle Chang parted the beaded curtain in the back of the store for Rogue to pass through.

"Thanks, Uncle Chang. I'll be in and out before anyone even knows I was here." Rogue said before walking through the curtain.

"Just make sure you use a door when you leave and not the window!" Mrs. Chang called after him.

There was an uncomfortable silence lingering in the SUV. The radio softly played the top ten songs of the week, but it was like white noise. None of the occupants were really listening. Azuma was standing on the backseat with his nose pressed against the window, watching the herb shop intently. Asha busied herself with a lighter that she had found wedged in the seat. She wiggled her finger this way and that, manipulating the flame like a puppet, while Morgan watched her in the rearview mirror.

Asha continued to manipulate the flame, each time coaxing it a little higher and a littler wider. Cupping her hand, she passed it between the flame and the lighter, coming away with a ball of fire dancing in her palm. When the flame looked to be growing out of control she closed her hand and extinguished it. "Is there a reason you're staring at me like that?" She caught Morgan off guard.

Morgan turned and faced her. "You're not like the other witches I've come across in my travels."

Asha blew smoke from her hand. "You might

say that I'm in a class by myself. What's taking him so long?" Asha craned her neck trying to spot Rogue through the murky window of the herb shop. He'd only been gone for a few minutes, but it felt like ages, and Asha was beginning to get impatient.

"You never can tell with that one. If you haven't noticed, he dances to his own beat," Morgan said.

"Well, I'm about to change the song." Asha pushed the door open and slid out. "Stay here," she told Azuma before closing the door behind her.

"Where are you going? Rogue said that we should stay here," Morgan reminded her.

"Rogue ain't my daddy. You can sit here playing with yourself all night if you like, but I'm going to see what's going on." Asha flipped her hair and strode toward the entrance of the herb shop.

"And you think whoever is running this front is gonna just let you stroll in?" Morgan called after her.

"Of course not. I'm going to wow them with my charm." She winked and slipped inside the shop.

Mrs. Chang had gone back to her trimming behind the counter when she heard the bell over the front door jingle. She looked up and didn't see anyone, but the door was flapping open and closed from the breeze outside. With a curse she walked from behind the counter and closed the door, locking it. Mrs. Chang returned to the counter, intent on finishing the potion she was working on, but the flower she had been trimming was gone.

CHAPTER SEVENTEEN

A dim light swayed overhead, barely giving Rogue enough light to see as he crossed the storeroom. Not that he needed the light. With his demon eyes Rogue could see in the dark better than most could see in the daytime. The spacious room was a mess of boxes and gardening equipment. The labels said the boxes contained herbs and cleaning supplies, but Rogue knew better. He knew that Mrs. Chang was surely watching him on the closed-circuit camera, but he still took the risk of peering inside a partially open box that was marked *Ginger*. Unless ginger had started sprouting with hundred-round ammunition clips, the labels were a ruse. The box contained several high-powered machine guns, and he was sure most of the others did too.

"Same old Uncle Chang," he mused to himself as he continued through the storeroom. In the far corner, hidden by several boxes, was a handleless door with the word *Private* scribbled across it with a black Magic Marker. Rogue banged on the door in a pattern that he knew hadn't changed since he had last been to the shop a few years ago, and waited.

There was the sound of footsteps behind the door just before the word *Private* slid to the side, revealing a peep slot. A pair of dark eyes stared at Rogue suspiciously. Rogue flashed the proper hand signal and the panel closed again. There was some sort of debate going on behind the door and then a second set of eyes appeared in the slot. Rogue flashed the hand signal again and the door swung open. Standing behind the door were two men. One Rogue didn't know, but the second one he was all too familiar with.

The man was built like an NFL defensive end and sported a mullet straight out of NASCAR. He wore a sleeveless T-shirt that looked like it would bust open if he moved the wrong way. There was a Confederate flag tattooed on his right bicep that stretched from shoulder to elbow, emblazoned with the words *Good Old Boy* and the number ten underneath. On his neck and in the crease of his forearm Rogue could make out small puncture marks, which would explain why the man was paler than Rogue had recalled. Across the bridge of his nose there were traces of a scar that hadn't healed very nicely. Rogue smiled to himself, remembering the night he had put the scar there with the broken end of a beer bottle.

"Johnny Boy, you cost me a hundred bucks. I bet one of the fellas that your black ass had gotten greased by one of your own people. Unfortunately, I was wrong," the tattooed man told him.

Rogue laughed. "Lester, you're about as funny as a hole in the head and twice as ugly. Let me explain something about gambling to the uninformed: always bet on black." Rogue brushed past Lester, but the other man grabbed him by the arm. Rogue turned slowly and looked him up and down. "I'm sorry. I don't believe we've met. I'm a headache in a world without aspirin, and you are?"

The man looked confused, but he eventually found his voice. "Everybody's gotta get patted down before they come inside. It's the rules."

Rogue jerked his arm away. "Let me say this slowly so as not to confuse you." He pushed his jacket open so that the two revolvers holstered under his arms were visible. "I don't like to be touched uninvited unless you're a pretty lady, and you don't look like you have a vagina." Rogue glared at him. "Then again, I could be wrong."

The man reached for the gun in his belt, but Lester wisely stopped him. "It's okay, Bart. Rogue is like family, ain't that right?"

"Yeah, your mom and me did kinda have a thing going on," Rogue remarked as he headed down the corridor toward the black curtain.

Lester clapped his hands. "Very funny, my chocolate friend. Hey, Rogue, please feel free to start something while you're here tonight so we can carve you up. From what I hear the boss might not be so quick to save your ass this time."

"Lester, if I were you I'd be more worried about the vampire you're letting feed off your dumb ass losing control and killing you by accident. If you need me, you can find me at the bar doing my best to give this dump a shred of class."

"Who the hell was that guy?" Bart asked after Rogue had passed through the curtain.

"A corpse that just doesn't know it's dead yet. Get back to your post," Lester ordered before following Rogue through the curtain.

The moment Rogue stepped through the curtain he found his senses overloaded. Lights blinked in different colors over the stage while a young fairy belted out a tune in a strange language. The vibration from the huge speakers mounted in the corners rattled the guns and holster beneath his jacket. The smoke in the air was so thick that it stung his sensitive eyes, leaving smears of black tears in the corners. Uncle Chang's back room was one of the most exclusive spots in the city; you could only party there if you were a member, which Rogue had been at one time. During his rebellious days, Rogue had spent more than his fair share of time and money in the back room, gambling until all hours of the morning and rubbing elbows with some of the most notorious men and creatures in the city. Trying to remain as inconspicuous as possible, he moved to the bar and ordered a drink.

From his perch at the end of the bar, Rogue observed the occupants of the gambling hall, reading their auras. All of the tables and booths were crowded with people, mostly mortals, but there was a sprinkling of supernatural beings here and there. There was gambling, drinking, and, of course, girls. As Uncle Chang had promised they were some of the most beautiful women he had ever seen. A girl who looked to be about twenty, wearing nothing other than a transparent teddy, approached him and offered him a dance. Rogue wisely declined. As tempted as he was, he knew nothing in that room came without a price, and money wasn't necessarily an option for payment.

A box being roughly dropped on the bar caught Rogue's attention. He peered over his shoulder and watched a brutish man dressed in a brown jumpsuit speaking to the bartender, wondering why he looked so familiar. Rogue wouldn't have to wait long to find out why.

"Got some good stuff for you tonight, Shelly. Me and my boys liberated it from a truck that was passing through the territory," the brute told the curvaceous bartender.

Shelly examined one of the bottles, which was filled with a brownish-looking liquid. "A-positive. This will go over well with some of our new members." She motioned toward a group of well-dressed businessmen in the front row enjoying the show. From their ghostly white skin, Rogue could tell they were vampires.

"I still don't see how you guys allow those stiffs in your places," the brute scoffed.

"Don't start that, Freddy. We cater to all kinds, as long as they pay. Besides, it's been almost a century since the Beast Wars. Let it go already." The Beast Wars had been one of the bloodiest conflicts in the history of the supernatural society. For three hundred years the followers of Tipua and Fang were engaged in a bloody battle that had almost wiped out both species. The war was technically over, but there were still great hostilities between the races.

"I will, once the last of their stinking race is wiped off the planet," Freddy said with disgust.

Shelly shook her head. "Why don't you relax and have a drink, huh?"

"As much as I'd like to stare at your pretty face all night, Shelly, I've got more deliveries to make," Freddy said, stacking the crates behind the bar. Suddenly he paused and sniffed the air. When he picked out the familiar smell among many, his eyes narrowed to slits and turned on Rogue. "You," he snarled.

Rogue raised an eyebrow, but didn't turn from his drink. "Do we know each other?" he asked coolly.

Freddy spun Rogue around on his seat to face him. "Oh, we don't know each other but we're about to get acquainted."

"Freddy, don't start that crap in here tonight," Shelly warned.

"This miserable piece of shit sucker punched me at the Triple Six the other night," Freddy snapped.

"It wasn't a punch," Rogue said sarcastically.

Freddy slapped the drink from Rogue's hand, splashing scotch all over him and the bar. "You stopped my fucking heart with whatever spell that was you cast on me."

"This was my favorite shirt," Rogue said, watching the liquor soak into the soft cotton.

Freddy snatched Rogue to his feet by the front of his jacket and rained spittle in his face when he shouted, "I'm gonna ruin more than your shirt!"

"Hey, calm that down," Bart ordered as he shoved his way through the crowd of spectators that was gathering around the bar. He placed a hand on Freddy's shoulder and regretted it as he was slapped halfway across the room.

Freddy shook Rogue violently. "It's easy to get the drop when you catch a man off guard, but let's see you try some of that magic while I'm paying attention."

Rogue sighed, knowing he was about to break his promise to the Changs. He slammed his palms against Freddy's ears, disorienting him. Infusing his arms with the power of shadow magic, he tossed Freddy across the room and through a table, disrupting the card game that was being played on it.

"Okay, now you've got to go." Shelly came up from behind the bar holding a shotgun. Without even turning around, he sent out a tendril of shadow and snatched the gun from her hands. By this time the room was thrown into chaos as people tried to get out of the way of the fight.

Across the room there was a low growling that got intensely louder. From the pile of people and overturned tables Freddy emerged, and he didn't look happy. "Sneaky little magician, I'm gonna maul you!" A foolish patron tried to play hero and broke a chair over Freddy's back. The larger man palmed the hero's face and tore a chunk of flesh from his chest with his teeth. Freddy closed his eyes, savoring the warm blood, and when he opened them again they had taken on an unnatural green glow. His lips drew back; his teeth had turned into fangs that seemed to be trying to burst from his mouth. Freddy threw his head back and let out a howl, tearing at his shirt as if it were on fire. His chest expanded and began to darken as thick black fur sprouted from it.

"Damn it, he's turning!" Lester shouted as he fumbled with the gun. He shot two rounds into Freddy's chest, but the lead only seemed to infuriate him. Abandoning the gun, he jumped on Freddy's back and put him in a chokehold. "Bart, get the kit!" Lester held on to Freddy for dear life.

Bart hurried to the bar and pulled out an iron box containing what looked like a tranquilizer gun and several syringes filled with silver liquid. Loading the gun as he went, Bart charged Freddy, whose face was stretching into a muzzle. He couldn't get a clear shot without risking hitting Lester, so he moved in for a better shot. It would be the last thing he ever did. Freddy's clawed hand tore through Bart's arm, liberating him of the gun and the limb. With Lester still riding his back, Freddy pinned Bart to the ground and tore out his throat.

Blood spilled down Freddy's misshapen face as his body twitched and convulsed in the thrall of the change. His fingers stretched three inches and sharp claws burst through the skin under his fingernails. When the transformation was completed, Freddy was gone and in his place was a hulking black wolf that stood on two bent legs. He reached behind him and raked his claws across Lester's back, cutting down to the bone. Lester collapsed on the ground with blood spraying out of his back like a water fountain. He tried to crawl away, but the wolf's massive jaws closed on the back of his neck, snapping it. Several more of the security staff joined the fray, but they were no match for the enraged werewolf as he tore into them with claws and teeth. When he was finished with the appetizer he turned his attention to the main course, Rogue.

The wolf barreled through people and furniture en route to Rogue, intent on ripping him to pieces. Rogue tried to slow him down with a web of shadow, but the wolf tore through it as if it were tissue paper. The wolf lunged, but just before he could reach Rogue he slammed head first into an invisible barrier. Rogue recognized the spell, so he wasn't surprised when he looked over and saw Asha standing in the doorway.

"Damn it, I thought I told you to stay outside!" Rogue barked.

"And had I listened you'd be Puppy Chow right about now," Asha shot back.

The wolf was down but hardly out as it struggled to its feet. It caught Asha in its gaze and immediately took off across the room after the new threat. Rogue was right behind it, whipping out tendrils of shadow in an attempt to keep the wolf from Asha, but the wolf tore through them faster than he could cast them. Rogue concentrated and slipped a double tendril at the wolf's legs, tripping him. The wolf hit the ground and skidded to a stop at Asha's feet.

Asha whipped out her dagger and made to plunge it into the wolf's back, but it slapped her arm away and sent the dagger flying across the room. It tried to tear out her belly, but she was able to spin out of the way and get behind it. Using her thumb rings, Asha dug deep into the wolf's flesh and pulled backward as hard as she could. Blood sprayed onto a nearby table as Asha ripped two long gashes in the wolf's neck. Asha called the words of power and the wolf's blood ignited beneath its skin. It howled and flailed wildly as she tried to boil it from the inside out.

Rogue came from the wolf's blind side and delivered a crushing blow to its chin. The beast countered with a strike that ripped through Rogue's shirt but fortunately didn't penetrate his body armor. As many spells as the mage knew, he had yet to come across anything short of death that would cure the lycanthrope infection. The wolf tried to take Rogue's legs out, but the mage went airborne, sailing over the wolf's back and drawing one of his revolvers as he went. Rogue fired shot after shot into the wolf's back, driving it into the bar.

Before the wolf could regain its composure, Asha pressed the attack. She flicked her hands, and three small discs sailed through the air and parked themselves in the wolf's chest. The beast shrieked and clawed at its chest as the silver began to burn. Getting cocky, Asha went in with her palm outstretched, trying to finish the job, but the wolf was prepared for her this time. Asha didn't see the bar stool until it was being shattered against her shoulder. She hit the floor and rolled to a stop against the bar, knocked senseless and at the mercy of the wolf.

Rogue cut loose with his revolver, trying to get between the wolf and Asha. The gun clicked empty just as the wolf grabbed him by the face and tossed him into the bar. Howling madly, the wolf slammed Rogue into the counter over and over until he finally lost his grip on the gun. Rogue tried for his other gun, but before it could clear the holster the wolf had pinned his arm to his side. With his free hand he grabbed the wolf by the neck, trying to keep the snapping fangs from making contact with his face, but the wolf was three times as strong as he was. Just before it sank its teeth into Rogue's flesh, something warm splattered across the mage's cheek. The wolf wore a confused expression on its face as its head fell off its shoulders and rolled across the floor. A few seconds later, its body collapsed into a heap at the feet of the shaken mage.

A few feet away, a man in a half-crouch held a katana blade that was slick with blood. The slender Asian man's eyes and sword glowed with power as the thick blood dripped from the edge and pooled on the floor. In a smooth motion, he wiped the excess blood from the blade and slid it smoothly into the scabbard hooked to his waist. A phantom wind wiped through his silken black hair, partially obscuring his boyish face and the tattoo that went from his temple to the line of his jaw. Rogue had seen the brand before, but never stateside. It was the mark of the Gammurai, victims of the fallout from the bombing of Hiroshima who were born genetically altered because of the radiation poisoning that had ravaged their tiny island of Gomorra. The warriors lived by the code of Bushido, the way of the samurai, and much like their cousins the Dragon Lords, they rarely involved themselves in the matters of the outside world.

Just behind the Gammurai stood a man who was as dark as the night itself, dressed in a midnight-blue suit with a black shirt and black tie. Hair that was such a deep shade of blue it almost looked black hung loosely around his squared shoulders and stopped just above his waist. The mortals who served him knew him as Mesh, underboss to one of the most feared crime families in both the human and supernatural worlds, and a skilled assassin, but that was only his mortal persona. What few outside Midland knew was that he was also Gilgamesh, prince of the dark elves and heir to the throne of the Black Forest, which was one of the last kingdoms of Midland.

Asha dangled limply from his hand as he dragged her across the room by her hair like a rag doll. He tossed the shaken girl at the mage's feet and regarded him momentarily before addressing the shocked patrons in the room. "What are my rules?" He began to pace. "No blood shall be shed in my house unless it is by me or my brothers of the Black Hand. And you"—he pointed a slender finger at Rogue—"are not one of us."

Rogue swallowed the lump in his throat. "Listen . . ." Rogue began but Mesh cut him off.

"Stay your tongue, mage." He pointed at Rogue. "You've got some pretty big balls, strolling in here and busting up my joint after I told you to stay away."

From the corner of his eye, Rogue could see the other members of the Black Hand moving in on him. Taking them individually, he might have had a snowball's chance in hell of getting out alive, but there was no way he could take all the executioners. "Gilgamesh, if I thought there was another way I wouldn't have come, but I need your help."

Gilgamesh and his men looked at each other and laughed. "You need my help? No, I think you need my mercies." Gilgamesh removed a piece of paper from his pocket and held it up for Rogue to see. When he read it, his blood ran cold. "There's a price on your head, Jonathan Rogue, and I'll give you three seconds to try and convince me why the heads of you and your little friend shouldn't be the next to decorate my floor."

CHAPTER EIGHTEEN

The unmarked hangar at La Guardia airport was quiet with nervous anticipation. In the corner a cube truck sat idling while the driver bit his fingers nervously. There was a twenty-foot mirror erected in the center of the hangar, held in place by rods of pure copper. The copper would help amplify the power of the spell being cast on the other side. A dozen uniformed police officers, armed with everything from handguns to assault rifles, were lined up on either side, watching as the mirror began to ripple with the first signs of the power being fed into it.

"Look alive," Riel told the police officers as he moved to the front of the line with an assault rifle cradled in his arms. Strapped to his side was the cursed blade Poison. His hair was pulled back into a ponytail and the scars De Mona had left him the night before were still visible.

The mirror began to pulsate as the reflective surface twisted in on itself and the first two members of the entourage stepped through. The robed figures moved like gusts of wind as they swept the hangar for signs of danger. When they passed close enough for Riel to catch their scents, he recoiled. He knew demons when he smelled them, and the two that had come through the mirror were of the worst kind. Beneath their robes he could see the tips of their swords dragging behind them—not that they needed them, since their entire bodies were weapons. When the demons were satisfied that there was no immediate threat, they took up positions on opposite sides of the mirror and stood guard for the others.

The vampire Helena oozed from the mirror, her golden eyes sending chills through the men as she looked around the room. After whispering something to the hooded demons, she stepped aside for the next wave of the convoy: women dressed in fatigues, carrying a box that was slightly smaller than a refrigerator and covered with a black tarp. When the box was secured on a rolling rack outside the mirror, they formed ranks around it to make sure that no one would touch it. The black covering over it made it impossible to see what was inside, but Riel could feel the power radiating from it.

Titus was the last to step from the mirror. He was dressed in a charcoal suit with a gray overcoat and black leather gloves covering his hands. The favorite son's soulless eyes swept over all in attendance; they bowed in unison. "Rise." He beckoned them with a wave of his hand.

The war demon Riel stepped from the sea of blue uniforms and greeted his master. "Lord Titus, favorite son of the dark lord and greatest of our lot, welcome to . . ." that was as far as he got before Titus delivered a bone-crushing backhand that sent him flying across the room.

"Buffoon," Titus hissed. "I trust my most celebrated general to pluck candy from a baby and all he comes back with is sticky fingers."

Blood trickled from Riel's lip and down his chin. He wiped the blood with the back of his hand and glared up at Titus. "It was a boy you set me on the trail of, but the Bishop who I stood against." Riel climbed to his feet. "The vessel is coming into the power faster than any of us anticipated, but I will part him from the cursed Nimrod before the Bishop is set loose on us again. Next time I will be prepared."

"And who says there will be a next time?" Titus's eyes flared with dark energy. Everyone in the hangar took a cautionary step back from the two demons. "Riel, you have failed thrice at your task tonight and failure is something that neither I nor the dark father take lightly." Riel's hand instinctively slipped down to the hilt of his blade, causing Titus to raise his eyebrow. "I welcome you to try, Riel, but we both know that even with the added power of your cursed blade I am superior here."

Riel quickly dropped his hands back to his sides and bowed his head. "Forgive me. I would never challenge your authority, Lord Titus." At least he wouldn't without his full demon power. Riel was an old and powerful demon, but on the earthly plane he was no match for Titus. "Though the Nimrod has managed to elude us for the moment, we have delivered a crippling blow to our enemies. The High Brother has fallen and with him the Great House."

"But the Spark lives. Therefore the house may rise again," Titus shot back.

This surprised Riel. "My lord, I assure you that every priest of the order was killed. I saw to this personally."

"So I've been told. If the priests are no more, he must have passed it to another. The question is to whom?"

Riel shook his head. "None of the mortals traveling in the group would have been able to hold it without being destroyed, and neither the elemental nor the demon could possess it."

"Then there has to have been someone you overlooked. Ezrah was said to have snatched someone from the aftermath of the battle; maybe it is he who carries the Spark? I shudder to think what the Spark could do in the hands of the wraiths. Have your Stalkers—"

"That's it!" Riel cut him off. "There was one at Sanctuary who I found very curious."

"How so?" Titus asked.

"He appeared to be a wraith, but he was alive.

Before the little coward fled the battle, I caught the stink of the fey folk on him, which I found to be quite odd."

"Maybe not as odd as you think." Titus's wheels began spinning. "Do you remember the tale of what was said to have caused the feud between the wraiths and nymphs?"

Riel thought about it for a minute. "I believe so. As it is told, Morbius had used the Efil spell to become flesh and violated a nymph princess." Riel looked at Titus with a raised eyebrow. "I know what you're thinking, my lord, but for that union to have produced a child is impossible, isn't it?"

"Nothing is impossible when dealing with the supernatural."

"But even if there was a chance that the Elif spell had allowed Morbius to procreate, the nymphs are so vain they surely would have killed the child at birth to hide their shame."

"Yes, they would have sought to hide their shame, but what if they gave the child away as opposed to killing it?" Titus suggested. "Over the centuries, Sanctuary has been home to orphans of many species. Who is to say they would not open their doors to a child such as that, if not to study him then surely to keep him from us? I could only imagine what kind of creature a union of life and death could have birthed. We need to search the ruins of Sanctuary. Where is the shadow master?"

"I am here, my lord," a voice whispered from

the corner. A shadow roughly the shape of a man peeled from the wall and glided across the floor to hover before Titus. The shadow was so weak and faded that Titus could barely see it.

"Yes, if *here* is what you can call what has become of you. I'm surprised that you are still able to hold any form at all on this side of the plane," Titus mocked him.

"It has been a task to hold on, but my thirst for revenge will not let me return to the oblivion of the shadows. There will be a reckoning with the puppet, Rogue." Of all Titus's agents, the shadow master Moses had come closest to capturing the Nimrod—until Rogue showed up. Moses had encountered spell-casters who could tap into shadow magic, but none with the command that Rogue had.

"Ah, yes, Mr. Rogue." Titus reflected on the tales he head heard of Rogue and his borrowed eyes. The eyes he had inherited from the shadow demon allowed him to tap the demon's power, but it also allowed the demon certain benefits of the mortal world. "I had always thought him to be a mercenary working for the highest bidder, but it seems that our little mage has chosen a side in all this. Don't worry; he won't live long enough to regret his decision."

"This I vow," Moses assured him. "Once I have claimed a new body I will destroy the mage."

"Your new body will have to wait. I have need of the shadows tonight."

"Ask of me what you will, my lord, and it will be done," Moses assured him.

"Gather your minions, go to the estate, and wait for me. Alert no one of your presence until you receive my signal."

"Right away, Lord Titus," Moses said, melting back into the shadows.

Riel waited until he was sure Moses had gone before addressing Titus. "Have you chosen the shadow master over me to be your right arm at the gathering?" he asked like a child who had just found out he was no longer his parent's favorite.

"You need not fear, Riel. Your seat at my table is secure. What I need done requires stealth, which isn't one of your strongest qualities. Moses will be our trump card in this little game. Now, has everything been taken care of?" Titus asked Riel.

"Yes, Lord Titus. Your messengers began arriving a few hours ago. It was short notice so not everyone whose attendance you requested will be there, but they've promised to send emissaries," Riel told him.

"No matter, there are only a few on the list who are important anyhow. The rest will be addressed when the time comes. Any word from Peter?"

"Yes, my lord. He will not attend the gathering, but will send one of his agents to the estate so you can present yourself and offer proper tribute to New York's vampire *king*."

The mention of the word made Titus's face twitch. He despised cowing to anyone but Belthon, but it would have been foolish to ignore the protocols of New York's reigning vampire king. There were many supernatural creatures of high standing in the city, but Peter controlled it.

"And how is the pride of Lamia holding up these days? Holding a city with such a diverse population as New York can't be easy," Titus said.

Riel laughed. "With the werewolves at his rear and most of the opposing vampire houses knocking on the other three sides, he isn't likely to hold it for much longer."

"Interesting." Titus rubbed his chin. "Maybe there will be something gained from this meeting after all. What's the latest with Orden?"

"Still as pissed as ever over the battle last night. Goblins don't lose face easily. I don't know if he's angrier at getting his ass kicked or the fact that he lost his brother in the process," Riel said.

This brought a broad smile to Titus's face. "Gilchrest is dead?"

"Don't know just yet. Seems he was left behind during the goblin's . . . withdrawal from the battle. Our people said he was taken by the Knights, but I couldn't tell you whether they offed him or not. If it were me, I'd kill the little bastard."

"Then it's fortunate for Gilchrest that the Knights have him and not you. But I see much to be gained from this. The Knights have killed in battle but they hardly have the stomach for murder. If Gilchrest is in any immediate danger then he likely put himself there, but Orden doesn't know this. Among the goblins, family is the only thing that is sacred," Titus explained. "They fought for our cause last night out of a sense of duty, but now it's personal."

"Sounds to me like we should just step aside and let the goblins have at it," Riel suggested.

Titus looked at his general. "Can you imagine what would happen if Orden got hold of the Nimrod and the Bishop started whispering dirty little secrets in his ear? No, we will spearhead this effort ourselves."

"Excuse me, Mr. Titus." one of the fatigue-clad women approached timidly. "The ladies are in the truck as you instructed."

"Thank you. My associate, Riel, will escort you to the next location," Titus said and dismissed her.

"My lord, I thought we were going to the house to prepare for the meeting with Peter," Riel said.

"Nothing has changed, but there's something I need you to do before you join me," Titus said.

"Ask of me what you will," Riel said confidently, but his gut told him he wasn't going to like what Titus was about to say.

"I need you to see my cargo safely to the Iron Mountains, while I take Helena to the house to prepare," Titus began. "When you get there, you will deliver my apologies to Orden for neglecting him and extend a personal invitation to stand at my side when I hold council with New York's leaders."

A shiver ran through Riel's body. No one

wanted to venture into the bowels of the Iron Mountains, especially when the goblins had war on their minds—which was most of the time. "Titus, I would never question your orders, but in light of the tensions festering in that place over all this, is it wise for me to go down there?"

Titus turned to Riel. He smiled playfully, but there was murder in his eyes. "Is that fear I detect in your voice, King Maker?"

"Never." Riel poked his chest out. "I would stand against one thousand goblins if it pleased my lord. What I mean is, they're already holding Flagg hostage until you honor Orden's request, so would it be wise to put them in a position to imprison two of your most valued advisors?"

Titus took Riel's face in his hands and looked him lovingly in the eyes. "We've offended our friends and so we must make them comfortable again lest they withdraw their support. Orden will see it as a great sign of trust and respect for me to leave something so precious to me in his kingdom for safekeeping."

"But why me?" Riel tried to keep his voice from quivering.

"Because you are my general." Titus slapped him lightly on the cheek. "But you have no need to fear, as I am even willing to send one of my honor guard with you to ensure your safety." Titus motioned toward the hooded figures who were both watching Riel intently.

"No thanks," Riel quickly said. "As vicious and

unpredictable as that lot is, I might have better luck going in with my Stalkers."

"Come now, Riel. Who better to safeguard you than a Valkrin?"

CHAPTER NINETEEN

Asha stood off to Rogue's right with her hands poised to call a spell when he gave her the word. They were up against impossible odds, but she had never been one to shy away from a fight. Rogue and Gilgamesh eyed each other from their respective sides of the room. The tension hung in the air between them like a dam that was on the verge of breaking and drowning everyone in reach.

"I'm waiting," Gilgamesh told Rogue.

Rogue took a deep breath. "Gilgamesh, rightful prince of the dark elves," he began, using Mesh's title out of respect, "if you and your men were to try to collect the bounty, and I was fortunate enough to make it out alive, I would regretfully have to tell your uncle who really crashed his Jaguar in 1992."

Gilgamesh could no longer hold back the smile that had been trying to creep across his face. "You rat bastard, I'll bet you would," Gilgamesh said playfully and hugged Rogue. Everyone in the room let out a collective sigh of relief.

"You know him?" Asha asked in disbelief. Her heart was beating so fast, she thought she could see it through her skin.

"We've crossed paths a time or two," Rogue said with a smile.

"A time or two? Johnny, have you forgotten how many fights I got into for trying to stick up for your skinny ass when we were kids?" Gilgamesh reminded him.

Rogue and the prince of the dark elves had a love-hate relationship that went back to when they were kids. Both the dark elves and the mages of Rogue's house worshiped the death god Thanos, so there was naturally a kinship, but Rogue's father and Gilgamesh's uncle were actually good friends. Many afternoons when their elders were out attending to their business, Rogue and Gilgamesh were left behind with the rest of the children. Much like Rogue, Gilgamesh had no patience for the study of the arts as the other children did, so he would find different mischief to keep himself amused. Rogue's siblings avoided the troublesome elf, but Rogue was drawn to him like a moth to a flame, joining in on his adventures in petty crime. Over the years their friendship would become strained as Rogue pursued law enforcement and Gilgamesh went to work for his uncle. Over the years they would find themselves on opposite sides of the gun, fraying the bond even more, but no matter what they would always be like brothers.

"Well, let's bore her with the gory details, Mesh. I was serious about needing your help," Rogue said.

"And I was serious about there being a price on your head," Gilgamesh shot back. Gilgamesh looked to his people, who were still trying to figure out what was going on. "Teko." Gilgamesh turned to the swordsman, who was still watching Rogue like a hawk. "Supervise the clean-up of this mess, please. I have to speak with Rogue and his friend in the back."

Teko nodded and went about giving the clean-up crew their orders. Rogue waited until he was out of earshot to pose his question to Gilgamesh.

"So when did the noble Gammurai become hired guns for scumbags like you, Mesh?" Rogue asked.

"Teko? He's no hired gun; he's my brother, here of his own free will," Gilgamesh told him. "Next to you, he's the only one I trust enough to watch my back. It's hard to find a good sidekick these days, Johnny. Hey, do you remember the time when we got invited to the Kremlin and you got drunk and pissed on the ice swan?"

"You took a leak inside the Kremlin?" Asha asked in shock.

"He sure did, and we almost spent the rest of our lives in a Russian prison because of his weak bladder," Gilgamesh told her. "But we'll speak of that later. Right now we need to talk about the mess you're obviously caught up in. Come on."

Gilgamesh led them to the back, where he made his office. It was a small room with little more than a desk, a couch, and a few chairs, hardly what you would expect from a mob boss and especially not from a prince. Gilgamesh was a man who kept an extremely low profile, preferring to leave the limelight, and the attentions of ambitious assassins, on some of the other underworld players.

Sitting behind the desk was an attractive woman with pecan-colored skin and dark eyes. She was dressed in a cream-colored blazer and brown wool pants that flared at the cuffs, partially covering her brown leather boots. She looked familiar, but Rogue couldn't quite place her. Standing just behind her, invisible to everyone but Rogue, was a ghostly figure. He was leaning over and whispering something into the woman's ear, but she ignored him, opting to watch Rogue watching her. When the mage examined her more closely, he could see the swirls of black and gray in her color.

Tamalla answered the question on his face. "Spare yourself the trouble, Mr. Rogue. I'm a clairvoyant."

Gilgamesh made the introductions. "Rogue, this is Tamalla P. Hardy."

"You're that chick who talks to the dead, right?"

Asha asked. She remembered hearing her name whispered by Dutch on more than one occasion.

Tamalla smirked. "I do more than talk to the dead, little girl."

"Yes, Tamalla is a broker of sorts. When there is business to be done between the living and the dead, she's the one who makes it happen," Gilgamesh explained.

Rogue raised his eyebrow behind his shades. "You planning on raising something, Mesh?" Like the mages of Thanos, the royals of the dark elves dabbled in death magic. Though not on as grand a scale as the mages, they had been known to cause quite a bit of trouble with their practices.

"Not unless it's your troublesome ass, Johnny," Gilgamesh told him. "I don't know who you've managed to piss off this time, but you've really stepped in a pile of it."

"Is that why you've brought her here? Come to barter for my soul, have you?" Rogue asked sarcastically.

Tamalla rolled her eyes. "I can't negotiate with you for something you don't really own, puppet. If you must know, I have business with the Black Hand and it just so happens to do with the little scavenger hunt you're on. Your do-gooder tales are legendary, Mr. Rogue, but this time you might've let your sense of nobility write a check that your ass can't cash."

"What the hell is she talking about, Mesh?" Rogue asked his friend. Gilgamesh reached in his desk drawer and dropped a sheet of paper on the surface for Rogue to examine. As he read the caption under a distorted picture of himself, Asha peered over his shoulder, trying to make heads or tails of the strange writing.

"Who wrote this, a two-year-old?" Asha frowned at the paper.

Rogue rolled his shoulder and nudged her back. "Unless you're fluent in the elfish tongue you wouldn't understand it." He read the wanted poster twice and shook his head. Rogue spread his hands over the paper and whispered the words of power. The poster shivered before crumbling into a pile of dust on the desk. "So two million is the going price for my head, huh?"

"If you ask me I think they're offering too much. I know some guys who would whack you for far less than that, my friend. You've built quite a list of enemies over the years working on the other side of the fence with the humans," Gilgamesh told him.

"So who's the lucky candidate they're sending to die?" Rogue asked.

Gilgamesh shrugged. "I don't know yet. They wouldn't dare approach the Hand for the contract, and most of the Dragon Lords have taken to higher ground to wait this thing out. For the kind of mess it's looking like you're caught up in, it could be anybody—"

"Including the Sheut," Tamalla interjected. "The wraiths have been up to something since this all started and nobody is quite sure what. What I do know is that something passed from the Dead Lands through to this side of the plane, something that wasn't a native of the Dead Lands."

"And you think this something is coming for me?" Rogue asked.

"I couldn't tell you who or what it's coming for, but it's coming for something and my intuition tells me that your little friends and whatever it is will cross paths before it's all said and done," Tamalla told him.

"Does it say who placed the price on his head?" Asha asked. Gilgamesh just stared at her.

"Who dropped the bread on me, Mesh?" Rogue asked.

"The same guy who sent these out." Gilgamesh tossed an envelope on the table. On the broken seal Rouge could make out the mark of Belthon.

"What is it?" Rogue asked, not even sure he wanted to know.

"It's an invitation to Raven Wood."

Asha scratched her head. "Raven Wood? Isn't that the estate of that Italian designer?"

"In name only. Raven Wood is the New York headquarters for Max Titus," Rogue informed her. "Mesh, what's all this about?"

"A gathering. All the underworld bigwigs in the tri-state are supposed to be there talking about something very heavy and very hush-hush. Rogue, what are you tied up in?" Gilgamesh asked seriously.

"Something more dangerous than he truly understands," Tamalla offered. "Mr. Rogue, Titus has got a major hard-on for this kid you're trying to protect, and the thing he's carrying. He's on the trail of the Nimrod and he'll stop at nothing to get it, including turning the leaders of the supernatural world against you."

"He wouldn't be the first idiot to try to kill me and I doubt he'll be the last," Rogue said sarcastically. "Titus is powerful indeed, but he still has a shitload of enemies. Even if he manages to sway a few of the more unsavory supernatural leaders, those loyal to the light will never go along with it."

"Which is why he hasn't extended the invitation to them," Tamalla added. "The others would either seek to claim the Nimrod for themselves or destroy it rather than have Belthon as the undisputed ruler of all. If he can get his hands on it before any of the other elders wise up to the Nimrod's presence, he can blindside them when he stages his little coup. Mr. Rogue, as long as you protect this boy you're going to be a walking payday."

"And what do you stand to gain by giving me the heads-up about what Titus is planning?" Rogue asked.

"Monetarily, nothing." Tamalla absently rubbed the scar around her neck where Titus had marked her. "I'm just one of the few who thinks that Titus coming to an untimely end is a far better option than hell on earth. Just something to think about."

Gilgamesh gave Tamalla a disapproving look.

"Johnny, these humans still don't get the fact that things like the Nimrod aren't meant to be controlled. The last time they poked their noses into something of this magnitude it let the likes of Belthon come over to this side of the fence, and you mean to tell me that they still haven't learned?" He shook his head sadly. "Johnny, leave these people to their business and come stay with us until it's sorted out. You'll be safe with the Hand."

Rogue studied Gilgamesh as he weighed his words. He could see genuine concern on Mesh's face, which was rare for the assassin. In his heart he knew that Gilgamesh was speaking the truth, but he couldn't sit idle while Titus made slaves of humanity. "Doing what's right isn't always the easiest thing, but it's the only way I know how to do things, Mesh. You know that."

Gilgamesh smiled, as he had known that was how Rogue would respond. "Indeed I do. So tell me, other than you having a death wish, what brings you to see me tonight?"

"I need to get into Midland," Rogue told him.

Gilgamesh looked at him as if he were insane. "Rogue, I've never known you to do drugs, but you've gotta be high for what you're asking. What's so important in Midland that you'd risk getting skewered to go after it?"

"The goblins snatched the kid's grandfather and took him to the Iron Mountains. Me and the Redfeathers go back too far for me to let him go out like that, Mesh," Rogue told him.

The name struck a chord with Gilgamesh. He hadn't spent as much time with the old scholar and his family as Rogue, and he had always considered them good people. "Damn." Gilgamesh let out a sigh. "Cracking the Iron Mountains isn't gonna be easy, Johnny. Even with my diplomatic status I can't march into the Iron Mountains without an invitation and that would have to be requested by my father."

"I'm not talking about being invited; I'm talking about busting in. Your people know the rifts that lead to Midland as well as anyone else, so all I'm asking is that you get me through one near the Iron Mountains and my people and I will do the rest."

"You're crazy, Johnny!"

"Maybe so, but that doesn't change the fact that I need to crack that mountain to try to save Mr. Redfeather. Mesh, I know the chances of me saving the old man and getting out are slim, but I gotta try. I owe it to him."

"Always the bleeding heart, Johnny. Okay, I'll get you the location of a rift in a few hours, but you're on your own as far as getting across. I love you, Johnny, but not enough to die for you," Gilgamesh said seriously.

"Thanks, Mesh." Rogue shook his hand. "So, what are you gonna do about this gathering that Titus has called?"

"I'm not gonna do a damn thing. The invitation was to my uncle, not me." Gilgamesh looked at his watch. "He should be on his way there as we speak."

Rogue looked surprised. "You mean he's actually considering whatever Titus is offering?"

Gilgamesh shrugged. "You know my uncle; he's a businessman before anything."

"But if your uncle and the rest of those guys side with Titus it'll bring this world one flush away from being down the toilet."

"And why should we care? Rogue, what you keep forgetting is that we supernaturals are only squatters here, because the humans forced us out of the equation long ago. This world is already on the high road to ruin so why not turn a profit from it? This isn't personal, Rogue, it's strictly business."

"Gilgamesh, this is a new low even for your uncle. I'd always thought of you guys as more than just leeches feeding on the weak and helpless, but I guess I was wrong. That's cold, man, *real* cold."

"No, cold would've been me letting Teko take your head and collecting that bounty. Friend or not, you are still guests of the Black Hand, so I'd advise you not to push your luck with me, Johnny." Gilgamesh removed a cell phone from his drawer and tossed it to Rogue. "I'll call you on that line in a while with the information you need. Until then, try to keep yourself from getting killed."

CHAPTER TWENTY

Procuring fresh clothes so that they could move freely through Midland proved to be more difficult than Gabriel and De Mona had expected. When they reached the marketplace, it dawned on them that US dollars would do them no good in Midland. With no way to pay for their items, they had to be liberated from one of the local shops. Luckily, Gilchrest was a far better thief than he was a warrior.

"I feel ridiculous," Gabriel said, stepping out from behind the bushes where he had gone to change his clothes. He had traded his jeans and sweatshirt for a pair of rawhide pants and a ratty burlap shirt. The shirt's sleeves were long enough to cover the tattoo on his arm, but it itched terribly.

"You look fine," De Mona told him, buckling the clamp at the shoulder of her green tunic. She had taken her braids out and let her hair spill freely over her tanned shoulders.

"Stupid cloak," Gilchrest grumbled, tripping

over the fabric every time he took a step. "I the only one of Midland so not see why it necessary to hide."

De Mona took a fistful of fabric from the bottom of his robe and cut it with her claws so it wouldn't be so long and Gilchrest could move better. "Because you would stick out like a sore thumb if you didn't."

"Could've taken a little off the sleeve," Gilchrest mumbled and stalked off into the brush.

De Mona shook her head. "Ungrateful son of a bitch." As she turned around to mention it to Gabriel, she noticed that he was giving her a very puzzled look. "What?"

"Nothing," he lied.

"Don't give me that. Why are you looking at me like that?"

"Well, it's just that . . . I dunno, you look like a girl," he said awkwardly. Now that she had shed her oversized jeans and T-shirt, Gabriel could really appreciate her beauty.

"You sure know how to make a lady feel special," she said sarcastically.

"I'm sorry; I didn't mean it like that. It's just that I've never seen you in anything other than boy's clothes, and I . . . never mind. I'm sorry if I made you feel uncomfortable by staring." He fixed his eyes on the ground.

De Mona lifted his head gently. "Its okay, Gabe, guys are supposed to stare at girls all goofy when they think they're pretty. Haven't you ever had a girlfriend?"

"No."

"Okay, maybe someone you were sweet on?"

Gabriel thought back to Katy. "Yeah, but she was killed back in New York when the Nimrod came to me."

De Mona covered her mouth in embarrassment. "I'm sorry for your loss, Gabriel."

"It wasn't really my loss. I liked her and she liked my best friend." He sounded defeated. "Listen, can we change the subject?"

"Sure. We should be trying to figure out our next move anyhow." De Mona was about to start hashing out her plan when her sensitive ears picked up on something coming their way through the brush. She stood with claws at the ready in case it was trouble, but it was just a little white rabbit that came scampering from the bushes with Gilchrest on its heels. He'd almost caught it, but it made a hard cut, causing him to stumble and fall flat on his face in the dirt. De Mona and Gabriel doubled over laughing at the spectacle.

"Not funny." Gilchrest spat out a mouthful of dirt. "Starving I am, haven't eaten in nights." he rubbed his stomach for emphasis.

"He's got a point; I can't even remember the last time I ate," Gabriel admitted. He had been so caught up in evading the demons and the police that food hadn't even been an afterthought.

"I could stand a meal myself," De Mona agreed. "But we had to steal these clothes, so where the hell are we gonna find a place to get some food for free?"

"I know a place," Gilchrest said slyly.

Gabriel stared around the marketplace like a tourist seeing Times Square for the first time. Even though it was dark, a few of the shops, catering to the more nocturnal creatures of the land, were still open. Goblins, dwarfs, and species that Gabriel couldn't identify roamed the streets bartering for goods and services, some with coin and others with steel. As Gilchrest had warned, Midland was a dangerous place.

"Stop your gawking before we are discovered, human," Gilchrest spat.

"I didn't mean to stare—it's just that I've never seen anything like this. There are so many different species and cultures represented here that it would take me a lifetime to study them all," Gabriel said.

"Lifetime to study them, but seconds to kill you if what you carry is discovered. Make no mistake, human; stink of black magic you do. If not careful you have trouble from more than goblins. Goblins eat flesh; some things in Midland devour soul," Gilchrest warned. "Now come, enough studying. Food not far."

As they neared the end of the market square De Mona could pick out the scents of animals and food cooking, which caused her stomach to curl up in knots. Gilchrest led them down an alley between a pottery shop and a tavern. He motioned for them to take cover behind a stack of barrels while he peered into the back of the tavern. In a small pen were several animals that looked like a cross between a goat and a pig, grazing on the weeds coming up out of the ground. A brutish-looking man wearing a bloodstained apron carried the smoked carcass of some sort of livestock, which he placed on a hook among several others of varying sizes. Neither Gabriel nor De Mona had any idea what kind of meat it was, but the smell made their mouths water.

"There." Gilchrest pointed at the meat, which sported stumps where limbs used to be.

Gabriel frowned. "I don't even know what that is, so you couldn't possibly expect me to eat it!"

"Unless you want to starve, suggest you stop complaining I do." Gilchrest hissed.

De Mona glanced at the meat and smacked her lips. "Dude, I'm so hungry that thing could have six legs and two heads and I wouldn't care."

"Not as stupid as you look, demon." Gilchrest snickered. "Wait until he goes back inside we must, then the human will fetch meat."

"Me?" Gabriel raised his eyebrow. "Why do I have to do it, when you're the thief?"

Gilchrest gave Gabriel an annoyed look. "Goblin

and demon stink of predator, frighten animals and make shopkeeper come. Human just stink, nothing fear you."

Gabriel looked at De Mona, who just shrugged. Reluctantly, he accepted the mission. "You know, I'm supposed to be the hero, but I feel more like the sidekick on this little adventure," he managed to muster a joke to hide his fear before making his way toward the meat.

Gabriel stayed as low as he could so as not to be spotted by one of the patrons of the tavern. He took a moment to peer into one of the open windows. Inside, dangerous-looking creatures ate, drank, gambled, and entertained themselves with what he assumed to be females. Abandoning his curiosity, Gabriel crossed the yard and made his way to the meat. Up close, he had to admit that the meat did look tasty. Even if he didn't know what it was, it couldn't be any worse than what he ate at the Chinese restaurants in New York. He selected a carcass that was slightly larger than a chicken from the hook, but when he tried to pull it down it got stuck. He looked over his shoulder at De Mona and Gilchrest, who were motioning for him to hurry up. Gabriel gave a final tug, but he put more force behind it than he meant to and ended up pulling down the entire rack, making enough noise to be heard all the way to the Iron Mountains and scaring the animals into fits.

"Quit with all the noise, you'll all get your chance to grace my chopping block soon enough," the brute in the apron said, appearing from the tavern. When his eyes landed on Gabriel lying in a heap amidst his meats, the man's misshapen lips drew back into a sneer. "What's this? Another one of you stinking river bandits come to steal from me again, have you?"

Gabriel looked around at the ruined meat and threw his hands up submissively. "Listen, mister, this isn't what it looks like."

"I thought when I sent the last one of your lot back downriver missing a hand it would send a message to all of your kind, but apparently it hasn't." He drew a meat cleaver from his apron. "Let's see if they get the message when I have your head delivered in a box!"

Gabriel managed to roll out of the way just before the cleaver made contact with the ground. He quickly scrambled to his feet and began backing toward the tavern door. "Buddy, why don't you take it easy with that thing before you hurt somebody?"

"I'll do more than hurt you." He rushed Gabriel. The cleaver whistled through the air, aimed at Gabriel's head, but ended up eating away a chunk of the tavern door as the fleet young man danced out of the way. The noise drew a crowd of spectators as the brute chased Gabriel across the yard.

"Listen, I'm sorry about your meat and if you just let me . . ." Gabriel's apology was cut off by the swipe of the cleaver. He managed to avoid it by doing a cartwheel that carried him back to the fallen rack of meat. The brute swung twice more, but Gabriel dodged both strikes while the crowd cheered him on. As he danced around the cleaver-wielding madman for the adoring spectators, he was taken back to his days as a part of his parents' carnival act. The memory excited him.

"Stay still so I can gut you, you wormy little bastard!" the brute huffed.

"You're more likely to die from a heart attack than to even come close to touching me with that thing," Gabriel taunted him. With a snarl the brute charged again, swinging the cleaver back and forth. Gabriel leaped into the air and landed on the brute's shoulders, where he proceeded to muss his already frazzled hair. "I'm sure a big strong guy like you can do better than that." Gabriel locked his legs under the brute's arms and threw himself backward into a summersault, sending his opponent sailing through the air and into the pen with the animals.

When the brute resurfaced, his face was covered in feces. "I hate you cursed river people," he gasped, before collapsing back into the waste in exhaustion.

The crowd erupted with laughter and cheers as they tossed coins at Gabriel's feet. Gabriel smiled and bowed gracefully to the crowd, scooping up a handful of the coins and the meat he had been trying to steal. Gabriel tossed one of the coins into the pen. "This is for the meat." He tossed another coin. "And this is for being such a good sport." Gabriel strode confidently from the back of the tavern with the meat tucked under his arm and the cheers of the crowd ringing in his ears. Gabriel wasn't sure what had gotten into him, but his pulsing arm told him it had to do with the Nimrod.

When Gabriel had gone, three short men wearing capes and hoods gave each other knowing glances and disappeared back inside the tavern.

"Seems you not so useless after all, human." Gilchrest tore into the portion of meat De Mona had carved off for him.

"Thanks, I think," Gabriel said. "I was scared shitless when he came at me with that meat cleaver."

"But you handled yourself like a seasoned veteran," De Mona told him while chewing a chunk of the rubbery meat. It was almost completely without flavor but it beat starving. "I didn't know you were an acrobat."

"I'm not . . . well, at least not anymore," Gabriel said sadly.

"Well, you could've fooled me. Good job, Gabe." De Mona kissed him on the cheek, causing him to blush. Gabriel, De Mona, and Gilchrest walked down a little farther, De Mona giving casual glances over her shoulder. From the look on her face, Gabriel could tell something was wrong.

"You okay?" Gabriel asked.

"Yeah, its probably nothing," she said in a less than sure voice. When they got to the mouth of the next alley, De Mona directed them to duck inside. Gilchrest complained, but she snatched him by the collar and dragged him along.

"Crazy demon, what problem now?" he asked in an agitated tone.

"Shut up and get out of sight." She shoved the goblin into a pile of boxes and directed Gabriel to lean against one wall while she took the other. Gabriel wasn't sure what the problem was, but he had learned throughout the course of their journey to trust De Mona's instincts. A few minutes passed with nothing happening, but just when Gabriel was about to question her, the three hooded figures that had been at the tavern appeared in the alley with their weapons drawn.

"Are you sure they came down this way?" one of the hooded figures asked the leader of the trio. In answer to his question, De Mona pounced on him from the shadows, knocking him to the ground. De Mona extended her claws with the intention of taking his head off when a golden ax came between them, deflecting the blow. The hooded figure with the ax drew back to strike De Mona from her blind side, but a crackle of lightning knocked him farther into the alley. When he looked up, Gabriel was standing over him with storm clouds rolling in his eyes.

"That young lady you tried to behead is a friend of mine, so unless you can give me a good reason I'm going to barbecue you." Gabriel drew his hand back with a ball of lightning resting in his palm.

Cristobel covered his face with the back of his hand. "I wasn't trying to hurt her; I only wanted to get her off my friend."

"Lies like the rest of his kind this dwarf does. Kill him and be done with it you should." Gilchrest spat.

"Hold on a second." De Mona placed a calming hand on Gabriel's shoulder. She looked down at Cristobel and could see the fear in his eyes. "Start talking or I'm going to let my friend make good on his threat. You've been following us since the tavern and I want to know why."

"Because of him," he pointed at Gabriel.

Gabriel gave him a confused look. "Okay, okay, I know I've made quite a few enemies over the last forty-eight hours but I've never met you before in my life so what could I possibly have done to piss you off?"

"Gabriel, I'm not your enemy. We are friends, friends of your grandfather. The moment I saw your face I knew you were the one he spoke of," Cristobel said in an attempt to calm Gabriel, but the statement only enraged him more.

Gabriel snatched the dwarf from the ground and hoisted him high above his head. Lightning crackled around him, illuminating the alley. "What have you done with my grandfather?"

"Nothing, I swear it! It was he who helped us escape the Iron Mountains," Cristobel explained as the lightning sent jolts of electricity through him.

"Fools to you we must look like. *None* escape the Iron Mountains," Gilchrest challenged.

"But we have, and it was thanks to the brave Redfeather." Cristobel insisted. "If you would only release me, I could explain."

Gabriel hesitated, trying to measure the truth of Cristobel's words. After quite a bit of internal conflict, he extinguished the lightning and placed Cristobel on the ground. "Okay, start talking."

Cristobel went on to tell them of how he discovered Redfeather and the young witch, then recounted their daring escape from the Iron Mountains. Gabriel was truly amazed at the bravery his grandfather had shown in the face of seemingly impossible odds. His grandfather had always been Gabriel's hero, but more for his wisdom and love than his swordplay. Gabriel had never been more proud to be a Redfeather than he was at that moment, but as proud as he was he was also saddened by the fact that his grandfather hadn't made it out with the others.

"Is he still alive?" he asked Cristobel, trying to hide the dread in his voice.

"This I do not know," Cristobel admitted sadly.

"Then we'd best go and find out," Gabriel said.

"Wait, we must first go to my village and tend to the witch." Cristobel reminded them of Lucy, who was living on borrowed time. "Even with the herbs and our best healers I fear that it will take more than potions to help her fight off the Slov venom. You're a wizard, so maybe you can succeed where the herbs have failed," he told Gabriel.

Gilchrest laughed at this. "Him no wizard, him dead man walking."

"As much as I hate to admit it, the goblin is right. I'm not a wizard, Cristobel, just someone dumb enough to accept a fool's mission."

Cristobel gave him a confused look. "But the magic you called . . ."

"It's not magic; it's a curse I've been forced to carry." Gabriel absently rubbed his arm.

"Waste of time to backtrack. Dead by now she must be, death the only cure for Slov venom. Go to the Iron Mountains we will," Gilchrest demanded.

Cristobel pointed his ax at Gilchrest. "Hear me and hear me well, goblin. I made two promises to Redfeather before we fled the mountains. I honored one by finding Gabriel and I intend to honor the other by trying to help Lucy. Whether you agree to help or not, I won't abandon her."

All eyes turned to Gabriel. Like it or not, he was the leader of their group, and the decision was his to make. "Fine. Which way to your village?"

CHAPTER
TWENTY-ONE

Cristobel's second return was worse than the first. The last of his people were marched through the streets in shackles, while whips crashed across the backs of those who were too elderly or weak to keep in step with the others. What was left of the already damaged structures were either in flames or destroyed completely. There were a few brave souls left who tried to stand against the invaders, but their crude weapons were no match for those of the warriors. With steel and arrows they cut the rebels down left and right, laughing mockingly as they did so. As it turned out, the goblins had returned sooner than Cristobel had expected and this time they showed no mercy.

"No!" Cristobel screamed as he charged down the hill with his ax drawn. The two brave dwarfs with him were close on his heels. Gabriel made to follow them, but Gilchrest grabbed his wrist.

"Foolish to rush into a battle you cannot win.

Let dwarfs throw away lives, you live to fight another day," Gilchrest suggested.

Gabriel jerked away from him. "I'll not stand by again and watch as innocent people are slaughtered, like at Sanctuary." Gabriel followed Cristobel and the dwarf warriors.

Gilchrest looked up at De Mona with his eyes pleading for her not to follow the boy to certain death, but he knew it was a useless effort. "Die young and leave a good-looking corpse," De Mona laughed before tossing the goblin over her shoulder and charging down the hill into the battle.

The goblin who was leading the line of slaves turned, hearing the battle cries behind him, and Cristobel brought the ax down across his chest, splitting it open. The second swing of the ax removed his head. A goblin who moved as swift as the wind rushed Cristobel from his blind side and delivered a blow with the force of a wrecking ball that sent him sprawling to the ground, knocking the ax loose. Cristobel looked up in horror as the goblin blade came straight at his throat. Before the blow could land, the goblin was incinerated. Standing behind him was Gabriel, holding the Nimrod.

"My thanks to you, friend," Cristobel said as he dusted himself off and retrieved the ax.

"Thank me when we're out of this safely," Gabriel told the dwarf as he turned to face the three goblins who were heading their way.

A few feet away, De Mona battled two sword-wielding goblins while Gilchrest cowered behind one of the legs of the water tower in the center of the village. The goblins were highly skilled warriors, but De Mona had been born to do battle. The first goblin launched an overhand attack with his broad sword in an attempt to take De Mona's head. She grabbed the blade in midair with one hand and slammed her other fist into it, snapping it as if it were made from plywood instead of steel. Discarding the broken blade, she raked her claws up the goblin's chest, spilling his insides onto the ground. The second goblin was more cautious with his attack, dodging in and out as he tried to find a weak spot on the Valkrin. He faked high but went low, taking De Mona's legs out from under her. When he moved in for the kill, she tossed a handful of dirt into his eyes, blinding him while she got to her feet. With unbelievable speed, she pounced on the goblin and snapped his neck before rushing to help Gabriel and Cristobel, who were being swarmed by the goblins.

Gabriel and Cristobel stood back to back, dispatching goblins with steel and magic. Gabriel could feel the Bishop's spirit deep within his soul crying for blood, and he gladly answered, tearing into goblin flesh with the points of the trident. A gangly goblin whose face was covered in warts and tusks managed to break their defense and grab Gabriel in a chokehold. The power of the Nimrod made Gabriel stronger than most, but the goblin's grip was like steel. Feeling his panic, the Nimrod flared to life. The shaft rooted itself in the ground and began to grow like a beanstalk, carrying Gabriel and the goblin several stories above the ground. The frightened goblin released his grip on Gabriel's neck and clung to his waist for dear life.

Gabriel looked down at the goblin with storm clouds in his eyes and a mocking sneer on his face. "Where is your legendary courage now, goblin?" he asked in a voice that was not his own.

"Please," the goblin begged.

"My god is merciful and so am I." Gabriel placed his hand on the goblin's forehead. "Be cleansed, my child." He forced power into his hand and through the goblin's body, turning it to stone. Gabriel blew on the statue softly, and what remained of the goblin crumbled and was carried away on the wind.

"There are too many of them," Cristobel shouted as he struck down yet another goblin with the ax. The invaders had forced him and De Mona back to the water tower and surrounded them.

"Keep fighting!" De Mona ordered as she tore out the eyes of one of her opponents. A goblin wielding a hammer swung for De Mona's head, but she dodged and the hammer ended up taking out the leg of the water tower. With loud snapping sounds the other legs began to break and the tower tipped forward. "Move," De Mona grabbed Cristobel and leaped out of the way to safety. But Gilchrest wasn't so lucky.

The small goblin cringed as the heavy tower sped toward him. The goblins had very thick skin but there was no way he would survive the impact.

Before the water tower could crush him, it exploded in a flash of light, and the water rained down harmlessly over the village. Gilchrest couldn't believe the gods had smiled down on a creature as unworthy as himself, but when he looked across the battlefield he realized that it hadn't been the gods at all, but the Nimrod.

Gabriel stepped into the center of the goblin invaders and his voice cut through the night sky like thunder. "Hear me well, godless spawn of the Iron Mountains, for I bring to you the gift of redemption." He slammed the shaft of the trident on the ground. The village was suddenly lit up like mid-afternoon, bathing everyone in the cleansing light of the Nimrod. When the flash died, all the goblins, with the exception of Gilchrest, had been turned to stone.

"Dead was I, dead I say," Gilchrest said, staring at the remains of the water tower in shock. His eyes roamed over the stone goblins and eventually turned to Gabriel. "Slain by my own I almost was. Great debt owe to you I do." He knelt at Gabriel's feet. The dwarfs looked on in shock; they had never seen a goblin pay homage to anyone except the goblin prince, and especially not a human. The act sent a wave of whispers through the crowd.

"Get up. You're embarrassing me." Gabriel tugged the goblin to his feet.

"Cristobel!" a voice called, drawing everyone's attention away from the awkward moment between the human and the goblin. Mavis came limping through the village, still wearing the goblin shackles with tears in her eyes. "Thank the gods you made it back safely. I thought the goblins had discovered you." She embraced him.

"We are safe." Cristobel lifted her arms gently and used the ax to cut through her shackles. "Where's Cassy?"

Mavis's face was sad. "Gone. She and the witch were among the first the goblins took when they stormed the tunnels beneath the chapel."

"No." Cristobel's eyes became glassy. "But how did they even know where to find you?"

"I fear Alec has betrayed us," she said sadly. The fact that one of the dwarfs' own had betrayed them to their slavers was a devastating blow to them all.

"Curse Orden and his lot." Cristobel banged his fist against the ax. He glared down at Gilchrest. "I should take your head and send it back to your brother in a box." He raised his ax, but Gabriel stepped between them, holding the Nimrod.

"No more blood will be shed here today, dwarf or goblin." Gabriel told him. Only when Cristobel lowered his weapon did Gabriel lower his.

"Now that's a nifty trick." De Mona came over, still trying to wring the excess water from her hair. Her tunic was soiled and tattered but she still looked stunning.

"That was no trick, child, but magic. Magic that has not been seen in these parts for centuries,"

Mavis told her, staring at the trident in wonder. She reached up to touch it, but Gabriel recoiled.

"Don't. I don't wanna hurt you by accident," he said.

"Nonsense." Mavis ran her hand along the shaft of the Nimrod. "This magic knows my blood just as well as it knows yours." The Nimrod pulsed softly and returned to its resting place on Gabriel's arm.

"What do you know about the Nimrod?" Gabriel asked, staring at the tattoo curiously.

Mavis gave a weak laugh. "Probably more than you do, young man. It was my grandfather's hands that crafted the mold for the trident."

"Your grandfather made this thing?" Gabriel asked in shock.

"Yes, he crafted the weapon, but it was the power of another that gave it life. Long ago, a stranger came to our village seeking the greatest weapon smith in all of Midland to help create a gift for King Neptune. For many nights, the strange magician and my grandfather toiled away in his shop creating the trident. The very angels of heaven came down to see the finished project and cooled the metal with their tears of joy, as nothing so beautiful had ever been seen on earth. When it was given back over to the magician to breathe life into it, my grandfather added his own blood to the enchantment so that his creation would carry a piece of him with it for all time."

"The plot thickens," De Mona said offhandedly.

"Indeed it does," Gabriel agreed. "So what happened to your grandfather afterward?"

"He was killed during the goblin wars, as were my father and my son," Mavis said emotionally.

"I'm sorry," Gabriel told her, placing a hand on her shoulder.

"Don't be, for it was not your blade that slew my family but those of the goblins. My grandfather has been dead for many seasons, but I wish he had been here to see that one of his greatest creations has been entrusted by the gods to someone as noble as you."

"I'm sure," Gabriel said. He was tempted to tell Mavis how he had really come upon the trident, but he didn't want to ruin her moment. "I wish that your grandfather were still here, because maybe then he could tell me more about the Nimrod. I'm afraid it's been quite the mystery to us all."

"Yes, only my grandfather and the magician really knew the secret of the weapon," Mavis said.

"I'm sure the magician has probably passed on too," De Mona said.

"Possibly, but I doubt it. Beings as powerful as he are not restricted by things such as time," Mavis said.

"So you mean to say that it's possible he's still alive?" Gabriel asked anxiously.

"It wouldn't surprise me. He stayed with us for a time and helped in the effort against the goblins when the war started, but he disappeared not long after. There were many stories about what happened to him, but the most common is that he retreated topside to the world of men, where he would be free of the constant feuding that has torn Midland apart."

The fact that the magician may still have been alive gave Gabriel hope. "Mavis, could you tell me what this magician looked like?"

"I'm sorry, but this I do not know. Even the eldest of us don't remember much about the magician except that he had hair as white as the clouds and eyes as blue as the morning sky."

For reasons that Gabriel was unsure of, his mind went back to the old man he had seen smiling at him in Queens. He was about to question Mavis further when the two dwarfs who had been with Cristobel at the tavern came over.

"We've picked up the trail of the goblins who've taken our people. They're headed for the Iron Mountains," the blond dwarf informed him.

"Then so shall we," Gabriel said.

"Sounds like a plan. Any idea how we're going to get in? I'm sure we can't just roll up and knock on the front door," De Mona pointed out.

"Know of a way I do," Gilchrest spoke up. "Enter through the sewers we can. Not most pleasant route, but least guarded."

"And we're supposed to just take you at your word on this, goblin? For all we know you could be marching us to our deaths," Cristobel accused.

Gilchrest sneered at Cristobel. "No love lost between goblins and filthy dwarfs, but not dwarfs

I do this for." He looked at Gabriel. "Save my life you did, so in debt to you I am. Gilchrest ensure you make it inside the mountains, but after that we even and our business done, human."

Gabriel nodded in agreement. "Fair enough. We'd better get moving," he told the rest of the group.

"Before you go I would like to give you something." Mavis waved Gabriel down to kneel in front of her. She took his hand in hers and looked at him seriously. "Were I still young enough to wield a sword, I would go with you and take as many goblin heads as I could. But since I can do nothing for you physically, I send you with my blessings and my wisdom." She kissed him on both cheeks. "The weapon you carry is more powerful than any of us truly understand. In your darkest hour it will serve you well."

Gabriel smiled at the kindly old woman. "Thank you, Mavis." When he turned to address his group his face was as hard as stone. "Let's go get our people."

"Five against the goblin army—I'd love to hear what Jonas would have to say about this suicide mission." De Mona shook her head.

"It's only suicide if we die," Gabriel shot back. "Besides, the yoga master is too busy with his meditations to worry about what the hell we're down here doing. I doubt if anybody has even noticed we're gone yet."

CHAPTER
TWENTY-TWO

Jonas's private chambers were far less modern than the rest of the high-tech facility where he made his base. There was a small twin bed, a writing table, and two chairs. The only light from the room came from candles mounted on the wall. Not so much as a spark of electricity ran in the room, which some might have thought was odd, considering how technologically advanced the rest of the complex was, but the wiring tended to disrupt the flow of power from the spindle when Jonas needed to consult the ancient thing.

The Medusan sat in the middle of the floor with his arms and legs folded. His eyes stared unblinkingly at the wall, but he saw nothing in the room except the strands of time in the spindle, which was resting on the floor a few inches in front of him. For several hours, Jonas's subconscious mind traveled the length of the strands one by one, plucking through now and yesterday in an attempt to come up with a solution to the problem that threatened the worlds of men and the supernatural. The mystery of the Nimrod was an elusive one, but he could not be denied the truth with so much at stake.

Between Jonas and the spindle sat a piece of bloodstained rubble that had been recovered from the remains of Sanctuary, which he used as a focal point. The deaths and lives of those who had been lost flowed in a reverse stream through his mind with the screams of the dying scraping across his brain like nails on a chalkboard. Cracking the particular block of time surrounding events during the Seven-Day Siege that he wasn't there to see for himself, was like solving a Rubik's Cube. Jonas spent a great deal of time trying to approach it from several different angles, and just when it seemed like a hopeless case he heard the telltale click of progress.

These strands were darker and much harder to weed through than the rest had been, but Jonas was both patient and persistent. In the strands he saw Titus standing over the fallen body of the Bishop while both Knights and demons looked on in shock. Concentrating, he crawled back farther along the strand and saw himself when the bargain was struck between him and Titus. Had he truly had mastery over time he would've undone the past, but that was outside the realm of his power. Focusing on the Bishop, he crawled back farther still. The strand's image became fuzzy, and when it cleared again he thought he had made a wrong turn because he saw the warlock king, Dutch, standing in the center of a massive crypt.

In the crypt were twelve ornately decorated sarcophaguses sealed with the same mark the Bishop wore on his breastplate. A wraith stood in the center of the room with twelve bound souls kneeling on a pentagram drawn on the stone floor. Dutch moved around the center of the room, chanting and etching symbols on the sarcophaguses in blood. Jonas could see the faces of the individuals inside the sarcophaguses, and they were familiar to him. Suddenly twelve sets of eyes sprang open and Jonas realized that the order had been horribly wrong about the Bishop's and Titus's plans.

When Jonas snapped out of his trance, he was disoriented. His legs felt like rubber, but he forced himself to stand. He knew that he would have to allow himself time to recover from the strain of the ritual, but time was something that none of them had.

"Twelve hosts for twelve souls," he muttered over and over as he staggered toward the door. When he threw the door to his chambers open he literally collided with Jackson. The otherwise cool and savvy warrior wore a very troubled expression on his face.

"We've got a problem. Gabriel . . ." they said at the same time.

"You first," Jonas told Jackson while he tried to compose himself.

"That idiot kid and the girl are gone and they

took the goblin with them. My guess is that they're headed for the Iron Mountains," Jackson told him.

"Oh no, we must get to them." Jonas's voice was filled with panic.

"Yeah, before the goblins send them back to us in little pieces. It might serve them right for being so damn stupid. Now what's got you so rattled?"

"I know what Titus means to do with the Nimrod," Jonas said.

Jackson raised an eyebrow. "Well, don't keep an asshole in suspense."

"Titus plans to finish what the Bishop started and raise the First Guard!"

Jackson's face went as white as a sheet. He knew the story of the twelve powerful warriors who gave their lives protecting Christ. "Sweet Jesus." Jackson leaned against the wall.

"Hardly. The souls Titus plans to use to reanimate the bodies are anything but holy ones. I shudder to think what we would have to stand against with the great warriors reunited with their weapons and animated by the forces of evil. Hell on earth would be a blessing," Jonas told him.

"We've gotta get to the kid," Jackson said.

"Agreed. Let's get topside ASAP."

"Get your gear and let's move," Jackson told Lydia and Finnious as he passed the dining area where they were eating sandwiches.

"Where're we going?" Finnious asked.

"It's time for a little on-the-job training." Jackson extended his blades. The look on his face frightened Finnious. Once everyone was armed and ready, they took the elevators back up to the hangar. "You guys stay close to me, and the motto of the day is to kill first and ask questions later."

"What's happened?" Lydia asked nervously.

"Your buddy Gabriel has taken us from the frying pan into the fire," Jackson said, pushing the hangar doors open.

The night was quiet—almost too quiet, in fact. Jonas and Jackson busied themselves loading the things they would need into the transport while Finnious clung to Lydia like a second skin. Something had the wraith spooked and she could feel him trembling.

"Finnious, what's wrong?" Lydia asked.

"I don't know . . . something doesn't feel right." He looked around nervously as if he expected the bogeyman to leap out from the shadows at any second.

"Don't worry. You know I won't let anything happen to you." She hugged him. Just then her sensitive ears picked up on something whistling through the air. "Incoming!" she shouted, and tackled Jackson out of the way just before several objects whizzed through where he had been standing. She swept her spear through the air and deflected the second wave of projectiles, embedding them in an abandoned Honda. The projectiles were black featherlike objects with pointed tips.

"Where are they coming from?" Finnious scanned the junkyard frantically.

A blur moved in Jackson's direction, and he raised his blade just in time to fend off the strike. He tried to counter, but the blur was moving again. "Stand still so I can hit you, damn it!"

The blur moved in Lydia's direction, but unlike the others she didn't move on sight but her hearing. She deflected the blow aimed at her and countered with one of her own. The blur staggered, finally becoming visible to them. It was a man, or at least something shaped like one. Large black wings flapped softly, dislodging the loose debris on the ground. A death's-head mask covered the creature's face, but they could see the milky blue eyes behind it.

"And who the hell are you supposed to be?" Jackson asked sarcastically.

"Death," Finnious whimpered.

The angel of death ignored Jackson's question and let his eyes roam over all of them, stopping when he reached Finnious. He could see the Spark radiating inside the wraith like a great beacon. "Give it to me," the angel said in a ghostly voice, reaching for Finnious.

Lydia knocked his hand away with her spear and stood between them. "If you touch him I'll kill you," she challenged. The angel tried to move around her and she cut him off again. His movement was so swift that she barely had a chance to raise her spear to deflect the strike from the scythe he was carrying. With a swipe of one of his massive wings, the angel knocked Lydia to the side and continued toward Finnious.

The wraith tried to scramble away, but the angel plucked him from his feet by the back of his shirt. "You must give it to me." He shook Finnious roughly.

"I don't know what you're talking about," Fin cried. Through the mask, he could see insane eyes staring back at him. The eyes were familiar, but he couldn't think why.

"Take your hands off him." Lydia rushed the angel. She tried to plunge her spear into his back, but his wings blocked the strike and knocked her backward. They flapped once and sent spearlike feathers flying at Lydia. She managed to dodge most of them, but one nicked her side and downed her.

"Give me the Spark, or I'll cut it from your dead body!" The angel raised his scythe over Finnious.

All Finnious could think to do to protect himself was raise his hands, and when he did they started to glow brightly. With a rush of air, light poured from Fin's hands and blinded the angel. Jackson seized the opportunity and struck the angel across the face with one of his blades, knocking his mask off. Beneath the mask was a spill of white hair and a face Jackson recognized from Sanctuary.

"Julius?" Fin gasped, turning the angel's attention back to him.

Julius's pale eyes momentarily filled with color as the light of recognition shone in them. Pain shot through his head as the voices of the restless dead flooded his ears, threatening to drive him insane. "I must have it! Give me the Spark!" Julius tried to split Jackson in half with the scythe, but he crossed his blades and blocked the blow. Jackson knocked the scythe away and delivered a glancing blow to the angel's stomach.

"Don't hurt him! He's a part of the order!" Lydia shouted at Jackson.

"Maybe he was a few days ago, but it looks like our boy here switched sides." Jackson moved in on Julius with his blades drawn.

"You don't understand. I must have the Spark to make the voices go away." Julius clutched at his head.

Jonas raised his hands toward Julius. "Let us try and help you."

"No, no!" Julius swung the scythe, nearly taking Jonas's hand off. "Only the Spark can make the voices stop."

"Then it sucks to be you, because the only way you're getting that Spark out of Finnious is over my dead body," Jackson told him.

Julius hesitated, and it almost looked like he was battling with the decision. There was another wave of voices and he lunged for Jackson. Jackson was a skilled fighter, but Julius had been trained in combat since he was old enough to hold a sword. The scythe moved with blinding speed, sending a painful vibration up Jackson's arms every time the blades met. Striking with his wings, Julius knocked Jackson's arms apart, leaving his torso exposed. The scythe came down, splitting Jackson's gut open. He staggered backward, watching his blood spill on the grass below before collapsing.

***

"I'd hate to have friends like yours," Asha said when she and Rogue were outside the herb shop.

"Shut up, Asha." Rogue stormed past her on his way to the SUV. He was more upset with Gilgamesh than he was with Asha, but she was the closer target. He was surprised to hear the dark elf's stance on the situation, but he couldn't say that he blamed Mesh. Rogue and people like him had been behind the scenes trying to save the asses of the human race from one self-inflicted disaster or another, only to have them create more problems for themselves. To top it off, the supernaturals were still treated like lepers by the few mortals who even acknowledged them. The sensible side of him had said to walk away from the problem before he got too deep, but by that point it was too late. He was in up to his neck, and the bounty on his head ensured that he would see it through to the end.

"How did it go?" Morgan asked, stepping out of the vehicle as they approached.

"My friend is gonna tell us where we can find a rift," Rogue told him.

"But he isn't gonna help us," Asha added.

"Listen, sweetie, I don't see Dutch busting down any doors to try and snatch your ass out of the fire, so you need to watch where you throw those stones. Let's get back to Queens to see if Jonas and Gabriel have made any progress."

Just then, Morgan's radio chirped to life in his ear. There was so much noise in the background that he couldn't tell what was going on, so he disconnected the earpiece and listened through the speaker. "Jackson, slow down, I can't understand you."

"Not Jackson . . ." the mechanical voice crackled.

"Finnious?"

"Get away, get away!" Finnious's frightened voice came through the speaker. In the background they could hear screams and the sounds of battle.

"Finnious, where's Jonas? Is Jackson okay?" Morgan asked frantically.

"Oh my God there's blood everywhere!"

"Where are you? Give us a location!" Rogue shouted.

Jackson's shaky voice came through the speaker. "Red, we're in a bad way out here. We're at the scrapyard getting our asses kicked by some dude with wings. Shit, he cut me up pretty bad, Red. Listen, man, you guys need to . . ." There was static, then the connection went dead.

Morgan's face was terror-stricken. "Jackson? Jackson!"

"We've gotta get to them," Asha said.

"You guys take my truck and I'll meet you there." Rogue took a few steps back.

"Rogue, this is no time for us to split up. Get your ass in the truck!" Asha barked.

"I'll get there faster on my own. I'll hold down the fort for as long as I can; you guys just make sure you get your asses there," Rogue said and raised his hands skyward. The shadows began to peel from the alleys and streetlamps, swirling around Rogue like a flock of sparrows. "If it hides in the darkness, the shadows will find it," he said, before melting into a pool of shadow and spilling into the cracks of the broken concrete.

"Sweet," Asha whispered in amazement.

"Quit your gawking and let's go before our friends are sent to their makers." Morgan grabbed her by the arm and pulled her toward the truck. He shoved her through the driver's side door into the passenger seat and got behind the wheel. He pulled out of the parking spot and immediately slammed on the brakes when two girls stepped into the path of the SUV. He slapped the horn over and over, but the girls refused to move.

"Hold on, I know them." Asha hopped from the car.

"Tend your tea party another time, girl; there are lives at stake here!" Morgan called after her.

"Just keep the engine running," Asha called over

her shoulder as she approached Lisa and Lane. There was something strange about the blank expressions on their faces, but Asha was so happy to see her sisters that she never noticed it. "Goddess be praised that you guys are here. Look, I don't have a lot of time to explain, but I need your help. Let's get in the truck and I'll fill you in along the way." Asha started for the truck, but Lisa and Lane didn't follow. "Are you guys coming or not?"

Lisa kept her eyes glued to the ground when she spoke. "Asha, we have orders to bring you before the council to face charges."

Asha couldn't believe what she was hearing. "Are the both of you high? We'll see what Dutch has to say about this."

"Who do you think sent us?" Lane asked.

Asha looked between the two witches she had once called sisters and her sadness was replace by anger. Magic flared to life in her hands. "I don't have time for this. Tell Dutch we'll speak about it later." Asha made to walk away, but the sound of a round being chambered froze her. She turned around to see that both Lisa and Lane had automatic weapons trained on her. "What are you guys doing?"

Lane grinned at her. "Like my sister said, we're taking you in. Alive or dead, it's totally your choice." Asha raised her hands and Lane aimed the gun at her face. "Asha, you're hands-down the best spell-caster I know, but I'd bet these shells against your magic any day. Now let's go. Our king is waiting."

CHAPTER
TWENTY-THREE

"Jesus, this place smells like ass," De Mona said as they walked through the sewers of the Iron Mountains. The ledge they were walking along was barely wide enough for them to walk shoulder to shoulder. A few feet below there was a river of some of the foulest water she'd ever smelled.

"What did you expect? All the waste of the Iron Mountains travels through these tunnels," Cristobel said, clutching his ax tightly. Though his face was calm, his heart was racing. They had barely escaped the Iron Mountains the first time and he could only pray that they would be able to do it again.

"I don't like this," said the redheaded dwarf who they had learned was called Suitor. "At least if we were topside we'd have room to fight should something go wrong, but in these cramped quarters we'll be at a disadvantage."

Gilchrest snorted. "Never make it within mile of mountain topside, especially carrying dwarf stink on us so heavy."

Suitor drew his blade and pointed it at Gilchrest. "If I cut your nose off, you wouldn't have to smell our dwarf stink, goblin!"

Gilchrest bristled. "Not be so brave if I free of this." He tugged at the collar.

"I would welcome the chance to take your head for what your people have done to us," Suitor said. The dwarfs and goblins hated each other, but they had made an uneasy truce for the sake of the mission. No one knew how long it would last.

"Arguing amongst ourselves isn't going to get us any closer to the Iron Mountains," Gabriel pointed out. Like everyone else, he was on edge, but as their leader he had to be the glue that held them together.

"No, but it provide Gilchrest with entertainment," the little goblin chimed in.

De Mona grabbed Gilchrest by the back of the collar and lifted him over her head. "Listen, you're supposed to be our guide, so guide us instead of running your mouth. How much farther?"

Gilchrest turned his head as best he could with De Mona holding him suspended and searched the wall until he spotted one of the hidden directional markers used by the goblins. "Not far, not far. Hardly used for more than waste these tunnels are, but inside the mountains they take us."

"Good." De Mona tossed him on the ground. "Lead on."

The goblin hobbled down the tunnel with his useless wings flapping behind him. A large rat darted out from the shadows and was swiftly snatched up.

Gilchrest stroked the rat's head and whispered something to it while the rat struggled to free itself.

"You'd better not be planning on eating that," the blond dwarf warned. He was called Jak.

Gilchrest squinted at the dwarf before dropping the rat back on the ground and watching it scramble away. He muttered something under his breath and fell in step with Gabriel. "Question I have."

"What is it?" Gabriel asked him.

"Why you do this, risk life for one too weak to fight own battles?"

"Because we are family, and family looks out for one another."

"Goblin law say they who too weak to fight either food or slave, even own family."

"Then the goblin laws are twisted. In human families we love and protect one another."

Gilchrest frowned. "At one time Gilchrest feel same about brother Orden, but much time go by and still no one come for me. Abandon Gilchrest I think he has," he said sadly. The moment quickly passed and he was back to his questioning. "Back at dwarf village almost killed by one of own I was, but you save. Why you do this, human?"

Gabriel sighed. "Because it was the right thing to do."

"But you human and I goblin, we natural enemies. Brother Orden try to kill you and take your grandfather and you still help Gilchrest?" The goblin shook his head. "I don't understand how you human think."

"Maybe after this is all done you will."

Gilchrest laughed. "Not likely. When this done, enemies again we are, yes?"

Gabriel thought on it. "Maybe, but it doesn't have to be that way. We have choices." He left it at that and moved to catch up with De Mona.

A few yards later, the tunnel curved left and began to slope downward. As they descended, the air became thinner and much fouler as the smell of raw sewage crept into all their noses. A little farther down, the tunnel opened up to a narrow platform that ran along a stream of murky green water that was thick with waste.

"I think I'm gonna upchuck," De Mona said, covering her mouth and nose with her hand. Being that her nose was twice as sensitive as the others', the smell was almost overwhelming.

"This way." Gilchrest led them farther into the recesses of the tunnel. The stretch before them was completely dark except for tiny lights that appeared once every few yards.

"I can't see a damn thing." Jak held the torch in front of him. A group of rats scrambled out of the tunnel and over his feet.

"I hate rats." Gabriel danced around trying to avoid the rodents.

"Rats plentiful in these tunnels. They get fat from goblins; grateful they are," Gilchrest said with a smug grin. "Come through here and we reach border of goblin territory." He urged them into the tunnel.

The darkness snapped closed behind them like a shutter when the last member of the group had crossed it. Gabriel felt an eerie crawling along his arms as he made his way through the tunnel. A curious rat perched itself on Gabriel's boot, and he instinctively shook his leg and sent the rat into the stream of sewage. The sound of the rat hitting the water was like thunder in the quiet tunnel, but the sound that followed froze everyone in their tracks. There was a high-pitched whining, followed by two more similar ones, with the last one coming from somewhere not far from them.

"More rats?" Cristobel turned to De Mona.

"Either that or someone is running a compactor down here," De Mona said.

"Something is coming," Suitor said nervously.

De Mona looked down the tunnel. At first all she could see were shadows moving, but soon the eyes were visible. Large red eyes glowing in the darkness and moving toward them. When the shadows crossed one of the tiny lights, De Mona caught a glimpse of the things. The pony-sized rats were hideous in appearance, with oversized heads and bulging eyes. Riding their hairless backs were the scourge of the Iron Mountains.

***

The goblin prince, Orden, sat at the head of the table drumming his fingers on the surface impatiently as Titus's commander and his entourage were shown into the main hall of the fort. He was initially upset that Titus had chosen to send his agents instead of addressing the goblin prince in person, but the message he had sent ahead calmed some of his hostility. Titus had invited Orden to sit in on a secret meeting he had called in the city, and the goblin prince was anxious to see what devious plan his favorite son had up his sleeve this time and how he could benefit from it.

Flagg had been on pins and needles while he waited for Titus to free him from the clutches of the goblin and the mission he'd been ordered to oversee. The mage's eyes registered both relief and concern when he saw Riel come in with the soldiers and the covered box trailing him. He didn't have to see what was in the box to recognize the magic securing it.

The first thing Riel noticed when he entered the main hall was the stink. He was no stranger to the scent of the rotting dead, but it seemed more concentrated down here. In the corner near the door, several of the largest rats Riel had ever seen fought over the remains of something that could no longer be indentified. The long wooden table that stretched down the middle of the floor was badly scratched and stained with blood, no doubt from one of the goblins' notorious feeding frenzies. The troupe guarding the covered box was visibly shaken, but Riel's face remained stern. Not because he wasn't disturbed about being within the mountains while outnumbered, but because he knew if the goblins picked up on his fear he would be as good as dead.

"Greetings, mighty Prince Orden." Riel bowed. "I bring my master Titus's apologies for his and your conflicting schedules as well as his thanks for extending your hospitalities to our friend." He motioned toward Flagg.

"You mean for not killing the worm when your master sent my men off to be slaughtered by the Nimrod, don't you?" Orden flashed a toothy grin.

Riel swallowed the lump in his throat. "Yes, the awakening of the Nimrod has taken us all off guard, but not to worry, great prince. With our combined forces under the leadership of Titus we will be victorious."

Orden slammed his massive fists on the table, spilling the goblets of wine that had been resting on it. "The goblins have *one* leader, demon. You'd do well to remember it if you wish to keep your head."

Riel lowered his eyes. "Of course, Prince Orden."

Orden's attention went from Riel to his Valkrin bodyguard, who hadn't so much as budged during his outburst. From behind the golden mask covering her face, her eyes bore into the goblin prince. Orden laughed and addressed Riel, who was still staring at the ground. "Your master must have a very low opinion of you if he has entrusted your life to a traitor." He spat venomously.

The Valkrin made to take a step toward Orden, but Riel waved her away. "The traitors among the warrior women have been weeded out and dealt with accordingly. I assure you that all here are loyal to the dark father. But let us not dwell on transgressions of the past, when the future is so bright. As a show of my master's trust in you, he has sent one of his prized possessions to be safeguarded by the mighty goblins during our stay here." Riel motioned for the soldiers to bring the box forward.

Orden watched curiously as the women placed the box on the table. He hadn't missed how Flagg moved away from the box when they set it down, so he drew his blade in case it was booby-trapped. "And what might that be?"

For an answer Riel removed the black covering, exposing the glass box beneath, marked with mystic symbols. Leah sat cross-legged on a pillow of satin, dressed in a hooded robe. Her golden eyes stared out from behind the glass venomously at all in the room.

Orden's eyes could not hide their hunger. "A sprite?" Even through the box he could smell her sweet flesh and so could the other goblins in the room. They all began to sniff around the box and salivate at the inviting smell of her magical blood. One goblin wandered too close to the box and received a backhand from the Valkrin that sent him crashing into the wall.

"Keep your distance, dog," she hissed. The goblin snarled and drew his weapon, but Orden stopped him.

"This meat is not for you, brother," Orden told

the goblin. "Demon"—he turned to Riel—"your master risks much sending you down here with such a rare gift." He wiped the drool from his mouth with the back of his hand. To the goblins, the fey were an even greater delicacy than magicians.

"And I have told him as much, but I'm afraid he has insisted," Riel said. "There are none more qualified to keep the sprite from harm than the goblins, greatest warriors in all the land. I trust that your men are obedient and fearful enough of you that no harm will come to the girl while she is with you?"

Orden thought on it. He was having a hard enough time controlling himself in the presence of the sprite, so there was no telling what some of his weaker-willed brothers might attempt when his back was turned. Still, he would risk it rather than admitting to the outsiders that he wasn't in total control. "Yes, we will keep the little fey from harm. I'll have Illini see to her personally."

"But I am to accompany you to the gathering," Illini protested.

"You will do whatever your prince commands," Orden shot back. "Besides, since Brutus's murder you are the only one trustworthy enough to guard the girl."

"One of your goblins was murdered?" Riel asked curiously. On his way in he had heard the whispers among the guards but was unsure as to what had happened.

Orden's eyes narrowed. "Nothing more than a

few of our slaves who have forgotten their places in the pecking order."

A young goblin appearing in the doorway saved Orden from having to explain further. He was thin with a rodentlike face and oversized front teeth. "My prince." He dropped to one knee.

"What is it, Musk, can't you see that our prince is having council?" Illini asked in an irritated tone.

"Forgive me, sir, but my pets have reported intruders in the old sewer tunnels," Musk told him.

"Then let the riders deal with them." Orden waved him off. "It's probably more of those fool scavengers who make their homes in the abandoned tunnels. They are a nuisance, but they keep our rats well fed."

"The riders are moving to intercept as we speak, but there's more. One of my rats says that they smelled a demon among them," Musk said timidly. This got everyone's attention.

"Invaders sent by the order?" Riel asked.

"Not in those tunnels. We hardly use them anymore, but we get the occasional displaced soul that's been cast from the outside world and foolishly tries to make a home in what we claim as ours. I believe you call them hobos," Orden said with an amused smirk. "Musk, take some men and assist the riders."

"I'll go with him in case the demon is right and the invaders are a part of the order," Illini offered.

"No, if we've been breached it's all the more reason why you must secure the sprite with haste.

Musk can have his pick of the men," Orden told him.

"I'll go." Everyone was surprised to see that it was the Valkrin speaking. "Enemies of the goblins are enemies of us all. I will go with your men."

Orden smiled broadly. "Looks like not all of your lot have lost their salt. Very well, if your master has no objections then neither do I."

The Valkrin looked at Riel, who seemed to be weighing it. "Go, if you must. I know how your kind loves a good battle, but be swift as we're expected at the gathering."

"I will help the goblins with the intruders and meet you at Raven Wood. I know the way."

"Very well, but be quick about it."

"As you command." The Valkrin bowed and followed Musk out of the hall. As they were leaving, two dwarfs came into the room pushing carts that carried serving dishes.

"Ah, we've been so busy I had almost forgotten that I'd ordered my finest cooks to prepare a feast for you," Orden addressed his guests. He waved the dwarfs forward and they began setting the table, placing a large covered dish in the center. "Please accept this meal as a token of my appreciation for your master Titus and all he has done."

"Great, I'm starving," one of the female soldiers said and helped herself to a seat. Riel gave her a disapproving look, but she ignored him. "What's on the menu?"

Orden removed the cover and revealed the

traitorous dwarf Alec's body on the platter. He had been gutted and stuffed with rat tails before they roasted him to a golden brown color. The female soldier pushed away from the table and threw up all over the floor, while Flagg and Riel looked on in total shock at the barbarism of the goblins.

Orden laughed, ripped off one of Alec's arms, and tore into it. "Eat up, my friends. There's plenty more where this came from."

CHAPTER
TWENTY-FOUR

"Goblins!" De Mona shouted, calling her change. A wave washed over her, hardening her skin and sharpening her fingertips to spearlike points. Moonlight shone in her eyes as she snarled fiercely, ready to engage the attackers.

"Found us the riders have, die we all will," Gilchrest said, cringing.

"Sorry, but I'm not ready to check out just yet." Gabriel manifested the Nimrod just in time to deflect an arrow that came sailing his way.

From behind Gabriel a rider came out of the darkness, moving at an alarming speed with his sword poised to take Gabriel's unsuspecting head. Before he could strike, Cristobel appeared with his ax flying in a high arc. The rider's momentum carried him directly into the blow and it cost him his head. Never stopping his motion, Cristobel brought the ax around and embedded it in the skull of the mutated rat. Before he could compose himself for another strike, a second rider flung himself from his mount and tackled the dwarf into the river of waste.

"Cristobel!" Suitor cried.

"I'll get him. You guys help De Mona," Gabriel ordered as he dove into the waste after Cristobel.

De Mona's claws tore through the face of one goblin and the belly of another as the frenzy set in. A third went for her head with his sword, but she swiftly ducked it and closed the distance between them. She raked her claws across the goblin's face, tearing through his eyelid and upper lip and causing him to stumble backward. She tried to take his head off, but the goblin evaded the strike, and De Mona's claws tore gashes in the stone wall behind him. The goblin drove his blade into De Mona's gut, failing to break the skin but knocking the wind out of her.

Before the goblin could take advantage, Jak was on him with his twin blades, launching a series of combinations, but the goblin was able to fend them off. The three blades interlocked as each combatant struggled to gain ground over the other. Unfortunately for the goblin, he was so focused on Jak that he never saw De Mona come up behind him. With a grunt the girl dug her claws into the goblin's back and ripped out his lungs.

By the time Gabriel made it down to where the tide had taken Cristobel, the dwarf was flailing about in the water while the larger goblin tried to drown him. Gabriel delivered a bone-crunching kick to the goblin's lower back to get his attention. The goblin spun on Gabriel with a roar and attacked. Gabriel plunged the Nimrod into the goblin's side and pushed with everything he had, pinning him to the wall. He expected the blow to kill the goblin, but to his surprise the goblin gripped the shaft of the Nimrod and pulled it free with a grunt. He tossed the Nimrod into the waste and pounced on Gabriel.

Gabriel was never a very skilled boxer, but he did the best he could, using his forearms to deflect the goblin's punches. Gabriel tried a roundhouse, but the goblin grabbed him by the ankle and slammed him viciously into the wall, knocking the wind out of him. Gabriel's limp body slid down the wall and disappeared into the waste. The goblin was peering into the water looking for Gabriel when he heard a splashing behind him. He turned in time to see Gabriel coming at him with the Nimrod. The points of the trident dug into the goblin's chest with a thud. Gabriel called the power and the Nimrod answered, stretching as it had done in the village and pinning the goblin to the ceiling. Leading with his fists, Gabriel propelled himself upward and knocked the goblin up through the ceiling to the level above the sewers.

Cristobel rejoined the fight just in time to see Suitor fall to a goblin blade. Seconds later, he avenged the death of his friend by hacking off both of the goblin's arms before taking his head. A commotion at the end of the tunnel they had come from drew his attention and he saw more riders closing in on them. "We're trapped!" he called to De Mona.

De Mona looked around with her brain working overtime, trying to find an escape. Her eyes landed on the hole Gabriel had created in the ceiling and she got an idea. "The hell we are," she said, pointing out her discovery.

"It's at least twenty feet to the top; we'll never make it before they cut us down," Jak said, deflecting an arrow that came flying out of the darkened tunnel.

Gilchrest dodged an arrow that was meant for him and scrambled behind De Mona. "All will die, all will die."

"Always the pessimist, aren't you?" De Mona picked him up.

"Let go, what you do?" Gilchrest flailed around in her grip.

"I'm trying to save your life. Now hold still," she barked. Before Gilchrest could figure out what she was talking about, he found himself shooting up through the hole like a rocket. Once Gilchrest was safe, De Mona turned to the dwarfs. "Circus time, kids." She cupped her hands at her waist.

"We don't even know what's up there," Jak said as he nervously placed his foot in De Mona's hand.

"Whatever it is has to be better than dying in a

sewer," De Mona said before tossing Jak up through the hole. "Your turn," she said to Cristobel.

"I won't leave you down here, De Mona," Cristobel said, opening the belly of a lunging rat, spilling its rider into the sewage.

"I'll be right behind you," she assured him.

Cristobel placed his foot in the cup of her hands and looked at her seriously. "If you're not topside in five seconds I'm coming back down."

"Then I'll see you in three and a half," De Mona told him before shooting Cristobel up through the hole. De Mona crouched and hurled herself upward. She had managed to grip the top of the hole when something snaked around her leg. She looked down and saw a hulk of a goblin holding the end of the whip and pulling her back down. She tried to pull herself free, but he was too strong. De Mona dropped like a stone back through the hole, smashing her head against the ledge before landing in the sewage. Before she could compose herself, she was swarmed by half a dozen goblins.

Claws, teeth, and blades struck De Mona on every part of her body that she left uncovered. So far her skin had withstood the worst of the damage, but she was taking a hell of a beating and wasn't sure how long she could hold her demon form.

She managed to shake the goblins off her, then

bounded out of the water and back onto the walkway. She made a mad dash for the hole, but a spiked club to the gut knocked her back down. She dispatched the goblin, but two more immediately took its place. Farther down the tunnel she could hear reinforcements coming. If she didn't get out of the tunnel ASAP she knew that she was dead.

A bug-eyed rat lunged from the darkness, narrowly missing her face as she ducked out of the way and split its guts open as it passed. Before she could get back to her feet, another goblin grabbed a fistful of her hair from behind and pulled, leaving her throat open for his comrade's sword. De Mona reached back to strike out with her claws, but found her arm pinned by another goblin. De Mona could do little more than struggle as the goblins held her suspended, preparing to take her head. Before the final blow fell, she heard a voice call from behind the swarming goblins.

"She's mine." From the crowd stepped the Valkrin who had accompanied Flagg to the Iron Mountains. She was carrying a longsword over her armored shoulder. The Valkrin looked at the helpless De Mona and shook her head. "You were a fool to come here, little one," the Valkrin said tenderly.

"No more a fool than you are to throw in your lot with Titus. I am ashamed to even be one of you monsters!" De Mona spat on her golden mask.

Something akin to hurt flashed across the Valkrin's eyes behind the mask. "I regret a great many things, but being here tonight is not one of

them. Die well." The Valkrin raised her sword and
struck.

Gabriel found himself in a small cavern just above
the sewers. It was almost completely dark except
for the bit of moonlight that shone in from the
mouth of the cavern. He looked to his left and saw
the bloody trident on the ground but saw no sign
of the goblin that had been impaled on the end of
it. He wondered where the creature had gone off
to, but he didn't have to wonder long as a thick
forearm snaked around his neck from behind, cutting off his air.

"Filthy human scum. I'm going to rip your head
off and use that fancy fork of yours to scoop out
your brains when I eat them," the goblin breathed
his foul breath into Gabriel's ear.

Gabriel tried to break his grip, but even with his
new powers heightening his strength, he couldn't
overpower the goblin.

Call it, the Bishop whispered in the back of his
head.

Gabriel tried to concentrate on summoning the
trident, but his panicked state made it hard to concentrate. "I can't," he rasped.

You must or you will die! the Bishop warned.

Gabriel tried again. This time the trident, which
lay a few feet away, rumbled but it would not come.
His throat began to constrict and spots danced

before his eyes. Gabriel knew he was taking his last breaths.

Suddenly the goblin released his grip and howled in pain. Gabriel dropped to one knee and sucked in precious air. He looked up to see Gilchrest with his legs wrapped around the goblin's shoulders, gnawing on its ear. Gilchrest's brave act was impressive, but also stupid since the goblin was nearly three times his size. The goblin reached up and plucked Gilchrest from his shoulder.

"Well, well, if it isn't the royal family's most hated son," the goblin sneered. "Normally Orden would have the head of anyone who laid hands on you, rodent, but since you've thrown in your lot with our enemies, I'm sure he'd understand." The goblin opened his mouth to devour Gilchrest. His teeth made it within inches of Gilchrest's face when Cristobel's axe cut through the air and opened up a nasty gash on the side of the goblin's face.

"Try me, monster!" Cristobel challenged.

The goblin tried to rush Cristobel, but he was too swift for the brute and managed to open up the back of his head and calf. The goblin dropped to one knee, grimacing. Feeling overconfident, Cristobel moved in for the kill, but the goblin had expected as much. He knocked away the ax, and grabbed Cristobel by the throat and began shaking him violently. The goblin was about to snap Cristobel's neck when he heard Gabriel call to him.

"Goblin, you wanted my trident so bad that I decided to give it to you," Gabriel said, before throwing the trident like a spear. The Nimrod buried itself in the goblin's back, causing him to drop Cristobel. Gabriel raised his hands and called on the power of the Nimrod and this time it answered. Bolts of lightning shot from the trident and swept over the goblin's body, frying both skin and bones. When the power finally faded, all that was left of the goblin was a pile of ash.

"Is everyone okay?" Gabriel asked, as he retrieved the Nimrod from the ash.

"I think so," Cristobel said, rubbing his bruised neck. "That was pretty stupid of you," Cristobel said to Gilchrest, speaking of him attacking the bigger goblin.

"No more stupid than you saving me. Roles had been reversed, let you die I would've," Gilchrest spat.

"And that's what separates monsters from men," Cristobel said.

"Where's De Mona?" Gabriel asked.

"She was right behind us," Cristobel said, looking around for the girl who was nowhere in sight.

Screams from the sewers below cut through the air and drew all their attention to the hole.

Jak peered into the hole. "She's still down there!"

"We've got to go back." Cristobel started for the hole, but Gabriel stopped him.

"No, you stay here and I'll go. If I don't make it

back, you must continue the mission and save our loved ones, do you understand?" Gabriel asked.

"You have my word," Cristobel agreed.

Taking a deep breath, Gabriel jumped down into the hole, with the Nimrod clutched firmly in his hand. He hit the murky water with a splash and took a defensive stance, anticipating the goblins would descend on him. When he looked over to where De Mona and the armored Valkrin were, he had to do a double take to make sure his eyes weren't deceiving him.

De Mona reflexively closed her eyes as blood splattered on her face. She expected to feel the sharp pinch of steel in her gut, but instead she was dropped roughly to the ground. When she opened her eyes, she saw the masked Valkrin driving her sword into the gut of one of the goblins.

"Traitor!" one of the goblins cried and rushed at the Valkrin, wielding a spiked club. The goblin swung the club, but the Valkrin's sword cut through it and his chest, and the goblin fell over dead. One by one, the goblins came, and one by one, they fell to the demon's blade. One managed to blindside the Valkrin and delivered a crushing blow to her jaw, knocking her mask off. The demon snarled and plunged her claws into the goblin's chest. Its eyes went wide in shock as she tugged and ripped his heart from his chest. Seeing that the battle was lost, the last few goblins retreated into the tunnel.

De Mona lay on the floor, trying to compose herself and make heads or tails of what had just happened. In the shadows of the sewer, she could see the glowing eyes of the armored Valkrin staring at her. Slowly the Valkrin made her way towards De Mona. Fearing another attack, De Mona got to her feet and took a defensive stance. When the armored Valkrin stepped into the light, De Mona saw her face and gasped. The Valkrin dropped to her knees a few feet away from De Mona and looked up at her with tears dancing in the corners of her dark eyes.

Looking at the Valkrin was like looking into a mirror. "Mom?" De Mona asked in shock.

Mercy composed herself enough to reply. "Yes, baby. It's me."

CHAPTER
TWENTY-FIVE

Raven Wood was fifteen acres of sprawling land on the outskirts of the sleepy town of Beacon, New York. Normally the estate was quiet with the exception of the occasional industry party thrown by its unofficial owner, but that night it was alive with activity. Luxury cars and limousines lined the driveway, while henchmen lurked in the shadows. The estate's owner, fashion designer Mario Bucaddo, watched nervously from the second-floor balcony as people dressed in everything from tuxedos to leather moved about his property.

The forty-something-year-old Bucaddo had gone from a relative nobody to one of the industry's hottest designers seemingly overnight. The media credited it to his hard work and cutting-edge style but there were some who knew better. When opportunity had knocked, Buccado eagerly answered the door, but he'd had no idea that it would be a gateway to hell.

A cool breeze on the back of Mario's neck caused

him to spin around nervously. He found himself confronted by a beautiful young woman. A jade green evening gown, with sequined hems, hugged her body like a second skin and gave an added boost to her full breasts. A spill of brown hair fell around her angelic face, partially obscuring one of her inviting brown eyes. "Nice place you've got here," the girl said seductively.

Mario had to swallow to build enough moisture to reply. "Thank you," he said, trying to hide the nervousness in his voice. She was by far the most beautiful creature Mario had ever seen, but he knew better than to take any of the guests in his house at face value, especially that night. "If you're looking for the party, it's downstairs on the main floor."

The young lady smiled and moved closer to him. Mario tried to back away but couldn't get his legs to work. The young woman ran her finger along the line of his jaw and breathed softly over his lips. "I think the party is right here." She opened her mouth and a monstrous tongue uncoiled from it. Along the edges of the tongue were suction cups with needlelike teeth ringing them. Mario was so frightened that screaming wasn't even an option. "Once you get past the pain, you might like it." Before the girl could attack, she was snatched roughly away from Mario.

Titus stood in the middle of the room with power radiating from his body like an overworked furnace. He held the succubus's head in a vice grip, slowly applying pressure. The girl struggled against his grip, but even her enhanced strength was no match for the favorite son of Belthon. "How dare you come here and disrespect our host by trying to make a meal of him?" The young woman whimpered a weak apology, but it fell on deaf ears. Titus squeezed and her head burst like a rotten tomato.

"Titus, I had no idea you were preparing the refreshments." Orden strode into the room with Riel and Flagg on his heels. The goblin prince had traded his bloodstained tunic for a brown toga and cloak. On his head sat a crown of barbed wire and glass.

"All must know their places in the order of things, good prince," Titus told him, wiping his hands on the girl's dress. "I trust that my parcel has been secured and all is well again between us, Orden?"

"I've had my own captain, Illini, attend to the sprite, so there's no need to worry about your precious young girl. However, the strength of our friendship will depend on why you've summoned me topside and how the empire can benefit from it."

"All will benefit from what I have to offer, Orden, especially our friends the goblins," Titus assured him.

"Then let us stop hiding behind formalities and envoys and speak as warriors."

Titus smirked. "All will be revealed once the gathering is underway. Let's go join the others."

The room Titus led his minions into was initially built to host meetings, but had been modified to give it a more intimate feel. The ceilings were carved in a high arc into the marble that served as the room's supports, with twin fireplaces carved into the wall like flashing eyes. The crackling flames played tricks with the shadows that seemed to dance on every wall. There were no conference tables for men to argue about who would sit at the head, only a great open space where the elders of several factions of supernaturals now gathered, speaking in hushed tones over refreshments. When Titus walked in with his entourage, all eyes fell on them.

Flagg stepped forward and addressed the guests on behalf of his master. "Friends, associates, and those who are just curious, we thank you for answering our invitation on such short notice. Welcome to Raven Wood."

"Enough with the pleasantries, wizard, tell us why you've called us here. There are only a few more hours left until daylight and I still haven't fed yet, so let's move it along." This came from a pale young man dressed in a graphic T-shirt and leather overcoat. His name was Murphy and he was an enforcer for the vampire house Sheol. Lounging on a beanbag chair behind him was a man who was paler still, dressed in a gray sharkskin suit. His lazy blue eyes rolled in the back of his head as he relinquished the young lady's wrist he had been feeding from and came up for air. Unlike the brash

Murphy, Spencer had a more subdued approach to things. He was an observant man who only spoke when necessary, opting to let his actions speak for him. Though Anglon was the house's official leader in Sheol's absence, Spencer called the shots on the streets and Murphy made sure the orders were carried out.

"Watch your tongue, demon, or risk losing it," Riel warned.

"If that isn't the pot calling the kettle black," Spencer mumbled.

"Gentlemen, let's not waste time fighting among one another. We are on the cusp of something that will solidify all our positions as masters of our respective territories as well as new kingdoms that will be like fruit for us to pluck when all is said and done," Titus told them.

"As you've already said more than once, but you have yet to tell us what this great revelation is," Croft said from the sofa where he was lounging. He was the voice of the dark elves in the mortal world and a noted crime figure. Attending him was his son Rol, a worm of a man who lived in his father's shadow. Titus had hoped that Croft's nephew Gilgamesh would attend the gathering with his uncle, but Rol would have to do.

"Yes, halfling, why have you brought us here?" Mongo questioned. He was a brutish-looking demon who had the body of a man and the head of a goat. Mongo's lot weren't the easiest on the eyes but they were quite deadly in battle.

"Yes, my reasons for bringing you here." Titus paused for dramatic effect. "Gentlemen, an opportunity has presented itself to me to finally secure my rightful place in this world, and as you have all been such good friends to me I have decided to share it with you."

"You mean the chance to help you become a god?" Merlin asked. He was an upstart young sorcerer who was always seeking a way to further his own gains, but even his all-consuming ambition didn't make him a fool. "I know that it's the Nimrod that has brought you here, Titus, and I think I speak for all of us when I say that I see nothing to be gained from becoming one of your slaves."

"And your people would be experts on slavery." Dutch came into the room. He was dressed in tight-fitting leather pants and a white silk shirt. He glared at the sorcerer, clenching his fists, surrounding them with power.

"Well, if it isn't the Black King." Merlin called his own power. "I can't say that I'm surprised to see you here, since you have long been more loyal to your own greed than you have been to your coven. We've been hearing some very interesting things about you, things that would surely make for an interesting discussion at your next meeting of the covens, Von Dutch." He called the warlock by his old name.

Dutch's face twisted into a mask of hatred. "Let that name be the last to ever cross your vile lips."

He flicked his hands out and sent two balls of magic flying at Merlin. Merlin cast his own spell and aimed his power at Dutch.

Titus sighed, stepped between the colliding magics, and raised his hands. Both streams of power altered their courses, collecting in Titus's hands and vanishing. "I would advise the both of you to remember why you are here and that you are my guests. You both know better than to abuse my hospitality, especially you, Dutch." He turned his glowing eyes on the warlock.

Dutch could not hold his gaze. "Forgive me, Lord Titus."

"This is a first, the Black King eating humble pie!" Orden laughed and smacked Riel jovially on his back.

Titus ignored Orden's outburst and continued speaking to his guests. "There is some truth in what the sorcerer has said. We have reason to believe that the Nimrod has resurfaced, but the reports have as yet to be confirmed," he lied.

"I've heard some nasty stories about that thing and I can't say that I'd wanna run into it," Murphy said.

"Speak for yourself. The elders say that it grants the wielder the powers of a god," Mongo spoke up.

"It didn't do Bishop Francisco any good, did it?" Spencer pointed out.

"That's because the Bishop, as powerful as he was, was mortal and therefore an imperfect vessel for the Nimrod's power," Titus said.

"And last we checked you were born to mortal parents," Croft pointed out.

Titus gave him a murderous look. "Yes, I was born a mortal, but I have since transcended my genetic deficiencies and become something more." He held his hand up and it began to glow brilliantly. "Something much more."

"And your half-demon status makes you a better candidate to command the Nimrod than some of us who are pure of blood?" Mongo asked.

"Yes, why should it not be one of us who takes possession of the thing?" Croft added.

"Because I have tasted its sweet nectar," Titus said with a starved look in his eyes. "This Nimrod has answered to my touch once and it will again."

"If it doesn't destroy you and us in the process," Merlin said.

"Gentlemen, you can side with me and become masters of the world, or you can cower in the shadows with the rest while my armies conquer all."

"Buddy, you're mad as a hatter." Murphy stood to leave. "If this thing is indeed moving around somewhere in the world and up for grabs, I think we'll try our luck without you."

"The dead man is right. Why should we hand over the weapon of ultimate power to you instead of trying to snare it for ourselves?" Rol asked.

"Because if you do not join me, then you become my enemies," Titus said seriously.

"The Black Hand does not take threats well, demon," Croft warned.

"I am not threatening you, only telling you the ultimate truth. Friends of the dark order will be embraced, while our enemies will be crushed under our boots," Titus told them all. Riel and the Valkrin bodyguard formed ranks around Titus while Orden watched the whole exchange with an amused expression on his face.

"If that's the case, we may as well do away with you now." Merlin raised his hands to work a spell, but they were immediately bound over his head by shadows. When he opened his mouth, it was invaded by shadows, eventually strangling him. One by one the guests found themselves bound by shadows. Moses's silhouette peeled from the wall and moved to a position beside Titus.

"I'm sorry to have to do this, but you leave me no choice." Titus moved down the line of his guests, now turned to captives. "I offered you a chance to be kings and you spit on my offerings, so now you must be shown the error of your ways."

"You offered us the chance to be slaves!" Mongo snarled. His beady red eyes stared murderously at Titus.

"And now you will be examples. Fear not, gentlemen. Your souls will surely be parted from you this night, but your bodies will remain to carry on your legacies. Your people will follow me, and it will be your voices that tell them to do so." Titus gave Moses the signal and one by one the guests were pinned to the walls by spears of pure shadow, all except Croft and his son Rol, who had backed defensively into the corner. Croft drew a pistol, but the Valkrin disarmed him and held his arms behind his back. Moses oozed toward the elf, shaping his hands into blades as he went.

"You know the shadows have no power over the dark elves," Croft reminded his captors.

"Which is why I have a special death in mind for you," Titus said. "Of all these fools I would've expected the dark elves to understand what I am offering."

"What you seek to do will have repercussions that stretch beyond just the mortal world, Titus." Croft struggled in the Valkrin's grasp.

"What I seek to do is cleanse this world and remake it in my own image. I knew that there would be some who would resist, but I did not expect the Hand to be fools also. Luckily I came prepared to deal with even the likes of you." Titus waved Riel forward. The demon stepped through the ground, with the great blade Poison hefted over his shoulder. "I'm afraid this is going to be quite painful."

"You bastard, you've been planning this double-cross since you slunk into New York!" Croft spat.

Titus smiled. "Foolish elf, I've been planning this for four hundred years. Finish him," he told Riel.

Riel swung the blade. Soundlessly Poison cut through the fabric of his clothing and left a thin scratch across Croft's chest. The elf's eyes went wide and he began to claw at his suit, tearing open his shirt. The flesh beneath was pink and oozing something akin to blood. Croft dropped to the floor and convulsed violently as the poison ravaged his system.

"Now for you." Riel turned his blade on Rol.

"I ain't going quietly!" Rol fired his gun, hitting Riel in the gut. The Valkrin tried to grab him, but he spun out of her reach and bounded over a chair. Moses whipped shadows after him, but the elf was already crashing through the picture window.

"Shall I go after him?" the Valkrin asked. Titus thought on it. "No, the die has been cast and there isn't much that even the Black Hand can do about it at this point. Get these bodies downstairs to the tomb. A few more hosts and we'll be ready."

Don't miss the first book in this spectacular new
series from

KRIS GREENE

THE DARK STORM

Available from St. Martin's Paperbacks

...and look for the next novel

THE RECKONING

Coming in 2011
from St. Martin's Paperbacks